Too Many Goodbyes

GLORIA COPPOLA

ISBN: 9781737660378

Printed in the United States of America
First printing edition 2022

Published by Powerful Potential
and Purpose Publishing Services

www.PPP-publishing.com

Hickory, NC

Each of us has pain in our lives and some experience great loss, grief and growth. There is not one person on the planet who truly understands the depth of your soul journey. While some want to tell you what to do, how to live your life, rip the band-aid off your heart and pour salt into it…will it help (heal) you?

Remember this…NEVER give up on you.
You have a purpose.

LISTEN TO YOUR HEART

Love ♥ *Gloria*

FOLLOW YOUR INTUITION

Dedication

For my mother
Your spirit lives within me daily
The shattered pieces have created a beautiful life
Wish you were here to share it with me
Always, in my heart - your daughter forever

Table of Contents

CHAPTER I

Italy

2014

Tapping the pen on the café table, She wrote, *what would have happened if I had made different choices?*

Alexandra's mysterious smile mesmerized her admirers. Her elegant stature revealed no hints of her aging, voluptuous body, even in her later years. The vibrancy she emanated had an element of sophistication as she wandered with grace down the Via Del Corso, a historical street in Rome where no one realized who she was *...or so she thought.*

Exploring the shops proved tiring, and after a few hours of walking, her feet became tender and sore. The shoes were quite uncomfortable and required her to find a place to sit. She stumbled upon a peaceful café down a narrow cobblestone street. The sound of her heels clicking heightened the awareness of her fatigue. She was hungry, wanting something to appease her palate. The thought of eating her undeniably favorite snack, pizza, sounded like a wonderful indulgence along with a glass of wine. She would love to engage in a conversation with a kindhearted person as she was exceptionally lonely today. If only to make her smile, she would be content. The perfect spot was available. She would relax for a while and engage in her writing—her memories and dreams. Removing her journal from a large Italian leather purse, she reviewed her last entry as the side of her lip quivered.

Many years of apprehensions and decisions have prompted me on a path, perhaps not the wisest, but full of adventure, no doubt, she reminisced. *Could it actually be almost five decades had passed? So many travel experiences in the world, so many love affairs, with merely fleeting moments fulfilled.*

With a sense of the melodramatic—she always enjoyed embellishing her words with extravagant sounds and senses evoked by her pen. This time she wrote to *him.* The aroma of homemade tomato sauce whirled through her nose as she waited for the server; her appetite was ravenous.

As Alexandra's hand flowed across the linen-like cream color page, she observed the handsome, older server through the corner of her eye. The pizza he carried was sizzling hot and juicy. Marcello, the owner of the delightful café, walked across the terra cotta tiles singing, *"Volaré,"* as he approached the ravishing patron of '*Non solo pasta.*' Her hat tipped gracefully over one side of her face, in elegant style. She peeked subtly at his midnight-brown eyes. He, on the other hand, became distracted when she lifted her hand in a delicate fashion to remove her wide-brimmed hat. Her eyes glistened like a sea of blue along the Amalfi coast. He lost his balance, nearly landing in her lap. She smirked, knowing she had a way of enticing men. *"Scusi,* I'm sorry. I clumsy. I be back soon. Ok to take your order?" "Thank you kindly, sir. I am going to just write while I wait." *Gosh, he has the cutest accent. "Si,* I mean, yes." Marcello was suddenly vulnerable and a little shy. There was only one time in life he had something similar happen. The memory popped in his mind momentarily. Always wondering, he mumbled to himself, "Where did she go?"

A series of events were about to unfold which Lexi never imagined. Life has a way of aligning in the right timing. Lexi reminisced how it all began. But… where would it lead?

I smile because I have survived everything the world has thrown at me.

I smile because when I was knocked down, I got back up

—BUDDHA

CHAPTER 2

New York City

1966

"Rise and Shine, Lexi!"
These words mean more than 'get up'.
Read it again and know this story is about seeing your
potential to shine your light in this world.

The metal doors echoed through the hallways of Washington Irving High School in New York City. Slamming her locker shut, Lexi was pissed, her heart racing excessively. Why did she have to read all those meaningless books required for learning? She created her *own* stories, spending hours writing in her precious red journal. It was no surprise when she was asked to share her insights on the assigned book with the class, she reverted to a story of her own. Everybody laughed and, as usual teasing, her pride was hurt. She had to meet with the teacher after class.

"What were you thinking, Lexi?" "Truly, if you need to know, I will inform you," Lexi sarcastically declared, boldly and with conviction. "I'm sick and tired of people criticizing me, mocking me, and that includes you!" "Lexi, you will never be a writer. You don't follow any guidelines. You don't read!" "You have no idea of my capabilities!" Lexi responded adamantly. Grumbling under her breath, she walked away from the locker doors. "No one is going to tell me what I can accomplish! No one!" Suspended for a week from school because of her sarcasm. There could be an upside. It would be the ideal time for her to daydream and write.

If I ever become a teacher, I would be certain
to encourage and motivate students.

"Damn," she said, banging on the door to the apartment. "Is anyone home?" Lexi kicked the door with annoyance as she slumped down gradually to the cool concrete floor. "Where is Mom?" she muttered. "No one is ever around when I need them. I swear, I'm leaving after graduation. I won't be missed by anyone."

Opening her backpack, she took the red notebook out and scribbled across the pages rapidly. "*I'm going and no one can say anything!*" Not knowing how she would turn her dreams into reality, she took rigorous notes, ones which might lead her someplace. Could it be more than a trip, perhaps a spiritual journey she would experience? "They laugh at me, even my family. Thinking I'm a dreamer. I've been called a drama queen. Well, guess what? I am a *queen!*" Suddenly, she overheard someone walking down the hall and closed her book. No one could read her secrets.

The only one who seemed to understand Lexi was her brother, Danny. He loved to travel as well, and his work took him to many places for business. He regularly shared his adventures with Lexi when she was younger. *Maybe this is how I became a dreamer?* writing across the page filled with questions. "Hi, Alexandra, you are home early." "Mom, quit calling me that. I prefer Lexi." "Well, why are you home? Suspended again?" Lexi stood with a grunt and a stomp of her foot. She assumed her mom knew her sassy attitude had gotten her into trouble once again.

She waited impatiently for her mother to unlock the door to the apartment. Lexi thought of crawling into her bed and locking the bedroom door.

"Alexandra!" yelled her mother as she dashed to her bedroom. "Leave me alone!" Lexi cried, slamming the door. Lexi's mother tended to her chores, unloaded the groceries, and prepared dinner.

Heaven forbid dinner was five minutes late. The old man might hurl a plate. Her father, not the most patient man, usually arrived home exhausted with not much to say. Her mother was definitely the caretaker and the compassionate one, a wonderful role model for Lexi.

Lexi threw herself on to the uncomfortable twin bed in a childlike manner. Her tears rolled profusely into her mouth. Never accepted, at least in her mind, she wept. Lexi joked once that her mom had the only available womb for her to come to earth, an observation she made at the age of five. No one was like her in the family. She regularly wondered, was she adopted? "Grr, being a teenager really sucks! Now to imagine where I can move, where no one recognizes me. Someplace I can be whoever I desire."

Fervently she wrote in her red notebook: *I can travel far and wide, across the oceans and discover my heart home. Egypt? I will go to Italy. Perhaps my own ancestors would understand me better? Now, how do I accomplish this? I need to save money. I can ask for extra hours after school at my part-time job. Figure out how to purchase an airplane ticket and study Italian. I will ask Dad to send me there for my graduation. I hoped this time he would at least grant me some help. I can hope there would be no disappointment in my heart this time.*

She knew he didn't have the means. "I bet he won't expect me to save the money and find my own way. I will show him." I wonder how scary it is to fly? I've never been on an airplane. Who can I ask? Lexi created an excessive number of questions, along with ideas about whom she might meet and where she could go. Would anybody be interested in traveling with her? It certainly would seem safer. The words scribbled across the page. *Freedom!*

Hours passed by, her dreams growing bigger and wider, when she heard her mother call her for dinner. "I'm not hungry!" "Get out here now and eat!" Her legs flipped over the edge of her bed and grumpily she wandered down the long hallway to the small kitchen where she plopped into a chair." "Alexandra, didn't you learn anything from charm school?" Eyes rolling, smirking, she remained silent. "Your mother asked you a question!" grumbled her exhausted dad. "Yes, sir!" Positioning herself like a private in the army. "Dad, I have a question." "Oh, you do? Shall I ignore you like you did your mother?" "I apologize."

Her father was consistently harsh on her. No matter what she did to please him, she invariably perceived herself a failure. Danny recognized her challenges and did his best to take her under his wing It wasn't much easier for him, though he seemed to excel at everything. "Now, pray," her mother said. Prayers were recited, but everyone remained on edge.

When Lexi's father had a tough day, he displayed his temper. You did not dare say anything, question him, defend yourself, or attempt to start a conversation. Eat quickly, wash the dishes, do your homework, and go write some more, thought Lexi. That was the plan for tonight. *He may have been hard on us so we could achieve more. Did he want us to struggle less in life? Maybe he has a hard time providing for us?* Lexi just wanted to be accepted and loved.

After the dishes were done, she slid down the hallway on the tiles, like an Olympic ice skater. She slipped back into her dream world, always peaceful for her. She called it her "bubble."

With the book on her chest, clothes still on, the morning alarm went off. "Hey sleepyhead, time to rise!" she heard her mother call. "Mom, remember…I'm suspended. I would love to go to the library today… please." "That is what I like to hear. A girl who knows where to spend her time. Stay out of trouble." "Thanks." Wrapping her arms around her mom tightly, she knew this woman cared deeply for her dreams. Pleased she had permission to go, she quickly rushed to shower, dress, and be on her way. *I cannot imagine a world without my mom. Who would I be if she was not here to encourage and support me?*

The New York Public Library

Lexi enjoyed long walks, people watching, noticing their gait, their grimaces and especially their laughter. Often, she would browse in shops too expensive for her high school budget, and always stopping at the most amazing pizza places. Every time she arrived at the library, she marveled in awe gazing around at the base of the marble stairs. Lexi never understood why it intrigued her so much but hoped to learn why someday. She found it interesting, this land, originally a potter's field, a burial site for poor people. She would often wonder *did they inspire the writers who one day would walk through these halls? I'm sure they had fascinating lives.*

Lexi read everything about traveling, especially about Italy, it became her favorite past-time. Perhaps someone could guide her. Where could she learn how to purchase a plane ticket, find a cheap place to stay, and explore to her heart's content? Of all the places in the world, this one called her the most. In this day and age, research would take her to meet many helpful people.

Her gaze focused upwards where she stood on the first step. Lexi saw fountains, statues, and three porticos, which invoked a triumphal arch in her mind. She took a huge breath, sucking in her stomach, filling her lungs, she sighed. Walking up the next step, a sense of *knowing* filled her little heart. Something gave her the strength and fortitude to climb higher. It compelled her to be a better person, and she knew deep inside, one day, she would see *her* book in the library with the millions of others.

Just then, Julia, an arrogant and obnoxious classmate, also on suspension, called out, "Hey, Lexi, trying to learn how to be a better student?" "Shut up, will ya?" "Lexi got suspended!" she melodically shouted across the length of the stairs. People stared at the both of them, snubbing them for their immaturity. Good grief, thought Lexi as she witnessed the reactions of the educated and most likely highly esteemed, successful people around her. I need to find new people in my life. Embarrassed, she entered the library, with her head down.

The library, which opened in 1911, became the place to launch Lexi's enthusiasm for travel and her passion to write. She saw the world through the minds of many authors' experiences. Fantasizing about her own world travels, she embraced the wonderment of this splendid world at her tender age of nearly 18. The massive door led her inside the library. Doors became a fascination for her and would continue to intrigue her for the rest of her life. *Could they be symbolic in some way?* As she entered the library room, the most majestic space, as large as a football field, it reminded her of cathedrals with side chapels she saw in picture books from Rome. This room was called the "*Rose Main Reading Room,*" a quiet place to study and conduct research. A trustee had gifted it to the library and named it after his wife. There were gilded curlicues, cornucopia, and cherubs playing flutes along the ceiling's celestial cloud of pink. "What is the significance of this coincidence?" she murmured to herself. "Grandma Rose and Rose Reading Room. I dare say a sign," she said with a smirk. Her grandmother always had a way of reaching Lexi.

Read, Lexi, she whispered, *and then write.*

"*Whoa*! This *is* a place I can write. I'm sure I can find many books to teach me to write with more sophistication. I am determined to find my place in the world." Lexi's enthusiasm was beyond anything she imagined. She had walked these halls dozens of times, but today was different, like a new reality. Scratching her head, tilting it to the side, she wondered, *why today?*

Soon she had piles of books in her arms, all intriguing to her, hoping she didn't drop any as she proceeded to a table. A curator asked if she needed assistance carrying all of them. "Why, thank you, sir," she said sweetly. He smiled and took Lexi to her seat, leaving with a gleam in his eye and a polite smile. *He most likely thinks I'm some kind of child genius*, she thought, chuckling to herself. *Little does he realize, I'm confused, timid, and seeking to find my way. Or perhaps he does.*

Pacing her steps with poise and grace, Lexi realized that the way she studied in charm school proved useful. This would be her world for the next year. Muttering to herself "I will plan my life, meet new people, and mature into a lovely young lady."

Julia appeared again. "Hey, hey, Lexi. I didn't know you could read. Seeking to impress us with all those texts?" "Julia, I'm in no frame of mind for this. Please stop." "Oh, the poor baby isn't into conversation today?" Lexi attempted to ignore the torturing from Julia. It wasn't easy. The curator wandered over to inquire if Julia needed help. She chuckled, gave him a sarcastic grin, glanced at Lexi with demon eyes, and walked away. "I apologize if she is troubling you, miss." "No worries, sir. She is a bully from my school." "That is undesirable in any situation. Perhaps she requires a book on etiquette." Lexi snickered faintly and continued to read and take notes. "Pardon me, sir, I wish to thank you for your kindness. What is your name?" "You may call me Charles." "Thank you, Charles." If he had a hat on, he would have indeed tipped it at the lovely lady in front of him. *Being here is like a source of water*, she wrote in her journal, *flowing around the continents and connecting the world*. With a deep sigh of gratitude for the ability to appreciate the writers of the world, Lexi was ready to find information to plan her escape.

One page after another, so many countries with interesting history. *Where shall I go?* she pondered. The next hours passed by as Lexi's imagination sizzled with ideas, her excitement building, and the intrigue of every country had her more confused. *How would she get to them?* She couldn't find information in these historical books to determine how one might pay for a seat on a plane and book a hotel. Just then, a librarian glided by. You barely could hear a footstep. "Ma'am, can you direct me to books that will teach me how to travel around the world? Do you know where can I find information about booking an airplane ticket?" The older woman with slightly gray hair responded, "Come with me, lovely child. I will show you a whole new world." Stunned and happy with her reply, Lexi politely followed the gracious woman to a huge section labeled "Travel." "You can spend hours here, I am sure, finding travel books with information on trains, planes, and boats," the librarian said with a smile. "Wow! I mean, I appreciate this so much!"

There were thousands of travel books for every country in the world. Her older brother had also mentioned researching Switzerland, a place he frequented for work. She would find a world atlas and learn about *National Geographic*. The numerous published articles of faraway places gave her the hunger to learn more.

Lexi soon stumbled upon *Europe on Five Dollars a Day*, a book by Arthur Frommer. Published in 1957, it became an instant hit. He put together a guide on how to travel across the continent economically and covered everything essential for Europe.

"This is what I need!" Lexi started to shout but covered her mouth quickly. Julia, around the corner in the next aisle, spied on her. She wanted to interrupt her moment of excitement. "You need more than a book, Lexi! You are such a loser!" With her nose in her book, she ignored Julia and went on her way. "Humph! You think you can ignore me?" retorted Julia. "I'm not going away anytime soon, you deathwatch out next week when you return to school." It took great restraint for Lexi to avoid this nonsense. She wanted to say, "Who invited you here anyway"? What would that accomplish? As she lifted her head, Charles, standing nearby, winked at her. For the first time, someone respected her, a comrade, possibly a mentor.

This serene environment lined with wooden tables and small brass lamps reminded her of movies she had seen. The sheer number of books aligned down each row was surely more than she could ever read. Nonetheless, it would be her haven for the next year as she planned her life. Each week she made sure she returned to the library to learn, study, and research, not only Italy and other countries but also every other topic she needed for school. She fell in love. It would not be the only time. Her school grades were improving, and she achieved the scholastic honor roll every month. Her life was shifting rapidly as she matured.

"Lexi," Miss Roland, her guidance counselor, called out. "I am pleased and impressed with all your efforts this year. I see you have considerable scholastic achievements. Congratulations!"

Did this just happen? Did the guidance counselor give me a compliment? Am I finally being seen for who I am? The kind words provided her with hope and courage. If only it had come from her dad.

"Hey, bitch, you rubbing shoulders with the guidance counselor now?" Julia was back. *Gosh, I'd love to punch Julia in the face!* With little attention to this remark, she happily strolled out the school doors.

Lexi remembered a quote from a plaque in the school's central hall penned by Washington Irving: *"There is in every true woman's heart, a spark of heavenly fire, which lies dormant in the broad daylight of prosperity, but which kindles up and beams and blazes in the dark hour of adversity."* This remained in Lexi's heart as motivation to push through her own misadventures and misfortune. Waving goodbye to Julia, she skipped down the steps, ready to buy her plane ticket.

CHAPTER 3

Switzerland

*D*ear *Jesus, thank you for constantly being my companion and guide. You have supported me through many challenges and decisions in my brief lifetime. I count on you to always protect me.*

Lexi prayed each day and night. Her relationship with Jesus was powerful. She believed she could see him, hear him, and talk to him, and she had, since early childhood. But it was always her secret, for fear she would be judged by this special gift.

At high school graduation day, Lexi received several honors for her grades along with a writing scholarship. Proud and surprised, she felt like a blossoming sunflower on a sunny day. She had serious dreams to help the world, have her own children, and be intensely devoted to her soul mate. Of course, travel was part of this vision.

When it came time to hand the ticket to the agent, her mother said, "You did not limit your dreams, beautiful child. My Alexandra...I know...Lexi," she said proudly. "You will have a splendid adventure in your life."

She hugged her mom, receiving a kiss which left a red lipstick mark on her cheek and teary eyed, because it was the first time her mom had called her Lexi. As she picked up her luggage to walk away, her mom waved, cried, and secretly began to live vicariously through her daughter. She also knew Lexi would learn more about herself. Her older brother Danny, who drove them to the airport in his brand new Chevrolet, gave her a heartfelt hug and wished her a wonderful trip. Her father was working, as usual. Danny had a surprise waiting for Lexi, which he knew would knock her socks off. He planned the whole thing with his colleague at the hotel. As he traveled frequently to Switzerland for business, he wanted his younger sister to experience a wonderful time on her first journey.

This is real, wow! How did I manifest this? Those hours in the library and studying everything led me to this moment. My part-time job to pay for it all since dad did not contribute. Initially I was furious dad wouldn't help me. I realize now he helped in other ways, perhaps more than I imagined. I became innovative, determined, and developed tenacity.

She presented the courteous airline stewardess the plane ticket and hauled her suitcase down to the gangplank and stepped on board. *This is much larger than I imagined.*

When Lexi informed the agent at the Trans American Airlines ticket counter that she didn't require the big jet, the lady giggled at her and replied, "Oh, yes you do!" Lexi wasn't sure what she was supposed to do next. A voice spoke from above, telling passengers to pay attention to the safety instructions. That's funny, she thought, since she had always heard voices. She followed along to understand how to fasten the seatbelt, wear the oxygen mask, and escape if necessary. *Oh, dear Lord, please tell me I won't need to escape.*

Once she got comfortable in her window seat she watched as the plane filled to capacity. One of the airline stewardesses stopped by to introduce herself and ask if she needed anything, like a blanket or a drink.

"Yes, please. I'll take a Coke and a blanket." "Coming right up."

Time to write; documenting this will be relevant one day.

Lexi had a brand-new red journal. When someone asked why her journals were always red, her answer was always the same. "It's because it's my least favorite color, and I want to learn how to love it. Everything I write in here will be my dreams and, like fire and passion, I will ignite them. Most things have always had a symbolic meaning, even if others don't understand it."

Daydreaming was Lexi's favorite thing to do, and she imagined listening to songs she enjoyed from her brother's era while the clouds, colors like raspberry sherbet, rolled by through the sky. Jotting some words down to the song *"Venus"* that Frankie Avalon sang in the '50s and humming, it brought pleasant memories of dancing with her brother. Exhausted from all the excitement, she drifted off into a comfortable sleep for the next few hours.

"Good morning, passengers. Breakfast will be served." Jolted from her dream, her head pressed against the cold window, it surprised Lexi to discover they served breakfast on a plane. She was quite naïve, but not for long. The stewardesses, all beautiful, handed out warm towels. This new experience most definitely would be quite thrilling for her.

What do I do with these? Silly girl, of course they are to wipe your face. Just at that moment, she had another thought, as she wondered what first class was like. *I wish I could peek up there…so mysterious with a curtain hiding them,* she thought, chuckling to herself.

"Excuse me, I need to use the restroom." The businessman next to her smiled, rose like a gentleman, stepped back for her to pass, and showed her the way, gesturing with his hand. *I'm really doing this,* containing her desire to jump up and down—a nearly impossible feat in the tiny bathroom.

"Geneva, Switzerland, here I come!" Danny suggested she visit this amazing place, though he understood her heart was set on Italy. His frequent business trips for his corporate job granted him these luxuries. Meanwhile, Lexi fantasized about the grand mountains, snow, villages, and, of course, the *chocolate*. Lexi learned about the Eurail train system from the lady at the counter where she purchased her ticket. A really cool, affordable deal students can obtain to travel in Europe. Then the person who sold her the Eurail pass told her about hostels. There was so much for her to learn. Nothing interrupted her process to fulfill her dream. Travel agents! Who knew people arranged trips for a living? How fun, she thought. She had to learn all the ropes, including how to apply for a passport. Walking back to her seat, she enjoyed a surprisingly superb breakfast and anticipated landing shortly.

"*Bonjour,* right this way," announced the man holding a sign bearing her name. Wow, this is quite cool. Her brother had reserved a chauffeur. He wanted her to experience a good life and encouraged her to strive for the best. The driver was well informed and held his hand out, providing Lexi a brochure to read on the drive.

"*Merci,*" she said.

Well, at least one word came out right, she thought, proud of herself.

Beau-Rivage Geneva Hotel, an iconic hotel since 1865, the brochure stated. *Welcome to the elegance and sophistication of a period building, its yesteryear charm passionately preserved.*

Immerse yourself fully in Geneva's cultural diversity in the comfort and art de vivre by Beau-Rivage. Explore. Experience your own exceptional private spa with jacuzzi bathtubs in our Suites.

She found herself a bit intimidated by the description as her brother did not warn her about the luxurious hotel. He just said she would love the old hotel with a view of the river. The only thing he mentioned, knowing his little sister had a flair for the dramatic, was to wear a beret. "You also may want to review some French you learned in high school."

"Mademoiselle, we are here." Lexi's eyes opened wide like a full moon. Luxurious yachts lined the river. A hospitality staff greeted her at the steps with flowers, and someone grabbed her luggage: she did not lift a finger. Brass railings, marble steps, and chandeliers in the elegant lobby, along with a fountain, live plants, pillars, and a concierge dressed impeccably only reinforced the grandeur of her surroundings. Here I am with a beret, scruffy clothes, tired eyes. I'm far too immature for this, she said to herself.

"*Bonjour*, Mademoiselle Caprio. My name is Suzette. Your brother has arranged everything for a delightful stay with us for three days." Boy, he sure knows how to live the high life, spinning her head around to take in all the sculptures, the art, and the fancy dresses ladies were wearing. "Merci, I am thrilled to be here." *Sheesh, Lexi, that's all you can say?*

"We will bring your luggage to the room along with room service. Do you prefer any beverages, pastries, or fruit?" "Umm...I mean, I'll be happy with your specialties and some Swiss chocolate, perhaps." Suzette smiled and said, "*Absolutment.*"

Speechless for once in her life, Lexi settled in, relishing the view of the city and the old-world vintage furniture adorning the junior suite overlooking the water. It was quite enchanting for this young lady. As soon as the guest relations woman, Suzette, left the room, she pounced on the bed, kicking up her legs and silently screaming in her head, *oh my gosh, this is magical! I feel like a fairy princess!*

The phone rang unexpectedly, and she jumped to lift the fancy brass and porcelain receiver. "Mademoiselle, your brother would like to greet you. I shall connect you now." "Hey, little sis!" Before he could say another word, Lexi incessantly began to ramble on with excitement and gratitude. "You didn't have to do this. Thank you so much. This is the grandest and most expensive place I could ever imagine. You are crazy!" "You deserve a little luxury in your life. I've arranged for a tour, all your meals, and anything else you desire. Just tell Suzette; she is your private concierge. I think you will connect well with her too." "You are a nut." "Lexi, now listen to me. Don't find any trouble because Mom will kill me." "Don't worry, I promise to be on my best behavior. I love you!" "I will be here if you need me. Just tell Suzette." "Okay, I really appreciate all you are doing for me. I would never have expected this kind of treatment. *Merci, merci, merci!* Thank you so much. *Bonsoir.*"

Lexi planned to bathe quickly. Then she and Suzette would schedule her three days before she took the Eurail to Florence, Italy. The thick velvet robe, plush soft towels, and the old-fashioned bathtub would be a most exquisite beginning to her new life. Much more than this girl could desire. The phone rang once more. This time Suzette called. "Miss Lexi, I arranged a massage for you this afternoon after you dine with us for lunch. Does this suit you?" "It sure does! I will meet you in one hour for lunch, okay?" "Yes, that will be fine. Shall I come for you?" "Come for me? Oh, you mean to show me the way to the restaurant. Yes, please, that is kind of you." "I shall return in one hour." *A massage too?*

Stripping her clothes off, running the bath, and thrilled to see how her day and life would unfold, she dozed off in the tub for a few moments when the phone rang. "Shit!" Carefully getting out of the tub, she rushed to wrap the towel around her and answer the phone. "Hello?" "Hello, I see you." The caller hung up abruptly as Lexi experienced an unpleasant eerie sense running through her. No accent, no operator connection, someone had to be in the hotel, she thought frantically. Dashing to put her clothes on and close the curtains, her breath deepened as she became even more concerned. *Perhaps just a wrong number?* Must be, she convinced herself. Remaining composed, she dressed promptly. "I can't discuss this with anyone!"

Maybe not the wisest decision, she noted in her journal. *I don't wish to alarm anybody and have them tell me to go home.*

Answering a soft knock on the door, she greeted Suzette, who was ready to accompany her to a divine lunch. All her worries vanished in an instant. Suzette, a charming escort, was sophisticated and tailored with a reassuring, cultured voice. "Lexi, is this your first holiday to Geneva?" "Yes, ma'am. This is my first international trip ever!" "Delightful. You will appreciate all we offer. Your brother has made certain of that!" "I'm thrilled to explore, learn, and experience it all." "You shall dine in Le Chat-Botte, the original hotel restaurant. It reopened to the public just recently. Our chef is outstanding. You may select anything you like. The chef's culinary creations are exceptional." "It all sounds incredible. Thank you, Suzette. Am I dressed properly?" "We can stop by the boutique, if you please, and find something perfect for you. Your brother has arranged it as a gift." "Wow, he considered everything."

Suzette demonstrated graciousness. She refrained from suggesting Lexi needed something more appropriate as she chose her words carefully. Classy, thought Lexi. This would be the first of many boutique expeditions this young woman would enjoy in life. Her taste for extravagance, fine dining, exquisite artifacts and jewelry, and let's not neglect shoes—would soon develop into one of her favorite pastimes in Europe. Suzette had an idea for a suitable place, one with the latest trends and leading fashion items, something she was sure Lexi would enjoy. The two had an enjoyable time wandering downtown, talking, and establishing a lovely bond. Suzette was like a good friend she had always imagined.

"Suzette, may I confide in you?" "Yes, absolutely." "Promise you won't reveal this to my brother?" "Okay, but I am here to take care of you." "I understand. I had a strange phone call today. Someone said, 'Hello, I see you,' and hung up." "Oh dear. Lexi, we must resolve this and investigate!" "No, please don't. I don't want to alarm anyone. However, I thought perhaps if it happened again, I would come to you." "Okay, but no further secrets? I'm responsible for you and your safety. I will contact our surveillance team and ask them to scrutinize the guests who are here. If they notice anything suspicious, we will investigate it. Sound reasonable?" "Thank you, yes. I'm more relaxed now, telling someone. Maybe a wrong number, right?" "Perhaps, but we shall pay attention."

Suzette found a cheerful yellow sundress with a pattern suiting Lexi's temperament. A fun wide-brimmed hat to accompany it and sandals completed her ensemble. The mirror's reflection revealed a joyful and confident youthful woman about to take on the world. "Come, we must feed you, and later you will receive your massage." When they returned to the hotel, Lexi saw several individuals roaming through the lobby. She heard a familiar voice in the distance, but when she turned around, she saw only one smartly attired woman checking into the hotel and her chauffeur tending to her luggage. *Maybe I'm imagining things.*

Lunch was divine, with linen napkins, crystal glasses, and Hors d'ouevres. Three servers tended to Lexi, which surprised her. However, she was delighted by their service. Each of them was extremely good-looking, certainly an added benefit. She beamed as they tended to her every need.

Thank goodness Mom sent me to charm school. I actually remember which fork to use, chuckling to herself.

"Miss Suzette, can we skip the spa today? I'm quite uncomfortable being alone in a dark space. I'm still a bit freaked out by the phone call." Lexi didn't mention the voice she had heard again in the lobby. "Sure, Miss Lexi. Would you prefer a helicopter tour?" "Are you serious? Yes!" "Come, we shall arrange it and take you in the air soon."

Pinch me, someone! Where is my journal when I need it? No one is going to believe this. A helicopter tour in Switzerland on my first day! An adventure of panoramic views dazzled her with snow-capped mountains, beautiful chalets, and flowers blooming in the valleys.

All too soon, jet lag settled in. She informed Suzette she would turn in early. Room service might be nice, she told her. Another new experience. Besides, she had lots to write in her journal.

"Miss Lexi, enjoy a good rest. I arranged to take you on a walking tour of the city tomorrow. Does that suit you?" "Yes. Will there be chocolate?" Suzette smiled. "A young woman after my own heart. I will take us to the finest chocolatiers, young lady. We shall enjoy a stroll in the old town and some fun girl talk. I know of a remarkable café, and anything else you wish to visit, just let me know. I shall pick you up at 9 a.m. for breakfast. Does that suit you?" "Yes, it all suits me, especially the girl talk." Lexi reached out to give Suzette a hug, and the two smiled. "Goodnight," they said simultaneously. "Gosh, I love this phrase. *It suits me.* Sounds so posh. I really need to get rid of my slang and become more sophisticated."

"Suzette, one more question before the night is over, if you don't mind?" "I suppose, Lexi. What is it?" "Are you my brother's girlfriend?" Suzette gasped for air. "Have you asked him, Lexi?" "No, but I can sense something between you both. I have uncanny insights like that. I don't quite understand them all the time." "Lexi, it is my job to provide our guests a wonderful experience." "Okay, I will accept that," she said, winking and waving good-night. Lexi had the gift of sense; however, she would let it go for now.

Fading into dream state rather quickly, she didn't complete her writing. The pen fell on the bed and her journal on her chest. A customary sleeping position lately.

The next two days would pass by swiftly. A whirlwind of fun, extravagance, her first taste of wine, exquisite chocolates, and pastries every day. Lexi could never have imagined such a fabulous experience.

While she gathered her luggage to get ready for her next adventure, the phone rang. Lexi jumped. The phone had not rung the last few days. Who could it be? she wondered. "Hello?" she hesitantly answered. "Hey, sis, why so quiet?" "Oh, I just woke up," she lied. "I had the best few days, and I can never thank you enough." "I'm happy for you. Suzette mentioned you are delightful. Sounds like the two of you bonded well." "For sure, she is exceptional. I'm in a rush now. The train calls. The next time I have access to a phone, I will call you. Tell Mom and Dad all is well. I'm really glad your job takes you to Switzerland. I enjoyed it so much." "Sure thing, sis. Love you." "Hey, Danny, wait, I have a question." "What's up?" Just then, the phone disconnected.

"Damn!" Apparently, the concierge had accidentally cut the call off when he dispatched someone to carry Lexi's baggage down to be loaded into the luxurious Mercedes. Suzette waited at the car to invite Lexi to breakfast. A last charming conversation together, and it was off to her next adventure, a less extravagant one; but one she anticipated with joy. "I'm glad everything pleased you, Lexi. I enjoyed our time together. Your company was charming. Your brother thinks highly of you, and now I can understand why." "Thank you, that is kind of you. I can understand why he has a fondness for you as well." They chatted, laughed, ate, and sipped their morning coffee together. Suzette shared a comparable story of her younger days, when she had a similar sense of adventure.

With breakfast served and done, the server came over and said, "I will see to it. All is taken care of for you, miss." A chill ran through her, the voice so familiar. She shivered and told Suzette she would use the ladies' room before meeting her in the car. *Should I go find him? No, don't be dumb. Leave now!* voices rambled in her head.

Lexi saw Suzette outside after saying *adieu* to all the outstanding staff members, hugs included, of course. The royal staff, which she called them, were invariably courteous, right down to the young gentleman who opened the door for her to the Mercedes limousine. Waving to the team like a queen, with a smile, off she went. "Suzette, I am indeed grateful for you and all you prepared to make my time here remarkable. I have something to tell you." "Sure, Lexi. What is it?" "At breakfast today, I recognized the voice from my phone call. The server who said, 'I will see to it. All is taken care of for you, miss.' It was the same voice on the phone that day." "Are you certain?" "Yes, but he doesn't speak with the accent like the rest of the staff." "My apologies, Lexi, we shall tend to this as soon as I return. Our company will tolerate nothing like this, and we expect the utmost professionalism, not to mention the safety and comfort of our patrons."

Suzette now had an idea who this could be. It had to be the only staff member from the USA who visited and worked with a visa. Without hesitation and any doubt, she would fire him immediately. "Will he get in trouble? I don't want to have him fired, but what if—" "You are right. I will attend to the matter."

"Now enjoy your journey and call me if you require anything. *Au revoir*," she said as she handed her a business card. Lexi stood in front of the train station, eager and apprehensive. She picked up her suitcase, threw Suzette a kiss, smiled, and walked away. Still concerned about the strange man, she decided to let it go…for now.

"A mind that is stretched by a new experience
can never go back to its old dimensions."
—Oliver Wendell Holmes

CHAPTER 4

Italy Bound

"All aboard!" The train was nearly ready to pull out of the depot in Geneva, Switzerland. The whistle blew, signaling the time for departure. Lexi was more than ready to launch the second segment of an adventurous life. Little did she realize the universe had a lesson for her. Spontaneous, since the age of five, she loved going places. If any relative planned to travel, she would gather a suitcase at once and announce, "I'm coming." Only this occasion had been arranged all on her own.

I am so excited; I can barely wait to arrive in Italy. My dream, well, one of them. She took a deep breath, her eyes scanning the numbers, and scurried to jump on board. Looking up, she saw #20. The porter took her suitcase and extended his hand to ease her climb up the enormous steps. Of course, with her independent personality and American swagger, she proudly declared, "No thank you, I got this!" "Okay, now to locate my cabin and begin this passage through the Swiss Alps. What shall await me during this expedition?" she asked herself. "*Scusi*, may I help you?" "Thank you. I'm looking for my cabin."

Smiling, he pointed to the number on her ticket. That's when she realized she was right in front of the cabin. The pleasant young man caught her complete attention, captivating her for a moment. He opened the door and respectfully obliged her to enter first. Lexi wondered if Italy had so many handsome men. "Thank you," she said, plopping into the leather recliner right up against the window. She would miss nothing on this excursion. The young Italian gentleman seated next to her spoke in Italian. Evidently, he understood barely any English, and Lexi knew little Italian. When she motioned with her hands to convey her inability to communicate, he just grinned. *Damn, if only I had pursued my Italian classes, but alas, I fell in love with French.*

An aging couple, short and stout with silvery hair, slowly waddled into the overnight cabin. The gentleman helped them situate their bags on the racks above the seats. They, too, spoke Italian. Lexi yearned to understand them. Everybody appeared to be pleasant. A small espresso cart rolled up to the window. Shouting out in Italian, the vendor waved his hands to the people looking out of the windows. Coaxing them to buy an espresso she instinctively responded yes. Handing him a lira through the window, she grabbed the small hot cup, saying, "*Grazie.*" The aroma was extremely potent. This would be a surprise to her taste buds, since she was not one to drink coffee. She waited a few moments to sip the cup of espresso. It was exceptionally strong for this novice. "YUK!" she blurted, spitting the espresso back into the cup. Lexi flushed in embarrassment. Her Italian travel companions chuckled, recognizing this was her first shot. The young Italian man, approximately 25, sought not to laugh and gave her an understanding smile. What a mess she had made on her blouse, completely feeling silly she rushed quickly to the rest room to clean it off.

Noticing the pillow on the rack above her, she reached to grab it, make herself comfortable, and settle in for the evening. Of course, the young man reached up to hand her the pillow. He smiled and established direct eye contact. It was strange and awkward for this teenager to be met with such intensity, but she cheerfully reined in her American style and smiled in return. She appreciated how gallant he was; he was certainly attentive. If only she knew his name. One other young woman showed up. Thank goodness she speaks

English, thought Lexi. This was going to be a lengthy trip with no one to understand.

The two young women sat across from each other and instantly bonded. Dina mentioned she was going to meet her friend in Florence. They were backpacking on their European holiday. The idea fascinated Lexi. Such a sense of freedom. She thought how cool it would be to backpack. She grasped her first lesson from Dina, to pack lightly.

The whistle blew one last time, and the train jerked a bit as it made its way out of the terminal. Twilight was approaching. Lexi peeked out the window, waving goodbye to the people standing on the platform, she laughed at herself. *How absurd. I am not acquainted with these people. So fun, nevertheless.*

"Is this your first time in Italy?" Dina asked in a British accent. "Yes, I'm so excited. I want to learn more about the country and my ancestry. I do not know if my relatives are alive, honestly. No one seems to have information about my immediate family." With a sophisticated air in her tone, Dina assured her Italy would not be a disappointment, as it was one of many amazing places in the world to visit. Obviously, Lexi demonstrated an air of innocence. "Why are you traveling alone?" "I wasn't waiting for anyone! Everyone had excuses. I made all my own plans. Where are you from?" "England, all my life. That is certainly adventurous for you to travel so far from home. I bet you will enjoy yourself. It will be a blast for sure."

The girls talked for hours. Mostly, Lexi listened, enchanted with the stories Dina shared about her travels. She could imagine one day telling her adventures. This had to be a sign. The train moved fast, and the scenery, trees, and farms were a mere blur as the ethereal beauty of blended reds and pinks settled upon the day. Quickly, the train proceeded through the Swiss Alps. It would arrive in Florence at approximately 3 a.m.

The Italian companions chatted, and the elderly couple would often glance at Lexi and smile cordially, as if they perceived something. The young man delighted listening to Lexi express herself with such passion and, of course, speaking with her hands as well.

She had to be Italian, and he wished they could communicate. Intrigued he would never forget her ocean blue eyes. Lexi, growing tired, reflected on her time in Switzerland—a brief stopover, a charming place of fresh air— and the finest chocolates and ice cream she had ever eaten. She *must* remember to ask her brother about Suzette. With that, Lexi slipped off to sleep.

A screeching jolt woke her a few hours later, as the train appeared to slow down.

"I'm sorry," she said to the young man, realizing with embarrassment she had slumped on his shoulder as she slept. He didn't seem to mind and motioned for her to rest her head. Respectfully, she shook her head no. Can anyone be so perfect? She questioned the energy running through her. Something unfamiliar. Perhaps just travel vibes, she concluded.

Boy, did Lexi dream. As usual, her grand imagination had her on quite the journey with someone. Visions drifted through her mind of them running through a meadow. Perhaps in Tuscany, sipping wine in a hot air balloon. Laughing so hard, they both collapsed to the grass and rolled down a hillside, landing on top of each other. Like most dreams, nothing had a progression. Everything was random and quick. Their eyes met, no conversation. A delicate touch of their lips, not a kiss. The warmth, an intensity, seared through her bones, her inhibitions cautioned her. He wrapped his hands around her waist and squeezed her closer to his body. She was aware of his breath on her face. He could sense her heart beating. Sweet serenity. Shifting his hands, he caressed both her cheeks and held her face. He whispered something in another language to her. With an intense kiss, he consumed her essence into his. The kiss lasted the whole night. However, she never saw his face.

Give or take twelve hours afterward, they drew into the station in Florence. Lexi was exhausted and could have slept much longer. The two girls stood up. The older couple smiled, and the young man helped both of them with their carry- on luggage. They waved goodbye to their companions, hardly awake this early. The two girls walked hurriedly to the steps to grab a taxi. They realized they had booked the same hostel at the Catholic school, which helped Lexi feel confident and a little safer.

Another little jolt. Then the train came to an abrupt stop, and someone bumped into her. She turned and recognized the handsome young man behind her. He tenderly took her hand and faced her. *What is he doing?* she asked herself. His deep seductive voice expressed something in Italian. If only she understood. Dina headed down the stairs and left her, leaving Lexi anxious. Their eyes engaged as they spoke to each other without words. Again, he repeated something in Italian, held her hand, as she attempted to catch up with her new travel friend. Lexi was frozen in time as people got off and hurriedly ran down the steps. "Young lady, he is proposing to you. Say yes!" a woman standing by revealed. Uneasy and not prepared, Lexi nodded her head and let go of his hand, charmed and scared. He kissed her on the cheek tenderly before she waved goodbye. Ciao. *The first of many goodbyes.*

His eyes watched her every step.

He would never forget, and neither would she. Surely, he thought, the intensity of their connection was mutual. Lexi would have a challenging time getting him out of her mind while in Italy, wondering always *what if?* "That was close! Imagine a complete foreigner proposing," she said to Dina. "It's customary," she said, laughing. "You will get many offers." The two ladies, tired but thrilled about their journey, seized a taxi and off they went to the Catholic school for a few days to explore this fascinating city.

"I don't understand how to manage the Lira yet. Can you help?" "No worries, I got it. You can buy me a cappuccino." "That is nice of you. Sure thing, I will, but not an espresso. I don't know how people drink it," said Lexi, puckering up her lips and shaking her head, causing them both to giggle.

Lexi rang the doorbell outside the big wrought-iron gate. Though it was dark and kind of spooky, the full moon shone in the courtyard, beaming a silver glow upon the marble tiles. Along came a nun shuffling her feet, greeting them in Italian, and motioning them to come and follow her. The mysterious, narrow hallway amplified the sound of each step and echoed with eerie reverberations. It was quiet and one could hear their own breath or heartbeat. The nun did not say a word. She showed the way, walking in her leather pump heels and holding her rosary beads, praying.

A dazzling beam of silver light blinded their eyes as they turned the corner. Good Lord, has Jesus arrived? Lexi wondered. The closer they strolled towards the light, an exquisite, enormous sculpture of Jesus appeared in front of them, all aglow. Their room was right there. Go figure, my pal is here guiding and protecting me again. *Thanks, Jesus.*

The girls walked into what appeared to be a classroom during the school season. Six cots were lined up in a row, as the room was now set up as a hostel for young adults. The sister did her best to interpret in English where to meet for a continental breakfast. "Hmm, cots, eh? One sheet and a modest pillow. This should be fun. I guess this is why it is only eight dollars a night. Breakfast included. I am grateful." She laid her tired body on the rickety old cot and dozed off. Sleeping was easy, especially since Jesus watched over her right outside the door.

Lexi scrambled to the restroom immediately upon awakening, squeezing her legs tightly together, when she abruptly stopped in her tracks. She was startled to see young men were likewise in line for the same facility. "Buongiorno," they all said courteously. "Where are the ladies' rooms located?" "Here," replied an American, a youthful man with curly blonde hair. "Oh, dear." He snorted, realizing they did not acquaint her with the coed bathrooms. "Why are there no doors?" she asked. "No worries, I can hold a large towel up if you like." "I like," she said, giggling. Adam was his name. A nice young man from Kansas, USA, and someone she would relate to during her holiday here, mostly in the bathroom. Quite comical, she mused. At shower time, the two would collide. Always polite, she expressed her gratitude for the "cover up." They talked about the cool people they met. Adam was a solo adventurer with a small backpack and leaving soon to explore Germany.

The sweet, tempting smells of fresh-baked pastries tantalized the young women. They followed their noses straight to the modest dining space with dark mahogany table and chairs. Continental breakfast consisted of a multitude of homemade, warm delicacies and coffee with warm milk. Everything was delicious and undeniably better than the espresso. "Is your friend arriving today?" "I expect she will be here tomorrow. If you would like to explore this city with me, I would gladly show you some impressive sights," Dina responded. "Yes, please!" Lexi's schoolgirl excitement bounced off the walls. The nun walked in with a stern expression. Dutifully, she poured each of them another cup of coffee. Lexi instantly realized eyes, smiles, and hand gestures are a natural form of communication. It would guide her through this country and her minuscule knowledge of the language. She politely bowed her head with respect and gratitude as the nun quietly walked away.

Swiftly, the girls hustled through the opulent city. The architecture and design blew Lexi's mind. She spun round and round, her eyes twirling in astonishment to assimilate it all. "You're going to get dizzy, girl!" Dina exclaimed. "I'm amazed! I never imagined such splendor all in one place. How does one take it all in?" "Purposely, like a slice of pizza. You take in it deliberately and lick your lips." "Pizza! That is my favorite meal, Dina! Ahh, to savor pizza all over the earth! That's a goal!" The two young women laughed. Dina enjoyed Lexi's wonder, charming expressions, and innocence. Something she lost way too young in her life.

"Andiamo! Come!" "Wait, I want to experience more!" "Come, we have much more to do! I'm about to bring to light another world for you. Let's go!" Ahh, such innocence, naivety. The time had come for her to know the real world, Dina thought, smirking. Undoubtedly, she had other things on her mind as she sashayed her curvy hips, catching the attention of the gentlemen.

Rushing across the piazza, Lexi stopped on a dime, peering up at the remarkably extraordinary bronze-colored doors. "What is this?" "The Gates of Paradise," an indifferent-sounding Dina said. In profound reverence Lexi evaluated every detail of each gilded-bronze sculpted story. The artist, Lorenzo Ghiberti, recounts a tale in moving fashion. One becomes part of the scene. The Bible stories revealed unforgettable accounts of love, soul connections, fates, and sacrifices. They were created during the early part of the Early Renaissance, which began in 1425. Lexi needed to know everything, but Dina had another agenda.

"My camera would never capture such exquisite composition. I shall feast my eyes upon each panel and devour it with my heart. I will never forget this moment! My eyes have witnessed the glory of one man's expressive abilities. The extent of his imagination, his brilliance to create. His interpretation will rest upon my soul forever." Lexi's passion and brilliance opened unexpectedly. "You are certainly the intense young lady. The Italians will adore your spirit." Lexi eagerly jotted in her journal details she could research subsequently. A faint breeze swirled, the sun casting a ray of light adorning each panel with a peace hue. Awestruck, it was hard to contain herself. "These doors will remind me of my pilgrimage." She left the page blank to explore one day.

Was she being guided to something? Is the door a symbol of life? Hmm, she thought, placing her finger to her lip. Bowing in devotion, she entered the cathedral of Santa Maria Del Fiore. Frankincense graced the elegant space with an ineffable presence. Her eyes swelled with tears. An emotional time, yet she was unable to identify precisely why this experience was so intense. Dina, on the other hand, didn't care and dashed around the cathedral. She remained restless. Glancing up, Lexi noticed the elegance of the dome, fascinated by every stroke, blended colors flowing with their brush and marveling at how the imagination of each artist accomplished this magic, yearning to do the same. "Dina, do you know where I can attend art classes?" Dina just ignored her. With a deep sigh, she knelt on the velvet covered wooden bench.

Thank you, Jesus, for guiding me here and teaching me a greater sense of reverence. It seems like I have been here. You graced me with your spirit as a little girl and I knew you were my protector. I always know you are with me and please protect Dina too.

"Come, Lexi!" "Just another minute, please." Dina rolled her eyes, saying, "I'll meet you outside." The organ player began manipulating the ivory keys from the balcony above. "Oh, to sing here would be such an inspiration!" Absorbing the melody within her cells, she reminisced of the time she sang "O Holy Night" at Midnight Mass. As she walked toward the exit, her eyes captured as much of the charm her soul could consume. She cherished every contour of the sculptures, so exquisitely defined, every brush of oil on the canvases. Never had she experienced such intense gratitude for art, not even in her favorite library.

Dancing down the stairs, she called out, "I shall return. I know it!" Yanking her hand, Dina said, "Yes, Lexi, I am confident you will. Now carry on. We have to go investigate those hot, suave Italian men if you wish to admire true anatomy. Lexi, reluctant, realized Dina had quite a different agenda.

"Ahh, Lexi, here are the delicacies I promised!" "Wait, can you slow down?" "No, young lady. You must become enlightened with God's diverse gifts, Italian men!" Dina demonstrated confidence, worldliness, and indeed was quite the flirt as she tipped her head slightly, coyly smiling, while running her fingers through her shiny dark brown hair. The men whistled as she flaunted her goods. She clearly basked in the attention and soaked it in. They heard music playing nearby, when Dina announced, "Come look at the statue of David and learn about anatomy, my friend. You appreciate elegant curves, right?" They took some photos, giggling like schoolgirls.

The two gals packed up their belongings and moved to another hostel in a nearby region, outside of Florence. Their host was a pleasant local woman named Gabriella. The type who takes you into their soft, comfy arms and welcomes you into their family. They both loved her instantly and were happy to have a real bed and their own bathroom. Their window faced a small alley where they could see the neighbors. They hung their laundry out to dry on ropes extending between the buildings. Neighbors chatted across the way and there was typically an older gray-haired woman leaning over the window, observing and examining everything. Gabriella had already chatted with Dina earlier when she arranged the reservation to do something wonderful to surprise Lexi for her birthday. "No problem, Dina. My cousin, he owns a local restaurant. He has a nightlife, you say, music and entertainment," she responded in her broken English. "We can make a party, yes?" Lexi had no idea this was the plan.

A Night to Remember

"Where are we going?" "Trust me, you will love it!" In the near distance, you could hear local music being played, the aroma of Italian delicacies swirling through the air, and the excited chatter of people assembling for a party.

"A party? What's going on, Dina?" "Just trust me, birthday girl." "How did you know?" "Don't be mad, but I saw you scribble it at the top of your journal." "No worries, but don't read the rest, okay?" Immediately, a striking, robust man with espresso-colored eyes, named Antonio greeted Lexi with his hand extended. "Bella, dance with me." Before she could react, he twirled her onto the dance floor, a place she enjoyed. Pumped with energy, vibrant and seductive, she moved on her tip toes across the floor, radiating her natural femininity, showing it off. Heads were turning. Her smile made everyone smile along with her.

The petite yellow lights graced the trees while subtle fragrances from flowers in bloom intoxicated her senses. Her love for dancing reminded her of a whirling dervish she saw in a movie that took place in Egypt. Intrigued, she practiced at home to spin every opportunity she had. It was better than being tipsy. She regarded it as another form of consciousness, she mused with her friends. Of course, they snickered and said, "Just smoke a joint." Lexi had no interest in anything but the natural high of life and nature. The tune merged into a romantic, slow dance. Antonio embraced this delicate beauty, feeling her heart pound excitedly. He imagined it might be for him. Alas, Lexi had never given her heart to any man…yet.

Lexi enchanted Antonio. She was now his new prey. He whispered in her ear, "You delight and fascinate me, young lady." Lexi giggled, drained from spinning. She honestly wanted to rest. She wasn't interested in being pursued. Antonio became persistent and kissed her on the cheek. Perhaps it was the time to stop dancing with him, she thought. Her mother was relentless in preparing her for how to protect herself.

My birthday is tonight. I shall enjoy this new experience. I shall celebrate my rite of passage and awakening! "Tell me, bella, what is your desire?" "I just want to dance!" "Then we shall dance the night away, together." Their chemistry was undoubtedly intense. They were an attractive couple. Locals were applauding and encouraging them to dance further. It appeared they were a perfect match, at least for dancing.

Antonio was worldly, experienced, handsome, and much older than Lexi. The owner and Dina were wheeling out an enormous birthday cake, decorated with festive colors, flowers and candles. On cue, Antonio twirled her around. She was stunned to see such a celebratory display. The entire crowd sang "Happy Birthday" in Italian. Lexi never expected this. She acknowledged Dina with a smile and thanked her while the crowd encouraged her to blow out the candles. Dina gave her a hug, expressed thanks for their journey together, not telling her she would soon escape to her next venture. She had a notion Lexi would try to stop her. It was time for both of them to move on. Her friend never appeared after the three days in Florence. Soon they would meet up in Greece once she made her impromptu exit. They chatted on the phone and had a plan for their next destination. Lexi expressed concern for her friend. It was a pattern for her to disappear mysteriously. Dina was expressionless and replied, "She is probably on her newest mysterious quest." Lexi was happy and caught up in the excitement of her party, she never saw Dina slipping away.

The dancing, the wine, and the cake all made her head spin. The moment came when she almost fainted. "Antonio, I must go to the hostel. I am exhausted. Do you see Dina anywhere?" "No, but I shall escort you back?" "I suppose, because I am not well." Antonio was a gentleman and literally carried her halfway, when, she fainted right into his arms. He would like to believe it was his charm. He knew otherwise and hurried to get her to the room at the hostel. Gabriella opened the wrought-iron gate and thanked him for bringing her home safely. They put her to bed and off to dreamland she went. Gabriella assured him she would take care of the young lady. "You, a nice man to bring her. Goodnight; now, go. She must sleep," waving her hands to push him out the door. Gabriella locked the wrought-iron gate and went back in to tend to Lexi.

The next morning, Lexi called out to Dina, to no avail. She looked for Antonio to see if he had stayed. He was nowhere to be found. She called out to Gabriella, and she rushed in. "You okay, child?" "Yes, but where is everyone? I have a headache." "No surprise. You had much fun last night, *si*? Antonio, he carry you back." "Did he stay the night?" Gabrielle chuckled and said, "No, no, babies last night," with a wink. "He came here this morning. He had beautiful flowers and a note." Lexi swooned over the elaborate flowers while reading his kind note.

Dearest princess, you are divine. My wish for you... to have many wonderful days in this beautiful country. You must explore. I would like to make you happy, but I know you must go.
Love, Antonio

"Wow, my first love note, Gabriella!" "I sure you will get many. Men will court you. *Andiamo!* Let's get breakfast. We must go to my cousin's. She has gift shop. Time to buy presents for your *famiglia*." "Wait, where is Dina?" "How do I put this?" said Gabriella, placing her finger on her lips, "Girls like that are *puttana*, you know...how you say, whore?" Lexi, being naïve, shook her head no. It sort of made sense how freely Dina acted around men. "Come, shopping, beautiful young lady, coming up." Gabriella may not have always spoken grammatically correct English, but she did her best and got her point across.

"That sounds so fun. I love shopping." After lots of laughter and a charming time together, Lexi thanked Gabriella for breakfast and her hospitality. Her bags packed; off she went to find Maria's gift shop. First, a long Italian hug, replete with tears, laughter, kisses, a big squeeze, and a snack bag. Gabriella initiated her in to the "family," with both of them giggling joyfully. Lexi followed the directions carefully and found a narrow alleyway with many gift shops.

A well-rounded woman with an apron said, "*Buongiorno*, you be Lexi." She spoke with a heavy Italian accent. "Yes, ma'am, I am. How did you know?" "Ahh, because my cousin, she described your cheeks, your lips, and your eyes." Her hands waved around while she talked. No one ever mentioned my round cheeks before. They were squeezable, and Italians liked to pinch them. Lexi had an annoying uncle who used to pinch her cheeks when she was little. She hated it and would run away. "Ahh, yes, that would be me," she said, laughing. "Your cousin Gabriella is a beautiful, kind woman." "They taught us to be kind. We make our guests like *famiglia*. Come, let me show you. You buy. It's good. Lots of nice things." Her chubby, soft hand grasped Lexi's and off they went into the overstocked gift shop. Colorful porcelain hot plates and teapots, linen towels embroidered nicely, Italian leather wallets, and gloves and shoes lined the shelves.

Maria watched Lexi peeking at the shoes. "Come, let's try. Here, some nice red ones. Every woman, she needs red shoes." Lexi, always polite, would oblige, though Maria didn't realize it was her least favorite color. The two ladies laughed, and Maria kept giving Lexi cookie samples. "Come, you buy some," she said, signaling with her hands. By the time she was done, Lexi had absolutely no room in her suitcase for air. "That was so much fun. Thank you for showing me all your beautiful gifts, and I love my red shoes," she said, lifting her foot coquettishly. I will surely have to learn to love this color red, she chuckled to herself. She never imagined in a million years she would wear red.

"Maria, I must get to the airport. I need a ride. Where can I find one?" "No problem…my cousin, he take you. He is good." Everyone is a cousin around here. I wonder if that is code for 'buy here,' she wondered. "*Grazie,*" she said. Maria called down the block, "Mario!" waving for him to come. "You take this lovely child to airport now. Get her safely to the station. She is a friend of Gabriella's." Everyone, of course, had to hug again, laugh, mushy wet kisses, and hug some more. Lexi waved from inside the car. She was ready to go home.

The following few months sailed by rapidly. Lexi had to decide what to do with her life next. Originally, college was the plan. Now she sought to explore the world. *What would Dad say?*

Perhaps the world will be my training, as she braced to break the announcement to her parents when she returned home.

*I believe every woman should own
at least one pair of red shoes.*

—Terry Tempest Williams

CHAPTER 5

Italy

Café 2014

An echoing impact, a pounding vibration, reverberated through the alley. Someone glided across the blue and white tile floors and jerked Alexandra out of her daydream. *What happened, where was I? I'm sure traveling back in time today. What provoked all these memories? I must finish my drink and pizza. Time to move on for the day.*

Poor guy. That was a dreadful fall. Taking another sip of her chianti, she had a vision of an incident when she had a dreadful fall, many ages ago, in North Carolina. *I'm trying to remember how old I was,* she wrote in her journal.

"Miss, you okay?" Marcello asked. He looked concerned. "No worries. I watched the man slip, and it reminded me of an unpleasant calamity I had when I was younger." "We will help him. Can I get something else for you?"

"I have eaten pizza around the world, kind sir. None was more satisfying than this one, the flavors bursting, the cheese dripping down my chin."

"*Grazie,* I am delighted you appreciate it. I own and operate this cafe for many years. I'm deeply honored. Take your time and later, dessert? My treat. Do you wish for an espresso?" "Oh dear, *no* espresso," she exclaimed, gagging and laughing. "Cappuccino would be splendid. Thank you for allowing me to remain here for hours and record my stories in my journal." "No trouble, bella. I'm surprised. You no like espresso. Yes, a splendid day, as you say, and wine," he said with a slightly turned up smile.

Alexandra was about to share the story about her experience with espresso when she was younger. At that moment, someone distracted her. A casual traveler passed by; a charming smile was exchanged. She returned to her experiences, writing about the loves she had and the ones that left, and completely forgot to explain. Alexandra drifted off again. Every little incident prompted a memory.

Times passes, memories fade. A heart never forgets.

CHAPTER 6

New York City

"Dad, can I get your opinion on something?" Lexi was worried he would discuss nothing with her if she asked a question. She learned a long time ago, he solely preferred to advise.

"What can I help you with?" "I have a dilemma and don't laugh at me." Of course, he couldn't contain a sneer. "Go ahead. What is the drama this time?" *Geez, why does he always say "drama?"* Lexi didn't dare allow herself to get annoyed at his choice of words. "I really loved visiting Italy. I learned so many things. It gave me a great abundance of knowledge, and I learned a lot about myself." "And?" he asked in a sarcastic tone. "I was considering taking extra time to explore the world. You know, mature before starting college? I wondered what you thought about this concept?"

"Absolutely not! You will not waste time and flounder around partying and probably running into trouble. We didn't waste money on etiquette school so you can go play. I didn't father you so you can take my responsibility lightly. It chose me to provide you a better way in life. Enough said!" "But Dad…please listen." "Listen to what? You have no basis, nothing to debate, you prefer to play around. I said, *no*!"

Her mother overheard the argument and attempted to settle her father down, but it didn't work. "Alexandra, your father is trying to do what is best for you." "How does anyone understand what's best for me other than myself? He never encourages me; he merely criticizes me. He constantly negates everything I desire and offers positively no help! I plan on working to pay for it all. He is not liable for anything!" she yelled.

"Young lady, you don't speak this way to us! Go to your room!" her father shouted. "I'm eighteen and you have nothing to say or hold over me any longer!" "Get an actual job and take care of yourself if you're so smart. Let's see how that goes!"

Lexi's mother broke down in tears, concerned that Lexi would do something drastic, and her father would shut her out. Frustrated, she ran to her room, and slammed the door. She vowed not to speak to "that" man until he apologized. "Fat chance!" Lexi cried for hours. Her passion ran so deep; her insights were coming in even stronger. Guidance was knocking at her door. She knew she couldn't avoid these messages. Perhaps Mom can talk some sense into him, she wrote in her journal.

It will all work out. I will take care of you, a soft feminine voice announced. *Grandma, is that you? Whose voice is this?*

A tap on her bedroom door woke her around midnight. It had to be her mother; her dad was working the midnight shift this week. "Come in." "Alexandra, please don't upset your father. He works extremely hard to take care of us." "Mom, I absolutely get it. I appreciate everything. You are the one who stands behind me. I often get a strange feeling he never wanted me." "That is not true, honey. Alexandra, it may take some work. Be patient and I will figure it out. What I can do is attempt to show him the value. You will mature through life experiences," she said with a wink. "I love you more than you imagine. Thanks, mom."

Over the following few weeks, Lexi's mom would find ways to show her husband how beneficial it would be for their precocious child to learn more about herself. She even suggested it might be wise to reconsider the investment for a college education. He surmised what she was doing and ultimately realized there was substance in her insights. "Perhaps you are correct, dear. This child needs to find out who she is." "Do you want to break the news to her? I think it would be good if she received your support in this decision." "Sure."

Lexi's mom knew all too well, she may find out things that were kept secret for many years.

CHAPTER 7

North Carolina

Several Months Later

"*A*dios, everybody! See you in a few months." Hugging her mom, her dad, and brother, like her survival depended on it, Lexi had her backpack, hiking boots, and a map of the Smokey Mountains in North Carolina. Looks like a perfect place for an adventure.

Lexi knew she needed private time to process personal concerns tormenting her. She borrowed a friend's jeep and had some extra cash saved from her last trip. Off she rode to determine what her future held. Dad agreed to allow her to explore even if she had to remain in the US. It was a fair compromise for both. Music blasting, belting out the tunes, in her own world, she drove for hours. There was a storm brewing this week, according to reports. She needed to arrive prior to the rain so she could enjoy a hike or two.

The trip on the interstate took her west. The North Carolina mountains crested over the asphalt pavement as the sun was setting, casting dazzling rays of orange and lavender hues. She was eager to get to Cherokee and drained from the long ride. "Practically there, I've got this," struggling to keep her weary eyes focused on the road. Lexi spoke out loud to herself a lot. It was almost as if there was always someone with her. Perhaps there was. "Well, I'm pleased I decided not to camp the initial few days. I wouldn't consider setting up a tent after this lengthy trip. Who am I kidding? This city girl has never gone camping." Spontaneous thoughts floated in her wild mind. Or was it exhaustion? "I would love to meet a shaman. I've only read about them." Random images popped into her overactive brain.

The deep forest-green jeep turned left on a gravel road, lined with a canopy of immense trees, producing shadows along the way. It was getting dark, and Lexi was hesitant. She was in no mood to get lost. Suddenly, an inner voice spoke up, *You will be fine. All is taken care of, my child.* Seems that voice shows up before I'm in trouble. I hope nothing dangerous is coming my way, she thought. "Where have you been?" she asked. No answer. Either way, she had a soothing sense. "Phew, I made it." She turned the engine off. Grabbing her backpack, she playfully skipped up to the door, where she noticed a note and key in the envelope.

Welcome, Lexi. We hope your stay is everything you wished for and more. Signed, Rosa.

Cool. Guess I just wander in and make myself at home.

Then she spoke out loud as the revelation hit her. "Rosa, that's kind of strange. That was my grandma's name. Hmm, another coincidence?" Signs would guide Lexi on this adventure, and one could only hope she would not overlook them. Her spirit guide was fully present to provide the education she required.

Opening the rickety old door gave her an eerie feeling. Lexi looked over her shoulder to be certain no one was there. One step in, the original wooden floors made creaking noises, alarming her. She was a little apprehensive about being out here alone. She sighed. Straight ahead, she saw a stone fireplace and a small round wooden table with two chairs. A glass jar with a flower had been placed on the table.

The strap of the backpack was poking into her shoulder, and Lexi started removing the extra weight, dropping it on a small twin bed with a green plaid comforter. It was cozy, musty, and clearly not up-to-date décor, but it had charm. "Nothing like ambiance!" After a brisk shower, she lay down, exhausted, on the squeaky old couch and was ready to journal. Tapping the pen on the cover, like she always does, she imagined what this adventure would bring and if she would meet any fascinating people.

Dear Diary, or should I add future novelist? I'm about to enter a dimension where no gal has traveled before. Well, this girl anyway. These mountains, which the Cherokee Indians have inhabited are sacred. Maybe I'm drawn to these peaks for a reason? Dare I declare divine alignment? Is it synchronicity? The person who signed the note is named Rosa. Grandma, are you here? Give me a sign. Maybe that was you?

Lexi wondered if it equally fascinated others--the unknown, the unusual, the metaphysical, philosophical, and sacred cultures. A free thinker, one could never surmise what she would blurt out randomly.

Wisdom, inner wisdom. Someday, I will write about it and the world will understand the possibilities.

Tired, as she was about to drift off to sleep, she scribbled these last words: *Who knows what artifacts, gifts, and people will cross my path on this adventure? What magic will I discover? Perhaps a manifestation of my dreams.*

"Holy shit, I see the light," Lexi squealed, chuckling as a striking yellow ray of sun flickered on her face. "Okay, whoever wishes me up, I got the message."

I wish I had known my grandma. I understand she was a unique person. If not for her, I don't believe I would have such a free spirit. No one else in the family has it. Perhaps I will connect with her on this trip, listen better, and learn what she has been trying to tell me.

Just then, Lexi was startled by a loud noise outside and practically jumped out of her skin. Stepping purposely towards the window, she drew back the old curtains and saw nothing. Presumably, it was just a squirrel in the leaves. At least she hoped so. "Hello?" she called out. "Hello, anyone there?" Not a peep. Lexi spotted a ceramic teapot, which reminded her of the one she had from Grandma. When Grandma Rosa passed, her mother gave her this gift. "This teapot is from Italy. The tin is yours with some coins. Oh, and this note too. It's all special and while it may not make sense, it will someday." "I never met her, but for some reason, I always feel like I did, Mom." There was no response from her mother as Lexi opened the gift. Secrets always seemed to exist, she realized.

Intriguing combination of presents. A chipped, multicolored ceramic teapot brought from Italy. I will keep it dear because evidently, she did too. A tin can. What, pray tell, could be the relevance of this? Well, with Grandma you never know the symbolism of her messages. I suppose I will learn one day.

"Oh, and one other thing I practically forgot." Her mom reached for a satin pouch with a piece of jewelry inside. "I wish for you to have this." "Isn't this yours?" "Yes, I am aware you have adored it since you were a little girl. I want you to have it." "Wow, it's been my favorite piece of jewelry!" "I know. I watched you admire it in the jewelry box for years. You were so cute, quietly sneaking into the room. You would dance through the curtains as the wind blew, like a ballerina." "You knew?"

"Yes, sweet child. I knew you had a connection with it. The cracked colored glass which created that lovely bouquet of light always intrigued you. I would watch your eyes beam, fascinated, dancing in circles like a ballerina." Hugging her mom and crying at the same moment, Lexi realized there was nothing more significant than receiving this right now in her life. For years, she prayed one day this would be hers. Why today? It will be a good luck charm, she promised herself. Lexi accepted the precious gift and would take it everywhere. Today was no different. Touching her hand on the pocket of her jeans, she noted, "Yup, there it is."

Ready to go, she yearned for a dog. Seemed fitting to travel with a buddy and have someone to protect her. "Canteen with water, check; journal and pen, camera and film, hat and sunglasses. I think I'm ready to go!" The map said the hike would be roughly three and a half miles. *Easy to do. Maybe I will meet an Indian.* All packed and ready to go in her jeep, she looked over to her right as if she were talking to a dog in the passenger seat. *I have to remember to be careful what I say and reflect. Speaking of symbols, I wonder which ones will appear today?* Her inner knowing was usually spot on. Most times, if she remained really in tune, something magical or entertaining happened. When she didn't pay attention, well, it could definitely create for an interesting adventure or encounter. Either way, she always had lessons appear.

The drive was about five miles to the national park. Since she would arrive early, surely it wouldn't be too crowded. According to the weather report, there was less of a chance of rain in those first few hours. Singing songs from the '70s, she happily went on her way.

Remember the "signs," Lexi. They are everywhere, a whisper from "somewhere" reminded her. *Interesting, this whisper differs from all the ones I've heard previously.*

The first sign she saw read, "Overlook on the right." Lexi didn't want to stop and besides, what did she have to overlook? She just wanted to get to the trail.

Enormous trees pleasantly embraced the drive, reflecting shadows on the road. Lexi looked for signs from the trees and the rocks. She could always discover faces, animal spirits, and ancient ones within them. It intrigued her, especially since most people were not aware of them. Nature was like a home for this young lady, one that mysteriously intrigued her. The sun was glaring directly in her eyes, placing on her sunglasses, she wasn't concerned because there were no clouds yet, in the sky. She was excited to see where she would be led today. Suddenly, thump went the tires, sending a jolt to her system.

She sent up a prayer that the rock she just hit didn't blow a tire. Jamming on the brakes, she jumped out of the car to examine the situation. "Damn, seriously, did I *overlook* something?" There was actually some humor in that, she smirked. "All is good. Perhaps a warning?" The road beckoned ahead, and she suddenly had a lighter sense of energy; in fact, it was almost magical. Without much concern, she was confident all would be fine, and she would be safe. A bird was tweeting as if speaking to Lexi, like she would understand. "That's pretty cool. What's up, dude? Will any of your friends visit me today? I would love to take your photo." Then the bird whistled.

He acknowledged her. Holding her camera steady, she peeked through the lens, hoping to capture a photo of this delightful new friend and perhaps others. She didn't see any, not even the one who had whistled.

The sun was still bright and warm as she scanned the trees slowly. She tiptoed, not wanting to scare any birds away. Looking up between the branches, she spotted something, a tinge of yellow. Imagining, as usual, words floated through her brain, thinking she would capture a stunning photo and submit it to *National Geographic. Yes, they will feature me on the cover. I can see it now. 'Young woman captures exquisite, rare bird.' Then I can tell others I'm a nationally recognized photographer.* Lexi always believed if she affirmed things in writing, out loud or in her head positively, she could achieve anything.

"I wonder if it was a yellow-throated warbler?" "Eww, was that bird poop which just landed on my arm? C'mon little guy, I know you are there. I sure hope this is not rain, because I like the idea of bird poop versus raindrops." She laughed at herself. "Damn, I lost it! Where did you go? You had to speak out loud, Lexi, right? Great, now I have to pray for another." She prayed to Great Spirit silently this time. *Oh, Great Spirit, I wish for you to send me a bird, not just any bird, but one which will stun the world when they see my photo.*

Just then, something made a "swooshing" sound and startled Lexi. "What the heck?" *Listen, overlook nothing.* "Who is sending these messages?"

As she continued, the trail became narrower and steeper. The mountains had a smokey haze and a mysterious depth to them. The leaves were brilliant and about to turn colors for fall. Deep greens blending with soft yellows and brilliant oranges were a delightful sight to her eyes. Lexi was happy she would have a few weeks to explore the mountains. Quite the opportunity to see many things in nature and make wonderful stories.

Slippery when wet. This time, Lexi did not pay attention to the sign; however, she wasn't concerned because it wasn't raining. Unfortunately, she did not have a device to stay informed of weather updates. A sweet scent captured her attention. It must be the pine trees, she thought, pulling her attention away from her focus. Was something warning her to slow down? "Holy shit!" Out of nowhere, big cumulonimbus clouds rolled across the sky while she was peering up through the pine trees. "Guess it wasn't bird poop." Laughing at her own sense of humor.

She realized she must find cover quickly or go back. Just then, a bolt of lightning scared the crap out of her, hitting the tree she was standing by. As the tree bark crackled and burned, she jumped back to avoid any further unwelcomed incidents. "What the hell?" she blurted out. "You trying to kill me, or did you need to hit me over my head to wake me up?" She slipped. Unable to stabilize herself, her body spun around. She threw her hands up, trying to balance herself. But the slippery mud on a rock rolled her over. She hit her head hard, leaving her dazed and disoriented. The rain poured in buckets and no doubt a flash flood could happen in this region, with a storm of this magnitude coming on so suddenly. Fading into oblivion, she would not recall much.

CHAPTER 8

Italy

Café 2014

That was quite a flashback. It's interesting, she wrote, *how an incident like the man slipping reminded me of this time. I had so many signs back then, now they are obvious. Hmm, am I being warned or guided again? Let me think,* she mused, with her pen resting on her cheek.

There was a great lesson in the Smokey Mountains, but how does this correlate, she pondered. "Don't *overlook* the signs." "That's it!" she shouted. "I'm being told again. 'Over Look,' two words or one? What does it mean this time?" Interesting, she continued to scribble, always a sense of humor from up above. Closing her eyes to reflect deeper, perhaps she could sense a message being revealed. She held her lucky charm and connected with her mother's mosaic brooch.

Pay attention to everything, the soft feminine voice intoned.

Just then Marcello ran over when the shouting from Alexandra startled him. "*Bella,* what is wrong? You call out? Did you need something?" Embarrassed, "My apologies. I was thinking out loud." As Marcello walked away, he began singing "Volaré" once again.

"*Scusi,*" Alexandra called out. Marcello turned around and acknowledged her. "Why do you love that song so much? My father also sang it all the time." "Ahh, your father was Italian?" "Yes, he would dance in the kitchen while cooking and sing this song. I would join in, and we would laugh while mixing up the ingredients for a fresh meal. It was the only thing we had in common." "I see your father was much like me. I dance in my kitchen too," he laughed. "Does it have something to do with blue eyes and the sky?" she asked. "*Si*, it does. I once fell in love with someone and I always think if I sing this song to the stars, she will return." "Please continue, I think it is very lovely." As Marcello's soft melodic voice entranced her, Alexandra floated away. She disappeared again to the sound of his voice.

Pay attention, Alexandra, the signs are here. This time, the whisper was faint.

CHAPTER 9

The Cave

North Carolina

Lexi jumped out of her stupor, wondering how she got in the cave. "Who are you?" she asked an old man, abruptly. "Where am I?" "I am the 'One.'" "The one? One *what?*" In a New York city tone, he replied, "I am the one who came to save your ass," humoring her. "Humph," she said. But as she went to put her hands across her chest, a sudden pain ran up her neck. "Ouch! What the—?" "You took a nasty fall during that sudden tornado when it whipped through the mountains. Do you remember anything?" "Not much. But do I know you? You kind of look like a photo on a brochure I picked up years ago." The two laughed. "Your name is Alexandra, correct?" "How did you know my proper name?" "Because I am the One who knows and was sent to you because you asked for me." "Stop. You looked at my driver's license, obviously!" He shook his head no.

"Alexandra is a powerful name given only to the courageous ones. It is a journey which brings much wisdom. You are the defender. When people hear the name 'Alexandra,' they perceive that person as someone who is impressive, elegant, and noble. You possess creative qualities as well, similar to actors, dancers, and performers. People admire your confident personality. Unfortunately, there are others who get jealous of you." "Oh great. But will it bring fun, my soul mate, and the chance to sing on stage?"

"Life has a way of bringing you things, yes? Not always, as one perceives it. Take, for example, the fact you overlooked the overlook and drove right by it. Then you overlooked the warning sign, 'Slippery when wet.'" "So?" "Well, perspective is everything. Perhaps, one day, you will see this as one of the most enlightening adventures you've ever had, opening a new world for you." "Huh?" "Is it possible you have already met your soul mate, or he is standing in front of you?" "You're nuts. Why would you say that?" she blurted. "Help me up, please. I need to get home."

He held out his hand, gesturing for her to stay. "Allow me to introduce myself. I am Atohi—ah-*toh*-hee. I walk between worlds. Do you know what that means?" "I read a book about a shaman years ago, it is some type of gift where one can feel or imagine being in two places at once. Like one foot lives now and the other one steps on the land one hundred years ago." "Have you ever had this experience, Alexandra? Like you just knew something or were so deeply touched by something? You just knew you would remember it in your heart forever. Déjà vu, some call it." "I suppose, several times. I often tune into a voice from another dimension. However, one memory is etched in the chambers of my heart. The bronze doors, the Gates of Paradise, in Italy." "Why do you think that impacted you so deeply?"

"I'm not sure. It was like looking at something I created with my own hands. That is impossible, because I am not a sculptor or metal craftsperson. However, I have this uncanny connection with Italy. Maybe, I did have another lifetime there."

The old man rubbed the left side of his head, pondering. "Am I overlooking something again?" she asked, the sarcasm ringing in her voice. He remained quiet, which frustrated Lexi. Her patience was wearing thin, as her head was pounding. It was like he sat there in stillness, waiting for her brain to burst. The old man sat calmly with his eyes closed. Lexi didn't realize he was projecting images, lifetimes, or perhaps, some sort of sign. Suddenly she felt an electrical burst run through her forehead, known as the third eye. She couldn't make out the symbols or numbers, and she found it quite confusing. An intuitive sense told her to let it flow and not focus on what she thinks she sees but allow what needs to be seen. Ocean waves, with the deepest blues, rapidly flowed into her head, followed by triangular shapes, trees, a man, a temple, and a cougar. They got faster until she got dizzy and passed out.

"Whoa, what was that?" she asked as she woke. *Trippy stuff.* "You didn't give me any weird herbal hallucinatory drugs, did you or am I dreaming?" "No, we don't need them when we open to our channels of wisdom. You will learn more. One day, it will be revealed to you." Lexi looked at her watch and said she needed to get back to her cabin. "Where can I wash off around here? Is there a pond or waterfall? I'm so muddy!" "Yes, you can find one down the path to the right. Follow the signs. I hope to see you again someday." "But wait!" he said, as he urgently stopped her. "I must cleanse you with sage and bless your journey." "Sure, whatever! Thanks for the help."

That was kind of cool. I feel renewed from the cleansing. What she didn't know was while she was unconscious, the shaman prayed over her soul. He performed a ceremony considered for initiates, and it was why she saw all those symbols later. He knew who she was. One day it would make sense to her, and she would remember.

Lexi took smaller, more deliberate steps this time. The path was narrow, windy and bumpy. "Geez, isn't anything easy?" The bushes and trees were getting dense, and the natural sunlight was diminishing. "Oh yippee, now I get to walk in the dusk, not knowing what lies ahead." In the distance, rustling sounds in bushes caught her attention as the rushing waters flowed down the creek. "Ahh, I must be closer. Hey little critters, stay away from me, please."

Just then, she saw a warning sign posted in bright yellow, "Avoid standing on the waterfall. Slippery." *I have no plans of standing on it, just washing off. No problem.* The gushing sound of the powerful water got louder. Lexi's excitement had her heart pounding. Waterfalls were one of her favorite things in the world. They brought her peace and took her back to a place where she always found herself as a young teen. It gave her solace and insights. She recalled a large slate rock beneath a waterfall, a place her parents would take her to in the mountains. It was then she began writing poetry. This place seemed similar to it. Was she having *Deja vu* or dreaming all of this?

Every step was diligent. She would not slip and slide this time. Shimmering rays of the sun, flickering out of her view; the sky would soon darken. Lexi had a sense of calm and understood this was where she needed to be at this moment.

I'm here with you. "I really wish you would tell me who you are. Am I going insane?"

"Anyway, I just love this!" she exclaimed. "I'm going to sit here and just allow the water to cleanse me. It's what I asked to hear, all the sounds of nature, communing in the oneness of creation." The bubbling sounds of the water flowing over the rocks made a loud hissing while tiny droplets fell to the next level like a chain of diamonds. It was magical. "This feels amazing. Nature's spa treatment, I declare. All of life can go on without me." As she swished her dirty feet in the cold creek below, the water was renewing her spirit.

Suddenly, a roaring, powerful gush of water pounded down with a ferocious force, knocking Lexi into the creek as she attempted to get out of the way. The creek was flowing rapidly. Lexi laughed as if this was part of her journey, but as the creek got wider and the rocks got bigger, she decided it was no longer fun. "Oh, dear heavens, what have I got myself into this time? Jesus, are you going to help me? Please!" Just then, she tumbled over, nearly hitting her head again. When she opened her eyes, the water was calmer. Only now she was headed straight towards another waterfall. "Shit! Hold on for the ride, girl!" Taking in a deep breath, she imagined she was the female version of Indiana Jones: Nothing was going to stop her or harm her. Her body pounded into the deep indigo pool below. Floating down further, a vortex of energy captured her in a cyclone or funnel of water...*going where?* she wondered. Remaining conscious, she was aware of glitter and sparkles rapidly passing her by. She wondered what the heck was coming next. Beams of soft iridescent golden light circled around her, when suddenly a hand grabbed her arm, pulled her out of the rapidly increasing centrifugal force, and found a place to gently place her body. "Who are you? Where are you taking me?" Her mind was signaling to someone. She received distinct telepathic messages. She calmed down, knowing she was going to be taken to safety. In a beautiful cavern of light and gemstones, she quietly waited. Standing before her was a goddess with flowing silver hair and sparkling blue eyes. The light she emitted was brilliant and blinding for a moment, almost knocking Lexi over. From her heart, a golden ray beamed straight towards Lexi. She tried to move, but something held her in direct alignment. She did not resist further. Something was familiar. Who was this being? An angelic voice said, *You are here, dear one, to learn about the depths of your soul contract.*

Lexi did not know what she meant and could not utter a word. She only listened and tuned into this dominant presence, which surrounded her with peace. This was a distinct new voice. Everything was serene.

The next morning Lexi woke confused. Was it all a dream? Did she really go for that walk and meet the shaman and goddess? She looked at her hands closely to see if she had scratches from the falls or a bruise on her head. Nothing. It felt so real, this could have been a dream! I remember everything so vividly. *Time to write.*

Child, it was not a dream; it was an altered state.

Lexi would spend the next couple months at the cabin contemplating. She had important decisions to make and one that included an option she never considered. For now, she could not tell anyone.

There is a reason she hides her tears...
A pain that runs so deep
she must hide from it herself...
In order to survive.

—GLORIA COPPOLA

CHAPTER 10

Italy

Café

"Madam, Are you okay?" "Oh, oh, I'm sorry. Yes, I'm fine. I was daydreaming again, and guess I floated off somewhere." Marcello was becoming concerned over how often she disappeared. He wondered if she needed medical attention. Alexandra continued to journal after reminiscing about the voice during her excursion in North Carolina.

If only I had known sooner. My entire life could have been different. I will never completely understand why they kept it all a secret. Continuing in her journal, she wanted to complete this note to "*him.*" *I believe now it was meant to be. If I were to meet you, would I recognize you?* How could it be? She thought about it, pen in hand, as her vision blurred. *Could it be I made a huge mistake that day?*

Alexandra leaned over while her hand scribbled across the journal page. Repeatedly, she asked herself the same question, always searching for guidance. *I've been a fool and perhaps confused my whole life,* she wrote. *Was my spirit so free I was blind to what love really meant?*

Little did she realize Marcello was watching her from the door. He had genuine concern about her drifting off. He did not understand what was truly happening. Upon finishing her meal, she wrote:

Dearest, if I never live to see you again--I will live, always wondering--and sadly leave this world without your love. If our paths shall cross before our time is up, I know it will be a union of two souls filled with a sensual and soul passion no other has known. -*Alexandra*

New York City Flashback

The time passed by swiftly, and most things calmed in her mind after those initial events. Once Lexi returned from her travels, she made a promise to her dad she would, in fact, go to college to earn her degree. She enjoyed learning and would go on to obtain her master's degree. She never told her parents about anything that transpired with the voices, the old man, and the goddess or angelic being she had met or why she needed to go away for 3 months. Her father would likely accuse her of doing hallucinogenic drugs.

The next few months were filled with quiet reflection, pondering her life and college. Childhood memories began appearing. She recalled a time when her father seemed happier, when a vision of a woman stood at the door of her mother's room. She always thought it was her mom watching her admire the brooch. Today, she saw an older woman, a familiar essence. There were many questions popping into her head, but she wasn't sure there were any answers. Why all the secrets?

Lexi was brilliant. She intrigued her professors, always questioning the universal laws, spirituality, and anything random that fancied her. One thing for sure remained a constant: her love to see the world and return to her heart home one day.

For the next several years, opportunities would come her way and open a new world. The best things that evolved for Lexi personally were the friendships she forged with some young women in college. She needed that even more than her studies.

*Someone I loved once gave me
a box full of darkness. It took me years
to understand that this too, was a gift.*

—PEMA CHODRON

CHAPTER 11

College Project

Choices for research spanned from extremely boring to bizarre, which was quite intriguing for Lexi's creative and inquisitive mind.

A few of her college classmates decided to make a day trip to the Philadelphia Museum of Art and explore the city. It was a long time since Lexi actually made friends with girls her age and enjoyed the company of other brilliant minds and fun conversations filled with laughter. There was a sophistication and an innocence they each possessed. They all vowed to make this research project fun, since their minds were overworked from years of diligent and serious studies. Everyone was agreeable. Marian's dad had bought her a new car recently, so the girls piled into the luxury BMW with tan leather seats and began their "play time," as they called it.

The museum, with the opening of seventeen painting galleries in the 1960s, expanded the Indian Art Collection to include Nepal and Tibet, completed a new Costume and Textile Library, and began work on a Hall of Armor and some additional South Wing galleries. The young women were quite curious as to what they might discover.

Excited by all the possibilities they had to explore, each of the four girls had completely different ideas, opinions, and levels of sophistication. The beauty of it all provided insights and deep conversations on new topics that engaged and challenged them to learn more about their particular areas of interest. First stop, however, was the coffee shop. Marian had to be extra mindful where she parked her vehicle, so she dropped the girls off in front of a local café and met them moments later. Lexi's eyes were always looking up, as she was fascinated with buildings. Sylvia just wanted her coffee and rushed the girls in to find seats. Patricia could not stop talking about anything and everything. Lexi waited outside for Marian as she continued to people-watch and enjoy the scenery. Sylvia called her inside with an annoying tone, and Lexi kindly asked her to save two seats. Once Marian was in sight, walking with ease, emanating an air of success, the two gals sat down with their friends for a cappuccino and girl talk. The time flew by. Suddenly, all four heads turned in synchrony as a well-dressed, suave, dashing young man caught their eye. "Damn!" Patricia blurted aloud, embarrassed as her thoughts were about to come out of her mouth. The girls tried not to chuckle. They didn't want to be portrayed as less than sophisticated in the presence of this aristocratic gentleman. Sylvia quickly decided he would have to be a successful snob who was a womanizer. Marian and Lexi remained quiet, observing his stride, his voice when he ordered, and his ability to command such a presence. Marian and Lexi began to bond deeply over the next few months.

Their ideals, dreams, and insights on life aligned in comparison to the others. They did not judge each other for differences of opinion. Fascinated with the psychology of the mind, art, science, and travel, they supported each other as friends and colleagues through the last few months of earning their degrees. The two young ladies took countless small adventures in the New York Tri-State area, learning about different periods of history, enjoying exquisite displays of art, visiting the planetarium, and laughing during a discussion about extraterrestrials, observing them at various exhibits. There was no limit to the conversations they explored together.

Marian's father, on the other hand, had bigger dreams for his only daughter. He wanted a bright, prosperous future for her. Little did Marian know he had arranged a marriage to an heir of a multigenerational fortune. He still had an old-fashioned mindset. It was his belief a woman's place was at home, taking care of her man. He believed if he could set her up with a luxurious lifestyle, she would always be happy.

Graduation day

Celebration time was here, all the graduates were excited. Lexi came to learn Sylvia dropped out of school at the last minute. It didn't make sense however, she assumed she had her reasons. Patricia, ran towards Lexi excited, holding her hat on with one hand. "Look, Lexi!" displaying a brilliant diamond engagement ring. The two girls jumped up and down joyously. Patricia always wanted to get married and now her vision manifested. "I'm thrilled for you Pat, seriously happy for you both." Patricia ran back to her family and fiancé. Lexi never saw her again.

"Lexi, help me!" "What is it, Marian?" "Take me far away with you, please!"

Marian was always the composed one. Something had her quite distraught and unnerved. Confused by this emotional outburst, Lexi grabbed her friend's hand and ran away from the crowd celebrating the graduates. A large maple tree stood around the hedges and the girls swiftly and quietly hid.

"Tell me what is going on!" Lexi said with concern for her friend. "I can't believe he did this to me. He lied!" Marian held her head with both hands, shaking uncontrollably. "Who?" "My dad. He pretended I could have the future I desired, but there was a catch. I could pursue my dreams while becoming highly educated, while he found me a husband!" she said, growling through her teeth, bawling her eyes out, and frantically pacing. "Wait, what the fuck? Is he insane?" Lexi comforted Marian while she cried, wondering what plan she might come up with to get Marian out of this predicament. However hopeless that plan would likely be going up against Marian's controlling, wealthy father. "Marian, where are you?" A stern voice called out to the young lady.

"Oh dear, he's coming, Lexi. What do I do?" Bewildered and shaken, Lexi didn't have an answer. She grasped Marian's hand to run and hide when Marian's father placed his hand firmly on Lexi's shoulder and announced in a scolding tone, "You, my dear, must leave my daughter now and never speak to her again." He pulled Marian away abruptly as she looked back at Lexi, sobbing in fury and frustration, helpless and distressed as her dearest friend had no solution. Lexi stood there frozen and numb. "Marian, we will figure something out!" Lexi shouted as Marian's father dragged her away. Marian's dad turned and gave Lexi the evil eye. He looked cruel and psychotic with vengeance in his eyes. She had never seen that side of him and didn't quite understand why he would end their friendship. This cannot happen, she kept telling herself. I must get her away from this insanity.

An elegant middle-aged woman approached Lexi, reached out her hand, and said in a sophisticated voice, "Come with me, dear one." When Lexi looked up, she realized it was Marian's mother, whom she had only seen once during a short visit. "Please understand, this is hard, but it's the best choice for Marian." "Best choice?" she hollered. "Are you crazy? Your daughter is brilliant and has big dreams." "Yes, she has a fantasy, as most woman do. In the end, we know we must make the best choice to be financially secure. We have duties in our lifetime and Marian must fulfill hers. Her time to play is over." "You have got to be kidding me! Tell me this is not true!" "I'm afraid it is all true. Now you must never contact her again. I know she loves you dearly, but she is easily swayed by your imagination and childish ideas." "Childish! Lady, you have gone too far. I'm an intelligent woman with great aspirations. I don't need a man to make them happen or change my mind. If I choose to partner with someone in life for a family, he will be supportive of my dreams too." "You are a silly young girl. I wish you much luck." With that, she strolled away to where husband waited to take his women home. "How dare that bitch call me childish!"

The crowds were separating, and Lexi had to find her mom and brother. "Where have you been?" "Danny, I'm sorry. A friend had a crisis and I had to console her." "You are always the compassionate one, my darling daughter."

Mom embraced her two children, smiled, kissed their foreheads, and said, "Let's go celebrate your success and future." Everyone agreed to make the best of this day and be happy. Lexi felt something was off with her mom. Maybe she was just tired. Intuitively, though, she knew something was not right. Danny was always the strong, gallant one. She wondered if he was tuning into anything but decided to enjoy their company. Her father, of course, did not attend because he said he could not take time off from work. He congratulated her that evening and never said another word.

How quickly six years went by and all for what? Lexi questioned herself while writing in her journal. *I have no solution for my friend, Marian, and my mother tried to explain for many families "that was the way." Dinner was fun with my brother and Mom, lots of laughs, which I needed and a sense of closure as the next part of life is entering. I will never understand Marian's father and hopefully someday I can connect with her. Life is crazy sometimes, and we can never make sense of it. Perhaps, I won't try to figure it all out and as Mom suggested, "Live your own dream, Lexi, and have fun doing it."*

~~~ Remember, tomorrow may not come.
Write your songs tonight~~~

The next morning, a somber energy hung in the air of the house. When Lexi didn't hear her mother say, "Rise and shine," something was *definitely* wrong.

"Lexi," said Danny softly. "Come here, girl."

Lexi sensed something was seriously amiss. Danny was never this serious. Maybe her father was sick? He always worked so hard.

Once Danny put his arms around Lexi, he cried so intensely, Lexi cried, not knowing why. "Mom, it's Mom, Lexi. Our rock, our inspiration…she died last night in her sleep." "Nooo! That is impossible Danny. Where is she?"

"Dad left after they took her body away early this morning."

"What? I didn't hear anything! Why didn't someone come get me? This is all a dream, a lie; please, wake me up!" she shouted.

The siblings sat on the couch in dismay, crying with no support from anyone. They had only each other.

There was no sense to it. Their mother was robust, perhaps not consistently happy, but she had no known physical issues. She was too young to depart this realm. A massive heart attack would take her from this world and break the hearts of her two children. She was the one to confide in, someone who held your secrets in her heart. Lexi never found out what her mother was hiding the night her father interrupted their conversation.

Danny didn't know where to find their father and assumed he was at a local bar with his buddies. He decided to go find him and told her to get some rest. They had plans to make for the funeral, and she would need to hold herself together. Lexi, on the other hand was furious, disappointed, and angry with God. The next few days were and still are a complete blur. Their beloved mother was buried, family came to share their condolences, and the darkness didn't lift for months. Lexi wrote every day in her journal, trying to make sense of life. Nothing made sense anymore.

No more late night conversations or advice. No more rubbing her fingers through my hair, rambling thoughts could not slow down. A tear dropped every time she wrote on the pages of her journal; no more yelling my name *"Alexandra"*. What will I do without her? It's not fair God! I need her, we need her. Who will I go to for help?

For months, she walked around in a daze, in total disbelief, imagining she saw her mom in any familiar-faced woman. Her father said nothing and didn't want to discuss anything. He sunk into his own depression, finding a way to cope by drinking more. He would rarely speak to his kids after losing his wife. Danny went back to work and took care of matters to help in any way possible.

Lexi decided it was time to leave. *Live your own dream, she heard.*

Surrender to grace
The ocean cares for each wave,
until it reaches the shore
You are given more help
than you will ever know.

—RUMI

CHAPTER 12

St. Lucia

"*I am so numb inside, I can't even cry. All I do is question why — now I find myself here.*"

Losing her mother after graduation was devastating, especially to a budding daughter who cherished guidance from her. Somehow, Lexi knew her mom was constantly guiding, prompting, and always looking after her. There was nothing like chatting at midnight and laughing about their days. She always encouraged her to travel, to be who she chose to be, to listen to her instincts. This was advice worth remembering. Yet, every day she continued to seek solace in those that resembled her mom as she walked around aimlessly

This trip to St. Lucia is for Mom, she believed. Not really sure why she chose this island, but something called her to go. All those countless discussions prepared Lexi for this destiny better than college and getting a master's degree. Maybe there was something waiting for her she never saw coming. *I know whatever the reason, mom will be by my side.*

For the last several years, Lexi's nose had been in textbooks, achieving milestones and realizing her capabilities. Genuinely bored most of the time, she dutifully attended college for her father. She required something to encourage her interest in life once again. This

vacation was definitely in order for a new perspective on life and some fun would be welcomed.

Her tan, slender body was radiant against the white, flowing dress for dinner tonight. A few days in the sunlight transformed her pale skin into an Italian delicacy. She left the suite for the dining room at the resort in St. Lucia. They had adorned the tall white pillars with fuchsia-colored flowers; it was beautiful. Within moments of arriving, two young, handsome Caribbean men appeared to accompany her to a table. Heads were turning; most were couples visiting. Yet they hardly spoke to each other. How strange, she thought.

There is a grace in singleness one must learn to embrace.

While many steadily admired her, she never actually had the assurance many suspected she had; inside, she was extremely bashful. Lexi didn't like people scrutinizing her Tonight, countless marvelous moments would cascade through her awareness while dancing across the wooden floor. It would light up her heart and rebuild the shattered self-esteem stored within. The soothing Caribbean breeze blew through her golden-red hair, drawing the attention of many to this vision of loveliness. It was traditional, she learned, when a woman dined without company, the greeter remained. She insisted there was no issue being alone.

"No, miss, we delight in accompanying you and making certain you are enjoying yourself."

This made her nervous but smiled at the charming young man. In truth, Lexi was squirming to conform to this tradition, feeling restless, nervous and lacking confidence. She wondered why this attention was not something received freely. Was it humility? Was it something that had happened in her past that made her react this way? Could she get over it and enjoy it? Oh, the speculations and reasons would not cease…until he walked in.

There he was, in all his majesty, but did not acknowledge her. His shimmering hazel eyes gleamed across the room. He stepped towards her table, exuding confidence in each step. Nervously, Lexi adjusted her dress and sat up straight: after all, if he should notice her, she needed to appear confident.

How absurd! Why would he notice me or come to my table?

Indeed, to her surprise, he drew out a chair to be seated at her dinner table to chat with the staff member who escorted her tonight. He did not glance her way. She felt extremely uneasy and a bit intimidated. The discussion was all business, concentrated on the details of serving the vacationers and the details of the nightly entertainment performance. Lexi listened attentively. She was dreamy-eyed listening to his French Caribbean accent and happily admired her view. Once the conversation was over, the young host excused himself from the table. Now finding herself face to face, alone, with the suave gentleman. Infatuated, neither one said a word.

"I apologize, miss. I did not acknowledge you. It was not considerate of me. Many urgent concerns on my mind to address made me unaware. It is still no excuse. Oblige me to make it up to you."

"No worries, I understand. I am grateful for the kind proposal, but you must return to your business." "Have you explored this charming property yet? Seen the stars at night? Inhaled the ylang ylang?"

"I have a little. Arriving barely a couple of days ago, I rested, mostly. The last few years have been exhausting."

"Ahh, I see. Then it is time to get familiar with my charming island. Like you, it has a mystique: it is captivating and evocative. You must visit the rain forest too!"

Bowing her head down slightly, shy, like a young girl. "Thank you. I will keep this recommendation and consider them. You are kind."

"No miss, I will be your escort, if you allow. I can sense it is time for you to relieve your stress and experience some pleasant times."

"Is it *that* apparent?"

He grinned and nodded. Reaching out, he stroked her hand affectionately. She could hear her own pulse. At this moment, nothing else counted. With his French Caribbean accent, he purred, "Come with me."

She finished dinner, and his proposal sounded tempting. However, she did not choose to interfere with his duties. "I am sure you have a lot to do. I would not want you to get in trouble."

"Trouble?" laughing wholeheartedly. "That is my middle name! Besides, you will come to work with me. You will be my co-star." Sheepishly she replied, "Okay."

Was she dreaming? No other response poured from her fuchsia-pink lips. One could merely inhale the intoxicating aromatic sweetness of the blossoming ylang ylang, a potent aphrodisiac, intensifying her attraction to this strong-bodied, beautiful male.

The moon rose as the indigo sky and stars set the backdrop for an amorous evening, and the golden sun disappeared into oblivion. The guests were showing up for the nightly entertainment and dancing. Lexi stood by his side, waiting, uncertain what her co-star role meant. The music got louder; steel drums filled the air. The people were served drinks and happy to be entertained tonight.

"Excuse me," she inquired, "What is your name?"

"I am the one sent to you by God to make you smile." She giggled and inquired again.

"My name is A'jay, the Invincible, and yours?" "Alexandra...but call me Lexi."

"Charming goddess, Lexi. I am exceedingly delighted to meet you." He kissed her hand.

"Good evening, ladies and gentlemen. It is my purpose to provide an exceptional evening of fun for you all. We hope to encourage you to reach the highest levels of our island joy!" His vibrant energy and charm had the crowd hopping. Everybody clapped and cheered. They were ready to party.

"It is further my delight to introduce you to my elegant and stunning co-star Lexi, who will be my dance partner tonight."

Whistles and claps galore, embarrassed her. She did not realize she would be in the limelight. As they instructed her in charm school, she bowed and smiled. A'jay spun her around, the pastel lights shimmering on her white dress and her charm exuding through the ether of the air--even if she didn't realize it.

Meandering thoughts rushed through her head as she recited to herself, *I'm not a little girl anymore. I am a charming woman. I can accomplish anything, and I asked to be on stage.*

The band played a collection of music: Creole, calypso, reggae, and more.

Exquisitely dressed, local women arrived on the dance floor in traditional colors of their flag: yellow, black, and white. Full flowing skirts embellished their lively presence, each one more beautiful than the next. Their male counterparts stood properly before them.

A'jay took Lexi's hand, trimmed her head with yellow ribbons, wrapped a colorful skirt around her waistline, and stood handsomely in the circle of dancers. Lexi did not know what to expect. Once the quadrille began, she adequately embraced a waltz-like folk dance. The tune was uplifting, fun, and elegantly performed. She had no trouble following A'jay's lead and was soon fitting right in with the locals.

She was happier than she had been in years. "This is the life!"

The audience applauded all the dancers. A'jay drew Lexi into the spotlight one last time for the local dancers to acknowledge her and show gratitude for her participation. The bright smiles melted Lexi's heart as they each regarded her willingness to experience their customs.

Back stage, A'jay quietly asked Lexi, "Do you sing as well?" "I do a little," she hesitantly responded.

"Are you hot, hot, hot?" He playfully grinned, grasping her hand to sing and dance with her on stage.

The music began, and the crowd cheered, "Hot, hot, hot!" The electricity was vibrant and building. Without a moment to respond, she shook her hips and drew excitement to the dance floor. A'jay followed her as she hopped off the stage and started engaging the audience to dance and sing with them.

Olé, Olé, Olé, Olé, Lexi chanted along with A'jay.

She was a natural. The crowd went wild, and everybody joined in the magical energy of the vibrant entertainers. No one could resist. It was an evening of undeniable delight! Once the music ended, the band played a medley of smooth, slow jazz songs while the guests caught their breath and grabbed a refreshment.

A'jay gave Lexi no chance to relax when he connected with her eyes and drifted across the dance floor alone with her. Lexi, for the first time, did not care. All eyes were watching. It was so romantic. She succumbed and relaxed into his muscular chest and strong, hard arms as he embraced her soft, curvy frame into eternal bliss. Time felt like it reached another dimension, stirring every sense, and she found herself craving more. The soft piano sounds, electric guitar and cymbals, bass, and snare drums lightly, setting a romantic tone for the evening. He whisked her away and, though she could not see the guests swaying in their seats, imagining they were dancing with their loves, she released herself to just him.

Moments later, one of the band members waved for the audience to join the couple for the next dance. They dimmed the lights as a pleasant breeze passed by, bringing with it the fresh, enticing essence of frangipani. It was as though something--or someone-- had divinely arranged everything for this singular moment. Three melodies later, the musicians faded their magical tones, and the room was in silent awe, with couples embracing their partners before returning to their seats.

Lexi and A'jay escaped for a while, and the younger entertainers joined the nightly review with cultural dances and music. It felt incredible to have his attention as she continued to allow herself to be fascinated by his touch and bewitched by his kiss. Oh, he *was* smooth. No other man had ever captivated her with such charisma. The sound of the night ocean, waves crashing lightly upon the sand in the distance, soothed her pounding heart. Kicking off her sandals, they raced together, hand in hand, down to the water.

A'jay lifted her up with his strong, athletic arms, draped his hands around her waist, swung her around, and set her back down ever so gently. Lexi was spellbound as he affectionately kissed her chest, pausing to kiss her chin, and stopping at her lips. The moonlight made her eyes sparkle in the dark while the dizziness intensified like the influence of a powerful hallucinogen. Clearly, she was not, although love has been described as intoxicating.

Intelligent conversation and far-out topics enticed Lexi, but tonight, she spoke barely a word. Yet a heated exchange was transpiring through her veins. That was quite unusual for her. She was surprised to find she was not at all bored with this gentle-man.

Deliberately, they both knelt in the sand, running their hands effortlessly along each other's arms and up through their shoulders. They stopped, gazing off into the eyes of their souls. A'jay could not resist any longer and, with his playfulness, broke the silence and rolled Lexi over into the sand, surprising her.

"What are you doing?" "Playing, my lovely. Is it not fun?"

All she could do was laugh as this man entertained her. Their giggling was infectious, and although nothing was funny to anyone who may have witnessed their playfulness, it filled them with joy. A'jay needed this equally, perhaps more. As their breathing quickened from laughing, they held each other and waited for the spinning to stop.

For a moment, Lexi tuned into her mom's presence, smiling over her and whispering, *Enjoy the moment, dear one.* So, she did, as they would lie in the sand for several minutes, quietly watching the stars. They didn't know they were both saying a prayer. Perhaps God brought them both to each other.

In the distance, A'jay heard his intro music. "Quick, Lexi, I must get back." The two rushed back inside. Lexi stood on the sidelines while A'jay jumped right back into action. Fortunately, he knew all the routines and could charm a snake if he had to.

"Let's give an enormous round of applause for our wonderful entertainers tonight." Motioning them to rise for an encore, everyone complied, while Lexi watched him adoringly.

"Now, for our last dance of the evening, I invite you to the dance floor. Look into your partner's eyes and it will sweep you away, enticed by the island magic."

He extended his hand towards Lexi to join him. A'jay whisked her onto the dance floor, her feet barely touching the ground, still catching her breath. "Come away with me." The two snuck away. No one paid attention. A'jay winked at one of the staff members and nodded in appreciation for covering the closure of the event.

What planet am I on? His sensual kisses ignited her entire being as they stopped to catch their breath.

"What do you mean, come away with you?"

He expressed his words with actions. Gently gliding and rubbing her body close to his, she could feel his firm pulsating body when he momentarily paused. They took a deep breath together while her feet sank into the sand. "Come," he said. She followed willingly as if he had cast a magical spell upon her. "What a tease you are," Lexi said, laughing. However, intrigued, she could not deny she was enjoying the foreplay.

This was new for her. She never randomly took off with a stranger. There was something exciting about this connection. She was comfortable exploring the evening with this romantic Caribbean lover.

Hmm, lover? Is that what he is?

Along the moonlight breezes, the sound of the steel-drum finale swirled in the air, intensifying the magical moment and Lexi's fantasy evening. Only this was real, and her heart was fluttering.

"Come, let us go into this cabana," A'jay said leading the way.

There awaited a soft white futon for two, sparkling little lights, flowers floating in a small water bowl, and the perfect setting for making love. She quivered with a little hesitancy but allowed herself to surrender to the moment. They had two glasses of white wine to wet their lips and the magic potion of love and lust to embrace their hearts.

Their passionate kisses extended for hours as his strong, yet soft hands ran across her back, pausing at her shoulders, up to her neck, and gently across her cheeks. It gave her chills. The night would surely be pleasurable. They wrapped their legs around each other and fell into a tantalizing, erotic world of dreams.

What if I stayed? she thought. *What would others think? Why would I care? Everyone has their own life and I'm just beginning a new one again.*

The next morning, A'jay awoke singing a popular song, "*Don't Worry, Be Happy*," saluting the morning sun after running on the beach for a half an hour as Lexi slept. With coffee in hand and a sumptuous tray of breakfast treats, he picked a few pink and orange local flowers to embellish the tray.

Sighing in satisfaction as she opened her eyes, she saw him standing in front of her. There he was, her fiery lover, offering her a cup of freshly brewed coffee with a grin on his face. Every woman should wake up this way.

"How long have you been up?"

"Many hours, graceful goddess. You entertained me with the soft, soothing echoes of your breath; your delicate skin as I placed my hands around every contour melted me. The rise and fall of your heartbeat connected me to your soul."

Lexi was seeking to assimilate this form of enchantment. A smile was in order and a thank you for sure. Her whimsical imagination wondered if someone was filming this as a surprise reality show. Rising to grab the cup of coffee, he swiftly propped the fluffy cushions behind her back to make his princess comfortable. He selected one flower and placed it in her soft, shiny hair and watched her sipping her morning elixir. A'jay swooned as he saw her lips pucker around the cup, her back arching slightly. He loved how her long hair draped across her back. To say he was hypnotized by her charm was an understatement; he never imagined someone so elegant would be in his arms all night.

"We shall go to the rain forest today. Does that sound fascinating to you? I have no work today." In a mellow voice, she said, "That sounds alluring, my love."

Lexi knew A'jay liked to smoke his marijuana, something that never appealed to her. When he offered, she respectfully said no, and he never pressured her.

Hours later, the two hiked the easy trail through the Des Cartiers Trail. Lexi became intrigued with all the melodies, especially those of the birds. She had never heard so many sing at once; it was like a symphony. Next, he took her to Dennery Falls. A'jay recognized her adventurous soul would appreciate this hidden gem, and they would most likely have privacy to bathe in the pools. There was no dissatisfaction for either of them.

She decided to begin a spiritual discussion with him, speculating he had considerable intelligence along with the undeniable physical attraction. The two bathed in the pools beneath the cascading waterfalls, and it was only the beginning of a whirlwind romantic experience...for a while.

"A'jay, have you ever considered why two souls connect so intensely?"

"Miss Lexi, yes, I have. Our eternal beings recognize each other from our previous incarnations. When intimate moments take us on a journey through and with another, it reminds us of our eternal moments together. An infinite abyss, like infinite states of consciousness, like many chambers in a house...we meet."

"Think of yourself. When you activate your awareness of these memories or the emotions, there are an inexhaustible number of possibilities. Do you agree? Everything waits for the alignment of these souls and their activation. The union results from the projection."

Wow! Lexi thought, *I did not think he could hold a conversation like this. I shall dive deeper and discover how this unfolds. I enjoy intriguing conversations.*

"If that is the case, would you conclude we have multiple encounters with soul mates, based on this explanation?"

"Oh, dear Lexi, of course we do. My lifetimes have explored infinite realities and dimensions. It has taken me far beyond to contact the spirit world. I have merged with frequencies in phenomena

84

beyond these three-dimensional earths. I have received the joy of God."

She wondered if his experiences were due to his use of recreational drugs. It was not the time to pursue that question, yet. They talked for hours. They spoke of the infinite universe, the probabilities which may exist beyond imagination, and what may evolve if they accessed considerable levels of consciousness than one presented.

Lexi realized she had aligned with a manifestation of her internal thoughts, enjoying intelligent and interesting conversations with passion, depth, laughter, and connection. Was this union magically aligned? Or were they discussing these realms from completely different sources?

"A'jay, do you believe we are soul mates?"

"There is no question, my goddess, we have shared many lifetimes and dimensions together. We know each other completely. I realize you want it all and your desire to be aligned with one who must have passion, playfulness, and intellect. I see it in your eyes. You walk alone in this physical reality, but your soul is multi-dimensional. Most will never understand your love. I already appreciate you."

They waded around the pools, playing like children, and splashing under the waterfall, all in pure innocence. Nothing interfered with their precious delights, and this miraculous kingdom granted a portal of love for them to explore.

Exhausted from their day in nature but filled with extraordinary gratitude, they showered simultaneously and shared a light dinner and a bottle of wine. The evening ended early in the arms of one another. The rhythm of their breath rocked them to sleep. She hoped this was real.

Lexi wondered how her mother would feel about all of this. She had cautioned her so many times in life about men. She was tired of not trusting men; however, maybe her mother knew things she didn't? It was time she had to find out for herself.

What young woman wouldn't enjoy a bohemian lifestyle with the Adonis of the island? Well, this gal was delighted to discard her jeans and wear sarongs, shorts, T-shirts, and straw hats. She enjoyed the tranquil lifestyle after the laborious years spent in school and at work. It was time for a new experience. One she would never forget.

That morning, the children's voices were squealing as their whimsical spirits joyfully filled the metal pails with sand. It was time for sandcastles and racing to the turquoise waters to dodge the waves. It was lively energy to begin one's day. She decided to stay. Months of fun filled her with a peaceful heart. They lived in a small old beach shack; but hey, who needs more when you have love?

The resort hired her to sing and dance, and she and A'jay would entice all the vacationers, tempting them lustfully onto the dance floor. Nights were hot, hot, hot! Her nights became exhausting and soon she would realize island evenings was definitely harder than expected.

"Lexi. Come, let's take a ride," as he moved the canoe into the shallow waters, stumbling awkwardly, hysterically laughing, as the local women giggled with him. Children bathing naked, splashing water on each other, and all the merriment was contagious. Mothers were making straw hats and baskets to trade at the market while they inspected the fair-skinned beauty. They often wondered what her motive was and if she knew A'jay's *secret*. They included her in prayers for her safety as part of their routine.

It didn't take long for Lexi to learn he was an extremely emotional being. It wasn't uncommon after a long day of entertaining patrons he would light up a joint to keep his temper at bay. Often, he would talk long walks without her and disappear into the sunset, sleeping on the beach without a care in the world.

Today he was calm and cheerful as he glanced down at the crystal-clear waters. "Look, me lady, I have a present for you," he said with a pirate's accent He scooped up some sand along with the *Eye of Saint Lucia*. "Aargh, 1 shall make thee pretty earrings. You will be proud of me when you wander through the markets and people are idolizing you. They know the magic of this eye." Lexi couldn't care less.

"I prayed for you to come," he continued. "Did you know? I prayed you would be my partner."

Lexi wasn't certain what he was referring to until he scooped up his palm and sifted the sand from the shell. Legend had it the orange face of the shell was the stylized symbol for the Blessed Virgin. He would tell the story.

"But you, my love, are no virgin! We, however, believe it is a lucky charm. Just like you."

The operculum shell had a white surface with a spiral and a vibrant orange coral. The warm orange surface resembled the human ear, and Lexi marveled at this gift of the sea. He took a drag of his joint, sat in the canoe, and arranged his feet on her lap, grinning; he had no cares in the world.

"I'm the king and you are my queen! My prayers have been answered."

Lexi had been working hard all week, and although she enjoyed singing and dancing at the resort, entertaining the guests, A'jay placed a lot of pressure on her and it was no longer fun. Passionate nights became limited, and she recognized he didn't genuinely care most days what she preferred, unless it served him too. She wasn't sure her prayer had been answered, so she did not respond to him. They apparently had prayed for two different things.

The sunlight danced upon the crystal clear, calm waters today, welcoming this glorious energy, since Lexi felt exhausted. Last night was especially challenging when A'jay lost his temper for no reason. Lexi clammed up like a youngster and stayed out of his way. He picked up a frying pan and clanged it on the counter. He claimed he was playing the drum. She thought otherwise and stepped back carefully.

"What's the matter with you, woman?!" he growled in a threatening tone. She jumped.

"I will make you jump," as he hurled a plate across the tiny shack. "Now you pick it up. I'm outta here!"

Because of her upbringing, Lexi grew up modeling codependent behavior, learning well from her mother as she endured her father's outbursts. A'jay never apologized, as if he didn't remember, and life continued.

A'jay dove into the water, suggesting his beauty come to play. She didn't feel especially well today, but he coaxed her relentlessly.

"Ahh, my divine, sweet darling, you are my mermaid today. Seduce me with your magic ways of the sea."

She had no strength today to serve his wishes. Obviously frustrated because she didn't choose to go in the water, he rocked the boat.

"Please A'jay, I don't want to go in."

The rocking became more violent, and she yelled, "I'm sick, please stop!"

"Sick? You have been pretending to be sick for days. I see nothing wrong with you. You are a liar." As he continued rocking the canoe briskly, he paid no attention to Lexi's' fright, and she began to cry. The canoe toppled and flipped, landing over her. She could hear him laughing, while she was suffering from a panic attack. Her body stiffened and drifted down. His voice became considerably distant. All Lexi could hear was the fading whisper of her own breath.

A few moments passed when A'jay realized something could be wrong, and he plunged deep into the water to recover her. Swiftly, he grabbed Lexi and brought her to the surface. Gagging, she made a small sigh and coughed. She was disoriented and confused. He pulled her body over to the small white-sand coast, where he pumped her chest to eliminate any water.

"Lexi, please, I'm sorry. I was merely playing. Come back to me."

Gasping repeatedly for breath, she opened her eyes marginally and saw a vague image of him. The fear was still rushing through her veins, as she assumed he had tried to kill her. A'jay placed his head against her cheeks, his hand on her heart, and pleaded with her to open her eyes fully. He sounded genuinely remorseful while sobbing and praying. Her breathing was shallow. Her body limp, shaking her to wake up. Lexi opened her eyes and muttered, "Home."

A'jay ran to retrieve the canoe without responding and brought it to shore. He took her hand as she stepped into the canoe slowly with her head down.

"Lexi, look, we didn't lose the shells. I had them in my pocket, and I will make you beautiful earrings when we get home. It will show my appreciation for you."

She did not respond. How can a man think of earrings when I nearly died, she thought to herself?

Once they arrived back at their home, she walked slowly, cautiously, queasy and regretting her decision. It had been five months on the island of St. Lucia, and she had no one but him. It was time to talk to one of the local women. Her estranged relationship with her dad did not warrant any outreach to him. Her brother was touring Europe with his sweet partner, Suzette, and not easily reachable.

As she walked up the old rickety wooden steps, one old woman glanced over. Her looked suggested: I'm here for you. Lexi could sense her message somehow. Her stomach was hurting, and she wanted to calm her nerves, so she settled down to rest.

"A'jay?" No reply. He was not there.

I must meet these ladies, she thought. I will need them, I know. Someone will have to help me. Within moments, she had to rush to the bathroom. Sweating, with a slight fever, she leaned over the toilet and threw up.

Shortly later, there was a gentle knock on the door. "I can help you," a woman's voice called out. She walked into their shack and found her way to Lexi lying on the floor. She placed her hand on her back and hummed a soothing song while Lexi sighed.

"No worries, Missy, we understand."

What was she talking about? Lexi wondered. But she didn't respond.

"I am the village medicine woman, and I am also pretty psychic. I sense you are with child." Lexi's eyes, obscured with tears, opened wider. She was shocked at the woman's statement. "Come, sit with me. Let us talk."

For the next fifteen minutes, the two women connected. "I am Julietta, the one who consoles those in distress."

Outside, they could hear some squabbling, which distracted them.

"Get out of my way, woman!" A'jay yelled. "This is my home!" Before he could thrust Nathalia, she stepped back.

"What are you doing with this crazy lady?"

"She came to help me. I was sick and throwing up."

"You come to me, not these crazy women! Stay away from them!"

"She was kind, A'jay. I required a woman who could understand my condition." "Condition? What *condition* do you speak of?"

Clearly stoned, he was oblivious to the situation, acting foolishly. "Get out of my house! It's none of your concern. She is mine!"

They all recognized his temper. It was not just from smoking pot; he had started doing drugs and drinking more frequently. The locals knew his patterns and it seemed he slipped back into them, unfortunately.

Lexi pleaded, "A'jay, listen. We are going to have a baby." Everything got quiet. He showed no reaction as he rubbed his head.

"Hey, Lexi, I'm going to lie down. No more drama for today. I need to sleep." "A'jay, did you hear me?"

He sat beside her, snot dripping from his nose, his eyes red and swollen, begging her to stop. He rested his head on her lap.

Outside, she could hear the ladies whispering. Tomorrow, she would connect with Julietta. She needed a confidante. Her concern grew about his outbursts, drug use and narcissistic behaviors.

The next morning, A'jay recalled nothing. He turned towards Lexi and asked her, "Do you have something to tell me?"

"A'jay, I don't know what happened to you yesterday. I lay awake all night, worried. You were acting strangely."

"Silly woman, I am fine. Stop making things up. I had a dream last night. You had some news to share."

Holding his hands, she somberly replied, "Yes, we are going to have a baby."

He hopped out of the bed, dancing and singing. He was the happiest she had seen him in months.

"Beautiful goddess of mine. No wonder you got seasick yesterday."

"Yes, A'jay."

"Let's go tell the village! I will be a proud papa and the best one!"

She reluctantly smiled and said she would be out as quickly as she could dress. He did not wait a moment; he grabbed his djembe, and began drumming, singing, and shouting to the villagers. "I'm going to be a father!"

The local children sang along, dancing around him. The ladies politely smiled. Lexi stepped out in a lovely pink sundress, appearing exhausted. The women could see she was; he did not. In typical A'jay fashion, he disappeared…again.

Later that day, she was alone cleaning the mess in the house. Sadness filled her heart. As she swept under their bed, a small bag caught her broom. She sensed something was not good. Opening the bag slowly, a white powder was inside, she assumed it was cocaine. She fell to her knees, her worst fears now realized. Life with him would be unpredictable.

He was an addict. She was confused. Perhaps, when she heard mom say, *"Enjoy the moment,"* it was only that moment that was meant to be.

She never confronted him about the drugs she found. He was missing for two days and never went to work. Her thoughts wandered; her concerns grew. It was time she made a plan.

In the meantime, Julietta and the local women took her into their confidence. They were already concerned for the baby, knowing the history of A'jay's drug addiction.

"He tries to be a good man, Miss Lexi. He works hard and has always been lonely until you made him smile. Sometimes, things set him off and he occasionally falls back into bad habits. He had a difficult childhood and no stability. But, please be alert," the woman warned her.

Nathalia remarked, "He has not lost his temper since you arrived. Allow us to be your family, your birthing sisterhood. We support our women because the men usually disappear."

Lexi's face showed no outward signs of concern, but inside, she was tormented. It was not the carefree island life she had envisioned. Reality was setting in. It was much harder than imagined, and tourists lived a fantasy through A'jay and her, all while envying her life. They didn't realize it was a show.

Over the following weeks, the two had limited conversation; when they did, it was mostly about work. A'jay was stoned frequently and no longer looked at his woman with adoration. Lexi needed help to make a plan. What would she do? She was concerned about taking his child away from him and providing a better life…or should she accept this as a soul contract?

Child, all is about to change. Have hope.

There was that whisper that had always guided her. Oh, if only I understood all these messages, she thought.

Tonight's performance would not go as planned. Lexi felt a slight fever coming on along with her stomach cramps. A'jay demanded his dance partner be present and that she should not disappoint him.

The music blasted, the infamous "hot, hot, hot" performance began, and the crowd was excited. Lexi leaped from the stage like always, although tonight, everything would change. While in mid-air, she grabbed her stomach in pain and fell to her knees, crying. A staff member quickly helped her to the ladies' room while the show continued. A'jay completely ignored her. He kept the crowd entertained and distracted. Looking down at her legs, she saw a blood stain when her cramps intensified.

"We must get you to Julietta." Lexi nodded yes.

As quick as they could, they met Julietta, knowing she would comfort Lexi and provide her a magic tea, cool towels to bring her temperature down, and hopefully explain to Lexi what was happening.

"Child, you are at significant risk of losing this baby," she said as she patted her hand. "You must rest and cannot dance any longer. A'jay needs to find a new dance partner."

The look on Lexi's face almost made Julietta cry. "Am I being punished, Julietta?"

"Dear child, no. Sometimes a fetus doesn't develop properly for many reasons. It is God's way of taking care of things. Understand all those drugs he takes can also create a weak embryo and cause harm to the fetus."

Angrily, Lexi made a fist and wished she could punch his face right then.

"Remain calm, child. You don't want to have further distress. Tomorrow we shall visit the doctor, okay?"

Lexi loved when Julietta sang soothing melodies and massaged her scalp. It was just like her mom used to do when she was a little girl and not feeling well. Drifting off, Julietta waited for A'jay to come home so she could talk to him. He never showed up after work.

The sun rose and a gut-wrenching scream came from the shack. Julietta and Nathalia ran quickly. There Lexi was, lying in a pool of blood, drenched in it all, while crying and screaming. They knew the baby was gone.

The two women cleaned her up. They took her to the doctor for an examination. Lexi didn't have any emotions. She fell into a somber depression, blaming herself and afraid to tell A'jay. What did she *overlook,* she questioned herself repeatedly?

Once the ladies got her back home and made her tea, they comforted her with their wisdom and put her to bed. All Lexi did was cry herself to sleep.

Later that evening, she woke up hearing the steel drums reverberating through the jet stream. She wondered if he would come home tonight. Too exhausted to worry, she had a cup of soup and fell back to sleep.

"Where are you, my love? Hello!" a voice called out.

A'jay walked into the room to find Lexi sound asleep. He was disappointed because he wanted to tell her about his plans for their family. Shaking her to wake up, she ignored him. He wrapped his body around her. It was like old times. He kissed her on the back of her head and fell asleep with a smile on his face.

Lexi was up quite early, surprised and nervous about seeing A'jay at home. She prepared morning coffee and sat on the steps outside. The children were always fun to watch, but today it only brought sadness to her heart. *I wonder if I will ever have my own child?*

No one knew she had to give one away for adoption. It was the reason she left for three months in North Carolina and now she lost one. Even her mom didn't know.

A half hour passed by when she heard A'jay singing in the house. He walked out with his cup of coffee to sit by her side. Placing his arm around her shoulders, he said, "I have some good news."

"Wait, A'jay, I must tell you something first!"

"No, no, allow me to share my joyful news. I go first!"

Without hesitation, he blabbered happily about a new position at work. It would pay more, so she wouldn't have to work the long hours. He told her his plans for a new home for their family, one of those tropical-style ranch homes with a picket fence. Lexi could not contain her tears.

"Don't cry, my love, it will be wonderful!"

"A'jay, please listen before you go further. It's important!"

"Okay, okay, but I have so much more to share. I am so happy!"

How do I break this news to him? I haven't seen him this happy since the night we spent the night on the beach in the cabana.

She paused, took a breath, and asked God for guidance. "You remember the conversation we had at the waterfall?" He nodded yes.

"Soul contracts aren't always what we think. An angel visited me in my dream. I didn't understand at first, but angels spoke to me."

"Of course, they did, my love. You have an angel in your belly!" gently caressing her stomach. "In this dream, the angels explained why a soul sometimes comes to us and doesn't fully incarnate," she said, sobbing.

"What are you talking about?"

"This soul entered my womb and decided it did not need to live in this physical reality." "What have you done?"

"God brought this angel home. They showed me my path, my lessons, and a greater love."

"You are making no sense!"

Uncontrollably crying, she leaned into his chest when he abruptly pushed her away and angrily said, "You aborted my baby?"

"*No!*" she screamed. The local ladies rushed from their homes to support her.

Madness was in his eyes! He was out of control, screaming and shouting, "You killed my baby!"

"No, I did not A'jay. I had a miscarriage."

"You lie!"

Julietta came by to explain and calm them both down. A'jay wanted nothing to do with this witch and pushed her away. One of the local drug addicts, a friend, heard the commotion.

"Hey dude, chill. Come on over."

Lexi begged him not to go. He threw his cup of hot coffee at her, pushed her down, and left. All her dreams shattered in that instant while she lay in the sand crying.

"God, I understand nothing. Why must this be part of my lesson?"

Julietta consoled her and Nathalia helped pick up the broken pieces of glass. The children ran up to wrap their arms around Lexi's legs.

You know what you must do, the voice whispered.

Yes, she did! She knew it was time for her to leave. *No man will lay a hand on me.*

That evening, the two local ladies helped her pack her few belongings and offered to take her to the airport. Everything was happening so fast! Lexi slept well for the first time in weeks. Another angel came to her.

The soul that entered your being will strengthen you and make you wiser. You needed this life force for yourself.

When she woke, everything seemed unexplainably healed. She didn't remember the dream. The three women set out to the airport the next morning. Everyone was quiet. Lexi was confused and deep depression was already setting in. The words *focus on work* rambled through her brain. So much disappointment.

"Perhaps Julietta and Nathalia, my time has arrived. To heal and to forgive. To really find my purpose." They both smiled though they would miss her.

"Please look out for A'jay. Maybe he will get help."

They smiled and nodded. The airport was close by, so they arrived quickly. When she opened the door, the steel band was playing, "*Don't Worry, Be Happy.*"

"Is this a joke, God?" The three ladies all burst into laughter.

Julietta said, "God sure has a sense of humor. Now beautiful, fair-skinned lady, go be happy! I know there is someone waiting for you."

Whenever things went wrong, Lexi always asked God, "Why did this happen? Did almost dying in the water, losing oxygen, cause an issue with the fetus? Was I being protected from a horrible outcome?"

Most people can *see* what happened, but they rarely question *why.* There is a level of consciousness when these lessons come. Few are willing to learn. She understood this was part of her purpose, even if she didn't quite understand it all…yet.

A whisper explained, *it was not the time for you to nurture a child. There is a plan for you. This time, you got distracted with desire. This is part of your early journey. You will understand one day more about this circumstance. An important person will enter your life. She will need to understand why we experience loss. I am preparing you to help one who will need the insight in order to save their own life.*

Lexi recognized the familiar gentle voice from her experience in North Carolina.

"Who *are* you?"

A'jay would never contact her. The ladies went on their way to take care of their village, and Lexi would begin a new chapter of her life.

Her heart had hardened. She found it easier to shield it. While she did not understand, there was no denying the consoling voices provided her a sense of comfort and wisdom. She trusted the voices.

Anxious arriving back home, she didn't know what the future held. Tossing and turning she tried to sleep. Hours went by when she finally faded off and received a message: *"Prepare now for the undoing of what never was – We know not – for a source more knowing has plans beyond our consciousness. Have faith in God and continue to love."* The morning sun greeted her with a new perspective.

> The secret of change is to focus all of your energy
> not on fighting the old, but on building the new.
> –Socrates

CHAPTER 13

Finding a Job

New York

*D*ear *Diary, Sometimes, I get so excited, I miss the hints you show me. But I promise to be extra diligent now. Something has to change. I can sense it. My emotions are protected, and I desire my heart to heal.*

The time eventually arrived. After several months of wandering in circles, Lexi was tired of moping around and feeling sorry for herself. Her tiny apartment was closing in on her and she needed to get a job. Nothing was aligning for her other than meeting a seemingly nice fellow who was a server at the restaurant. They had a few informal dates but nothing serious. She wasn't ready anyway and kept her heart protected. Lexi realized she needed to meet with her brother for guidance.

Danny took her out dancing. Puzzled, she wondered why he side-stepped advising her, to go dancing first. "You will understand."

It was a marvelous evening in New York City. The air was crisp, the energy high, and the twinkling- colored lights on the streets created a magical setting.

Danny taught his sister how to dance when she was four. He would have her stand on his feet and waltz around the apartment. It was a love they both enjoyed. Every wedding or family event they attended you would notice these two were the first out on the dance floor. It wasn't until this day when Lexi realized this magnetic bond was also a motivating force for her passion.

The two danced for about an hour. Lexi suddenly realized the purpose of the dance.

"That's it!"

"That's *what?*"

"You knew this could ignite my inner flame, build my life force, and put a smile on my face. Dancing would open my creativity and desire to find my purpose."

"I did? I figured we were just going out for some fun," he said with a smirk.

On the way home, they had a heart-to-heart chat in the taxi. Danny needed to understand what she enjoyed and suggested to her he might have a way to help. After all, he had contacts everywhere.

He arranged several interviews in various companies, which didn't go smoothly. They just weren't a fit for her. She required something highly stimulating. It had to involve her imagination and fondness for travel. Danny reminded her she may have to pay her dues for a period. She understood but was not willing to settle.

Job Assignment

The next few weeks, she continued to submit more job applications. Determined, she was not giving up. Most of the interviews disappointed her until she got a call.

"Danny! You won't believe what just developed!"

"Do tell, sis!"

"I got hired to write!"

"If anyone could manifest their ambitions, it's you, sis. I'm so thrilled for you. So how did this happen?" "You had a magazine on the dinner table one day. I scanned through it, marked off the articles of interest, and afterward sent them my resume. I never expected I had a chance. I prayed for an angel to guide me. Then, it happened! I received the call!"

"You certainly have ample angels watching over you. More than anyone. I have a good feeling about this."

Danny never mentioned to his sister he had a relationship with the magazine editor, Marty. They had been friends since college at Pace University in New York. He was not surprised to hear his colleague was impressed with Lexi. The two met for cocktails and caught up on life. Marty and Danny were always ambitious and enjoyed a few laughs together about their college days.

"Well, she really does have talent and a broad imagination. Not only do I owe it to her for the pranks years ago, but I'm glad she didn't recognize me." The two fellows had a good laugh, toasted Lexi's success, and chatted until midnight. Danny was appreciative she had Marty as a mentor and the two vowed to never reveal their secret, unless of course she figured it out.

Lexi was hired to write articles in a national magazine about travel and one of her dream locations in the world. This would yield her credibility in the field. Her dream was now reality. For now, she had to prove herself.

"My assignment is in Egypt," she shouted to the world, even if no one was listening.

I shall pretend I am Cleopatra, sailing the Nile where men will bow at my feet and embellish me with gems. Oh, such an imagination. A young woman could fantasize, she mused.

Of course, there would be months of internship, trainings, and she must prove herself capable to handle the project.

It was a warm, muggy week in New York. Lexi was eager for the opportunity to travel, excited to find out what insights this experience may provide. She appreciated the salary and the bonus she would receive for writing an impressive feature story. She worked long hours and mentored with everyone who supported her inquisitive mind and hone her skills. Her boss observed her dedication. It paid off, for sure. It was unusual for a new team member to get such an offer. It helped that her professors sent shining letters of recommendation and of course Marty, knew she was a great kid, like her brother.

One of the team members, Tina, got along well with Lexi. They became buddies at work and close friends in their personal lives. Like Lexi, Tina had been obsessed with Egypt her entire life. They chatted for hours about past lives, aliens, and speculations on how the pyramids and other structures were built. These two could float away literally to a time before theirs, as if they lived in those moments with each other. Their minds worked together, even on projects.

They confided in one another that they could smell frankincense when they were deeply involved on the projects. The intrigue became deeper. The two began to research the significance of frankincense, wondering if it was a scent that would spark a memory for them. The connection was unusual, as they could read each other's mind, finish each other's sentences, and even travel in dreams together. Lexi's desire for a close friend was always out of reach...until now.

Lexi begged her boss to see if there was any way Tina could come to Egypt as her assistant. He placed his index finger to his temple and said, "Let me consider it for a moment." He closed his eyes, leaving Lexi to anxiously await his decision. After what seemed like an eternity to Lexi (but was probably only a matter of seconds), he reached his decision.

"Lexi, this is a fine idea. I've seen you two collaborating. Tina's editing skills undoubtedly will move the project along quicker. Let me talk to the board and I will get back to you."

"Oh my God, thank you so much. This will be awesome. Tina and I often feel we are there together." She scooted along and back to her desk, barely containing her excitement.

Tina and I will be able to explore the ancient sites and perhaps find out how far our friendship, our past lives have gone. There must be a reason we crossed paths. Tina was smart and Lexi looked up to her. However, it wasn't about this worldly connection they had at work; they both knew something else was meant for both of them.

Everyone in Lexi's life had a purpose; some unfolded later, others were warnings, and many remained to evolve. Over the next year, Lexi learned a lot more about teamwork. First, she worked on developing her skill sets. Then she learned how operations at a popular magazine were carried out to produce quality stories for publishing. At moments, she was uncertain. That good ole "Impostor Syndrome" kicked in. Editing simple articles was a challenge. She was required to learn basic editing skills. Could she accomplish this feature article? Tormented day after day, Tina became her rock, her support and cheerleader.

One of her mentors, Stella, pointed out that her doubt was natural. Stella was older, wore glasses on the tip of her nose, and had observed Lexi for months. She was a reserved type of lady. It did not mean she didn't value the devotion and diligence Lexi displayed. Periodically, she corrected or recommended, but essentially, she allowed Lexi to enjoy the fun exploration of creating. It was this freedom that allowed Lexi to use her talents to explore beyond basic facts and grammar edits. Stella wasn't concerned with those details, for now. She knew her creativity was unique, and her style brought excitement when storytelling, even at the employee lounge.

"Lexi, you are absolutely competent in achieving your goals. Your fondness for travel is undeniably a bonus. I have been paying attention, and you have what it takes to bring forth *a fresh vision and insights* for our readers. With your experiences, it seems you are destined to visit Egypt."

"Thank you, Miss Stella. This means more to me than you realize. I wasn't certain if you recognized I was qualified. I positively have a connection with Egypt. I always have, and I'm not clear why. I will find out soon. I'm different and most people may not recognize it as gift that could open one's imagination. I've been frightened all along, failing is not an option. I've been studying and research-ing for years about the ancient schools and the power of initiations one goes through. It's fascinating how they believe knowledge is 'revealed' in levels and it will be earned. What's really cool is the connection with symbols. I've been paying attention to them my whole life. However, what really intrigues me are the laws of time, death, and resurrection and the alchemy they speak about. I've had so many losses; I'm about to gain a new perspective on it all."

"Lexi, trust deeply in yourself. I recognize in my heart everything is preparing you for this journey. I look forward to publishing your article. By the way, Tina was authorized to join you on this trip." Lexi had no words to describe her anticipation for this adventure, approached Stella for a tender hug, and waved goodnight.

"I've got to call Tina and let her hear the news. In a few months we will have a trip of a lifetime or a previous life experience together."

Love yourself first and everything falls into line.
–Lucille Ball

CHAPTER 14

Another Goodbye

New York

Dear Diary, Finally, something grand! This is going to be a meaningful part of my life, thanks to my angels and guides. I've been preparing since childhood and every sign was always there, even Grandma's Egyptian coin. Every unit of grace you have bestowed upon me, God, at the moment of my incarnation, has served me, and I am ready.

Their flight was to leave in forty-eight hours. Lexi had some last-minute shopping to do for those important items a girl does not want to get caught without. She wrote all the details of their expedition in case someone needed to contact them. After a sip of Merlot and a stressful week, she went to pick up her phone when it rang.

"Oh, that must be Tina! She beat me to it," she said.

"Lexi, where have you been? We have tried to reach you all day."

"I've been working my buns off nonstop to get prepared for this huge feature story. No time to stop for anything. Why are you crying, Danny? Who's *we*?"

"Your friend Tina, well, she was in a car accident," said Danny, crying through his words. "Your boss, Marty, called me. He gave me the heads up and thought it would be best for me to share the news."

"Where is she? What hospital? How is she?"

"Lexi… Lexi…she died," his voice cracking.

"That can't be! No, God, you did *not*! This is impossible! Why?"

"Why did you go? Please tell me, Tina," she called out to her bestie. She dropped the phone, barely hearing her brother. Lexi was so busy; she never retrieved a message Tina left on her phone earlier that day.

It might have thrilled Tina to go on this adventure to Egypt, but she decided at the last minute she could not make it. None of it made sense. There was a little disappointment in Tina's voice, but she relayed on the voice mail there was a reason. She just didn't know it yet.

"Silly girl," Lexi screamed while listening to the voice message from Tina. "What do you mean you can't make it? You got the time off from work and our boss loves the idea of having you keep me on task with the project."

"You freaking *knew*, and you didn't tell me?" Lexi was beyond her sane mind, questioning everything, screaming, crying, throwing things, and falling to her knees in prayer. "I'm so fucking mad at you!"

Her last words took her final exhausted breath, and she fainted.

Someone was banging on the door a bit later, calling Lexi's name, shocking her back into her numb body.

"Umm, wait a minute, I'm coming," she barely mumbled. "Tim, what are you doing here?"

Tim was the waiter Lexi had met several months ago. They became friends and hung out together frequently. She wasn't exactly sure what their relationship status was, although he was kind and available.

"Lex, I heard what happened. I want to be here for you. How can I help?"

She just fell into her new friend's arms and cried her heart out. There was nothing else in this moment.

Tim was a person who was just there. It was like he was always watching over Lexi. Part of it was comfortable and sometimes it felt weird. They were more friends than lovers. However, she enjoyed the scrumptious prepared meals, after a long day at work, and a soothing foot rub he offered frequently. Lexi asked him several times, "How did you learn to cook like that?" he would never give her a straight answer.

Resting in his arms now, reminded her how safe she felt when she was with him. *He is almost too perfect*, she thought. A few moments later, she remembered she had a flight to catch in a day and would have to call work to cancel the assignment. Tim, who also worked with Lexi now, told their boss. Tim surprised Lexi one day and told her he was working for the same company. It did indeed shock her a little, but it appeared all good.

Marty totally understood and had already rescheduled her flight for after the funeral, in two weeks. A deep sigh of relief and more tears burst from her eyes. Gasping for breath and grieving for a loss so deeply, it was as if a part of her died.

Tim just held her, saying nothing, as any wise man knows, and continually handed her tissues to blow her nose. "Old reliable," always taking care of Lexi. But what was it about him? Lexi often wondered. She could not put her finger on it. He always seems to have everything taken care of.

The next morning, Lexi and Tim went to assist Tina's mom with the funeral arrangements. Her mom, Jessie, could barely stand. How does one handle the loss of a child at any age? Tina was a few years younger than Lexi, but somehow, they "clicked" and knew each other's secrets. Oh, the adventures they had in their brief time together…they would never be forgotten.

"I'm going," Lexi later blurted out to Tim later. "After this assignment to Egypt, I'm quitting my job and going back to Italy. There is no more time to delay and this I know." He tried to get a word in edge wise, quite shocked. He had something up his sleeve, but couldn't mention it at this moment.

The arrangements were all made. Everyone agreed this would be a celebration of Tina's beautiful life and laughter. Lexi would sing some of her favorite songs. As she hummed the song "*Stairway to Heaven*," the lyrics jumped out, "Sometimes words have two meanings." What was the message here? Surely, she wasn't doing drugs, or did she? The universe always had a way of sparking her curiosity and hoping she would look deeper into the truth.

Jessie encouraged Lexi to rebook the flight and leave sooner than later. Lexi wasn't ready, though her friend would probably have said the same thing. Losing your twin soul creates a deep, dark emptiness and she did not know how deep into the abyss this would take her. She felt lost, disconnected, with no one who truly understood this level of soul connection. It felt like jumping from a plane without a parachute, learning to trust you will be supported…falling.

Two weeks flew by. Lexi rarely came out from under the covers. The phone kept ringing, but she didn't answer. Behind the clouds, there was a light but all she could do was cry for help. She didn't want to talk to anyone but Tina. That's exactly what she did for days and nights. Tina would smile and make her laugh. She would tell her jokes and Lexi would laugh until she cried herself to sleep. Today, however, someone was pushing her out of bed, forcing her to move and get dressed.

"Tina, what is the message in that song, the lyric about words and their meanings?"

Out of nowhere came a thump. "Is that you?"

I am always beside you, dear one.

"Mom? Jesus? It sure doesn't feel like you." She didn't recognize this voice.

"I have nearly died; I've traveled in both worlds, and I still don't understand. I lose everyone I love and now this…my best friend? God promised me I would understand the why of experiencing loss. I do not understand why my friend also had to end her journey."

You will, very soon. Your wish and soul contract were to learn wisdom and seek the truth. It is now you will gain greater understanding of life and death. There will never be fear or questions about it. These grand losses had to affect you deeply, enough to learn your purpose and the meanings behind it all.

"Oh, goodie, are you going to show me the stairway to heaven?" No response.

"I want a life with ease and grace…please?" Nothing but silence.

It's all a reflection of reality. Words.

"Anything else?" Again, no response.

Go figure, she thought to herself, always, they leave me hanging. *Well, this time, Jesus, I'm going back to Italy.*

"I plan on singing or dancing or something! Something different! You heard me; I'm going to learn how to sing opera. They will recognize me for my arias. The crowds will cry with me as the melodies flow from the gut-wrenching pain I store deep within. Somehow, I will find *him*, the one I walked away from a long time ago," she promised Jesus. "I will create my reality!"

Just then, Lexi remembered the tin box handed down to her by her grandmother. Why now? she wondered. I've completely forgotten about it. Just a bunch of old coins. Could she have left something else in there?

"Grandma, what are you up to? You are in my head directing me right now. Where did I put that box?" She scrambled around in her closest. Blurting out loud, "There it is!" Lexi dumped all the coins on her bed, when a tiny piece of paper fell from the bottom. "There you go again, Grandma."

The note said, *One day, my beautiful angel, you will go to your special place. The time is now. Look for the coin I brought back from Egypt in this pile. You will know.*

How the heck does she do this shit? I have looked at these coins many times, but I guess I overlooked the fact one was not from America. Oh, shoot! *'Overlooked.'*

Take the coin with you.

Lexi added the coin to her pouch of good luck charms she had gathered.

Charms? The Egyptian pharaohs wore pieces of jewelry recognized as charms. Amulets, a protective shield to ward off evil, she said to herself. That's it! Something about this Egyptian coin is protecting me from something or someone.

Silence

Silence ~ nobody knows I am here... That I breathe...
In the silence there is oneness... there is love.

Potential
The life essence undefined
We live our lives to actualize and reach it
Truth, Faith, Hope, Understanding
Time to activate
With joy and strength
I communicate my sense of self..
—G.Coppola

CHAPTER 15

Egypt

A deep gold ray blinded her vision as She stood on the balcony of the Mena House.

How could I be here? I don't remember the flight. Oh wait, did Tim propose to me at the airport, or am I dreaming? Dear Lord, what did I say? I don't remember.

"The freaking Great Pyramid? What are my eyes witnessing? This can't be. So surreal. It's massive and I'm standing on a balcony. This seems impossible."

The phone rang and startled Lexi, hypnotized by the structure before her eyes. "Hello?" No one responded.

"Hello, who is there?" There was a long pause. There was no response, but she knew who it was. A phone call, a sign from Jesus.

"Lexi?"

"Oh...Tim." Her voice dropped a tone, sounding disappointed

"I wanted to make sure you arrived safely."

"You freaked me out at first with the silence."

"It must have been the connection," he lied.

"I'm going to get dinner and go to sleep. I'm so exhausted. Let's chat soon, okay?"

"Call if you need anything." Tim liked to keep tabs on Lexi. His unusual mannerisms could be unnerving and often Lexi wondered if he was a control freak.

After a lovely light meal of lentils in the Mogul Room, an Indian restaurant at the hotel, Lexi called it a night. Tossing and turning, she suddenly felt as if someone had transported her somewhere else.

Hello, bud...pretty fucking amazing, don't you think?

"You bitch, you came anyway, didn't you? A free ride."

Sort of, but I'm here to encourage you to move beyond the bounds of the physical and enter another dimension.

"How come I can touch you?"

We met at the same frequency. We are not different here.

"That is cool. I wonder who else I will meet in this dimension." *You might just be surprised. Stay open to the gifts you are about to receive.* The room grew dark. She heard a voice say, *You are Alexandra!* "Who said that? Tina, is that you?" No response.

"Wait, Tina, I need to know something! Were you taking drugs?" Again, silence. The rest of her night was restful. Lexi would never have her answers, but knew she had to trust and believe the guidance she received. This would be how she would learn to deal with all her losses...an inner knowing.

Her employer, Marty, had arranged numerous tours and special access to some temples and the Great Pyramid. Lexi researched about it for years, the time had come for answers. The ringing phone woke her with a pleasant surprise.

"Madame, we have a lovely breakfast for you on the way. Is it a good time to deliver it?"

"Yes, please," she said as she wrapped her soft white Egyptian cotton robe around her. "And thanks, boss," she added, as she put her hands together in prayer, acknowledging her gratitude.

She opened the door for the young waiter. "Good morning, come in. You can place the tray on the table."

"Allow me to serve you, madam."

"Absolutely, yes, thank you so kindly."

As she consumed her eggs and falafel, she read the laminated paper that stated: *It is considered impolite to point the toe, heel, or any part of the foot toward another person. The Egyptian culture highly values modest dress. Greetings often occur before any form of social interaction.*

Oh, dear, I'd better call Tim, she remembered.

"Operator, can you please connect me to this number in the USA?"

The phone rang several times before she heard his deep voice.

"Tim, we need to talk."

"I'm so glad you called; I was thinking the same thing."

"I said *yes*, didn't I?"

Tim lied to her: "Yes you did."

"Oh my gosh, we are going to be married?!"

"I believe so, beautiful one."

"I remember nothing, Tim. I'm so sorry. The Sleepy-Time Tea made me forget my worries. Everything has been happening so fast. By the way, can you do me a favor?"

"Sure, what do you need?"

"You have the key to my apartment. Please go to the teakettle Grandma gave me. Look inside and take all the money and deposit it in my bank account. I completely forgot with all that happened. There is a deposit slip there too."

"You want me to deposit Grandma's money for you now?" "Yes, please!"

"Okay, you got it!"

"Thanks, I may need it."

Tim thought that was kind of strange. What is she going to do with thirty dollars? This girl is not thinking straight, but I will pacify her. He also did not let her know there was more in the tea. He had knocked her out, adding a muscle relaxant and sleeping pill.

The anger soared, and the tears bottled up ~ tightness around my chest ~ Release, it needs to escape.

I asked God for help ~ I trusted ~ the emotions flared ~ you encouraged me, never once judged me. It was the first time, you see, I could feel all of me. ~ You loved me anyway.

The next morning, she went down to the gift shop to pick up snacks to take on a scheduled tour to the temples. Just before leaving, the gentleman who served her said, "You must meet my cousin. He can heal you."

Well, strange and interesting, she thought. Also, a bit odd for me to believe him.

"Really? How does he do that?"

"He was born with a healing gift. His eyes can see into your chakra system. He just knows what energy is draining someone or if their heart is broken." His voice was soothing and calm.

"And what does he do?"

"Honestly, he would have to explain it. It's not something I entirely understand."

"So, you expect me to meet a stranger, your cousin (gosh, everyone has a cousin, she thought), and just allow him to heal me?"

"No, he can come here tonight, and you can meet him. You decide." Remaining calm and encouraging, he did not want to scare her away.

"Okay, what time?"

After all, what did she have to lose? It could be an excellent piece for her article. "I will meet you here at six o'clock. Is that good?"

"Yes, Mahmoud will meet you here. His name means 'faith.'"

That didn't surprise her at this point. Words, meaning, reality, double meanings ...Lexi was understanding the signs more now.

It was an intense day in the scorching desert sun taking photographs. She learned about the history of each temple. Yet all Lexi could think about was the appointment with the healer. She ran back to the room as soon as the tour ended, cleaned up a bit, changed her clothes, and grabbed a snack and water while running down to the gift shop.

A tall, slightly pudgy Egyptian man stood before her with emerald eyes that cut right into her heart. His presence felt magnificent. He motioned to her with his hands to turn her palms up. She questioned nothing. It was like some powerful force overcame her.

Gently, he placed his hands on top of her palms. She almost fainted from the intense energy circulating around her palm which then shot up into her heart center. She had no idea what was happening. However, there was an innate sense of comfort.

While she had little knowledge of this 'healing' process, he stared through her eyes, as if he was looking into her soul. There was absolutely no fear. He spoke in Arabic and his cousin interpreted.

"He feels your deep grief in this lifetime."

Is he guessing? How could he possibly know?

"He says the energy in your body is not yours or your responsibility to own. He says he could release it for you. He has healed many, and he wants to gift you a healing session."

It was strange, but she agreed.

Without knowing where she was going and who he really was, she got into a car with him, a perfect stranger. There was no verbal communication. Lexi felt as though she was moving into a different frequency of energy and time was not the same. She really couldn't express it when she wrote in her journal.

As they drove up and down the small, narrow streets of Cairo, practically on the sidewalk, nothing phased her. Suddenly, the car stopped. He opened the door and summoned her to follow him.

They walked up a dark flight of stairs with exotic scents exuding from the wood. She had the sensation of being under the influence of a hypnotic aphrodisiac.

Politely, he held a heavy wooden door open for her to enter the room. The walls were lined with Egyptian glass perfume bottles emanating the scents of frankincense, sandalwood, and other unfamiliar fragrances. She could not feel her feet touching the wooden planks she walked on as she observed people sitting on red velvet cushions sampling the oils.

Mahmoud motioned her to follow him to a smaller room. There was a mat on the floor, with only a little natural light peeking through a window. The room darkening curtains dimmed the room. Stretching open the palms of his hands, he motioned for Lexi to lie on the mat. With no idea what to expect, she followed his directions, completely fearless and with faith.

There was a shelf by the door with various little blue and brown bottles. He picked up a few, poured a drop or two in his hand, and placed the precious oils on her body--from the top of her head to back of her neck to her heart, along with one drop on each foot. Then he left the room.

It was relaxing and soothing, but beyond that, Lexi didn't know what to do, except breathe and observe.

Moments later, he came back into the room. This time, he prayed over her body. He applied several more drops of oil to other parts of her body, including her palms and her heart once again. He stepped out of the room quietly. And in a flash, the room went dark.

Lexi saw an opalescent aura--a powerful presence of *someone* who loved her. Her eyes welled up as a floodgate of tears flowed. She felt the depth of her pain, stored for so many years. But who was this person hovering over her?

The healer walked back in several moments later and prayed over her body once again. This time, he did something with his hands. As if to clear her aura, he waved them through the surrounding energy. He paused, applied more oils, and left the room. The scent of frankincense caught her attention.

"Tina, is that you? Is the frankincense a sign you are here?"

Lexi wasn't questioning anything. She remained fully present at the moment--experiencing her grief, the longtime depression--when everything arose from her prior lifetimes. No one came to help her when she moaned and screamed. She lay there, waiting. Everything hurt. She felt pain through her entire being: physically, mentally, emotionally, and spiritually. The alluring light called and remained within her, reassuring her on some level that all was safe, and she was protected.

Lexi murmured softly, "I know I know you, but I don't know you."

Nothing made sense as she drifted through lifetimes. But Lexi was familiar with unusual circumstances and insights.

Every time Mahmoud entered the room, Lexi drifted off further while he prayed, anointed her, and mysteriously disappeared.

For decades she carried a heaviness, now lifted. She could feel a heat, an unfamiliar sensation building up within. For a moment, she thought she saw her mom standing in the corner. She closed her eyes. The room appeared like a gateway or portal, as if she could see an opening to somewhere. Her body floating like a feather through the ethers. Apparitions appeared, and she experienced a heightened sense of love extending through her entire being.

Not quite able to understand what would happen, she allowed herself to surrender. Joy embraced her like a fetus being protected in the uterus. She opened her eyes and saw angels above her, and her mother stroking her hair. The pain she was experiencing cut through her loss of her unborn child, the soul that gifted her the strength to make a hard decision in her life, one that remained a secret. Her heart full with compassion for herself, she realized God placed something in there she needed more than anything: a new life.

A sense of peace and calm came over her. The room was aglow. She felt different. *Free.*

The healer came back and remained quiet. He extended his hand to help her up. Not knowing what was customary, she just stood there in silence. The communication from her heart to his said more than words would ever describe. He held her hands once again. Palms up, he scanned her soul once more.

In this moment, she *knew*. He had healed her of her past. A few moments later, the energy in the room grew dense. He showed her the way out and smiled. He asked for no money, however she purchased a few of the powerful oils just in case she needed them again.

There are no limitations to the love that can expand in your heart.

The car was waiting outside, and the polite man took her back to the hotel.

That night, another dream. Tina came once again to say goodbye. All felt serene, and there was an understanding without words. It was time for Tina to move on her soul journey. Lexi waved to her friend, and, like Mahmoud, she now had a powerful presence of a soft pink light around her, a wisdom with no words and a heart that reflected a vibrant love for her friend.

Waking up, feeling renewed, she was excited to visit the Great Pyramid that evening. The hotel specially arranged for an intimate group to visit after the regular tourist hours. For now, she would have her coffee and journal her experience with Mahmoud. It all started with faith, she wrote. I always knew I was from somewhere else. The obsession to look up, never-ending.

Dear Diary,

Soon, I will stand before one of the Seven Wonders of the Ancient World. The oldest monument, supposedly. I say supposedly because it is only speculation and perspective. Like most things in life, there is always something hidden, I've come to realize. The Great Pyramid, completed before the birth of Christ, was slightly off, misaligned with the other two. Why? Some say it took more than twenty years to complete. I'm sure glad my mother told me to believe nothing of what I hear and half of what I see. I'm about to tune into something beyond what the physical eyes can see.

The Great Pyramid

It was the night of the full Blue Moon, an auspicious moment to be granted entrance to this sacred monument. The moment Lexi entered; she was drawn to the King's Chamber. A palpable force of energy took over her physical body. It allowed her to run faster than she could imagine through the dark passageways and up a plank leading to the doorway of the chamber. This part of the pyramid was under construction, but not for a single moment did she worry if the old wood plank may break. Heaven forbid, because she would surely fall to her demise. That was not in the plan.

At the speed of light, she consumed questions and insights on the truth of this structure and how it was created. Lexi felt some stories were not truthful. How did she know? Or was this just a fantasy? How much of the knowledge was speculation and how much truth was withheld? Lexi placed her hand in her pocket and touched her lucky charms: the mosaic brooch and the Egyptian coin. She silently prayed for guidance as she squatted down to climb through the small opening to the chamber.

Grant me the insight, the reason you brought me here and to learn the truth. Please and thank you.

The only lighting came from tiny half-burnt-out bulbs, enough to project a subtle yellow glow. Four people in the group sat, one at each wall, like the four cardinal directions. Alexandra, who finally at that moment decided to own the power behind her name, was drawn to a magnetic area within the chamber. She wondered if it was the "true north," as she had read in many books. Since something pulled her there, she believed it be so.

Sing, Alexandra, from your soul voice, a voice she didn't recognize whispered.

She remained still, breathing into her heart center, asking to be shown how to connect with her soul voice. She was no longer thinking; she could hear every echo in the universe and her sight became clearer and more vivid. Guided to open her lips, a deep resonance escaped from the pit of her belly, as if to charm the ancient guides to come join her and open the gateway portal. Each tone blended into another, bouncing off the stone walls, hitting one in the heart center like a laser, cracking open the light we hold inside. Within moments, the four people in the chamber began to chant random tones. It was a mystical moment, a connection with a God source, an unexplainable dimensional shift.

Suddenly, the lights went out. In the absence of stimuli, one could imagine hearing the molecules of air vibrating, a conscious communication not familiar to most humans.

Alexandra fused into time and space and didn't question anything at that moment. She experienced the veils lifting (or, at least, what she thought was this phenomenon). Her eyes were open in the utter darkness of the space, yet she could see swirling lights, auras, and higher dimensional beings in light form. She sat and observed, knowing on some level she was being guided to connect with these beings. It only felt like seconds before she heard a form of communication. She later learned two hours had gone by, but there was no time as we humans understand it.

The first whispered tone was unidentifiable and not in the English language. Alexandra was aware she was receiving a gift and allowed it to happen. She could never put it into words because there were none in the human language, at least, as we know it. The closest explanation was euphoria. Absolutely nothing distracted her, and she wasn't seeking answers. It was pure mindfulness of spirit.

I'm here, Alexandra. She recognized *that* whisper.

"Mom, is that you? Where have you been? I've looked for you everywhere."

I never left you. I have always been here. Only my physical body moved into a parallel frequency where you were unable to see me with your eyes. Alexandra said nothing.

You see, Alexandra, you can hear me clearly and sense me because you removed your mind chatter. You found me because I never left while you were searching. Now, you will learn more. Answers will come. The time has come for you to step into your gifts and live your life.

Alexandra understood and, telepathically, as she communicated to her mother, it made sense. She was ready and open to receive. Silence.

Sweet child of mine, I'm here too.

"Grandma? That doesn't sound like you. Maybe the frequency shift makes you sound different."

No, I am not Grandma. I'm your birth mother. Alexandra didn't seem shocked. She always had a sense she was adopted.

You will find out more. Be patient. I will come to you again in the right time. Silence.

"Grandma, are you here too?" No response. Lost in an abyss, supported by a greater source of love, trust and faith, she waited.

"I've guided you, protected you, and shown you the way. Now it's time for you to find your own path."

"But I want answers. Please don't leave me."

Child, all the answers are already within you. I will always be here, Alexandra's true birth mother reminded her.

Just then, a small light illuminated the room.

"Birth mother? I have so many questions."

The group sat there in awe, quietly assimilating their own experiences. Once Alexandra decided to rise, an incredible surge of power propelled her out of the chamber, down the wooden plank to the stone entrance way. She stood looking out, ready to fly.

For the next seventy-two hours she needed no food, no sleep, and was in tune with all being shown to her. She didn't need to speak, and it wouldn't have mattered anyway, because no one was able to see her. She realized this one afternoon when she spoke to a woman who nearly passed right through her, never responding. It would happen many times during these three days.

After sitting inside the Kings Chamber, she wondered about many things, including how the stone was laser-cut for this massive structure. Twenty thousand people came together, it is written, to construct this site and move stones that weighed thousands of pounds. How did the sound travel, and was this a communication tower to higher dimensions? The questions would linger for a long time.

Perhaps the greatest insight was the veil lifting through the dimensions. How easy it was to communicate with the souls that had passed on and to learn about her birth mother. While it didn't quite surprise her, always feeling she was not of her family, she did delight in knowing her intuition was real. Now she looked forward to finding out more about her birth mother and tying up the loose ends that left her confused through life.

Dear Diary, I'm seeking the words to describe this wisdom passed to me, this mind-blowing experience. I know I will never be the same. My heart has been healed; my mind expanded. I now have clarity in my vision and a burning desire I've yet to comprehend.

Alexandra realized every sign had a meaning and, perhaps, a deeper one to decipher.

When she returned from Egypt, her boss sent a limousine to take her home. How was she going to write an article on these experiences? She wanted to provide greater depth and insight to the readers.

However, she didn't anticipate the many unexpected things waiting for her when she arrived home

CHAPTER 16

New York City

Lexi assumed Tim would greet her at home.

Something is amiss, she sensed it. She tried calling him on the drive home. There was no answer. She called her employer to announce she had landed back on American soil and was ready to create an amazing feature about her Egyptian experience. They chatted for a while. They were both excited about the story concept. Next, she asked for Tim. "He didn't tell you? He quit." Startled, Lexi had no comment. What the heck was up? Perhaps he had a surprise for her at home.

"I was not reachable for most of the time. I didn't get a message he left," she said, forcing a lie. The driver brought her baggage to her residence. She thanked him and he would not accept a gratuity. "It's all taken care of, Miss Lexi." Unlocking her door, she couldn't shake the deep sense she was stepping into an unfortunate situation. Maybe he is sleeping, or he has a surprise engagement party awaiting me. No one was there as she walked into the apartment. It was cold and deserted. Tim was nowhere to be found. No note, no voice message. How odd!

I will unpack and worry about him afterward.

It wasn't common for Tim to be missing. Many theories drifted through her head since she had just lost her best friend.

"Damn it, Tim, where are you?"

What was it about him, that consistently had her curious? A gut sense caused her to race over to the teapot Grandma Rosa had left her. All the cash was gone. "Well, I told him to deposit it," she declared out loud. Suddenly her eyes detected a piece of paper laying on the floor. It was the deposit slip for the bank.

"Damn, you did *not* do this, Tim. No way! Calm down, girl," she told herself. Tim would do nothing like that, assuming he never deposited the money! She opened her computer to log onto her bank account. Her heart sank. No *fucking* way!

"Seriously, Tim, you ran off with Grandma Rosa's money and my savings!? I better contact the police." Lexi began calling everyone. All her friends sounded uncertain, and some were stunned, except one.

"Bob, where is he? You two are like twins," she screamed. "Settle down!"

"What did you say? Do you comprehend how much money is missing from my bank account? Calm *down*? I'm going to murder him if he's not dead already!"

"Lexi, Tim moved. Actually, we both did. I mean, we took off together." "*What?*" "We ran off together. Goodbye." "Wait, what did you say?" The phone connection dropped, and no matter how many times she dialed, he would not respond.

"Those sons of a…now I am calling the cops. Damn, if Tina was here, she would come with me to find their sorry asses and knock the crap out of them."

"How could you do this to me? You were constantly kind and caring and suddenly you slip away with my savings after you propose to me!" Frantically talking to herself.

Screaming, frantically talking to herself, sobbing, pacing, and infuriated, Lexi didn't know what to do. She sank down on her couch, placed her hands over her eyes, and moaned, "I'm sorry Grandma, I'm so sorry."

No worries, my baby girl, there is a reason for everything.

"Grandma, it wasn't just thirty dollars! Those silver certificate bills and rare coins were worth money to a collector. I also saved an enormous amount of money to go back to Italy. The son of a bitch took everything. Thank God I didn't leave *the key* in there."

The police were knocking on the door, Lexi quickly dried her tears and allowed them in. They received a full statement from her and a complete description of Tim. They said they would notify all his contacts he was missing. She mentioned Bob and provided his former address, though they allegedly had escaped the country.

"Ma'am, we will look at everything and do what we can to recover your property. However, if they left the country, it may not be hopeful. If there is anything else you remember, here is my card. You can call me anytime. Do you need any other help?"

"No, thank you, officer. I'm exhausted from a long trip and deeply disheartened that a dear friend and fiancé would walk out on me and with my money." The police officer acknowledged, tipped his hat, and showed himself out with his associate. "Check to see if he took anything else and inform us." She locked the door, sat on her couch in dismay and tried to make sense of things. "I need a glass of wine to calm my nerves." She opened a bottle of merlot, teary eyed, breaking out in hives from nerves and doing her best to remain grounded.

She couldn't understand how a man like Tim could be so evil. "What did I *overlook?*" She questioned herself, remembering the wise words from the shaman so many years ago. Perspective is everything. Perhaps, one day you will see this as one of the most enlightening adventures opening a new world for you.

You never saw who he really was, Lexi, a voice called out in her head.

Just then, she found a piece of paper on her dresser.

"You never said yes. Signed, I see you." "No freaking way!" she exclaimed out loud. "Why would he say that? It *couldn't* be!" That's all it said, nothing else, not a name, but it was clearly Tim's hand-writing. She recognized it well from all the cutesy notes he had left her in the past.

Several weeks had flown by when the officer showed up at her door.

"Miss, I think we should chat about your incident." Lexi showed him into her apartment, and he asked her a few questions.

"Sir, this is everything we have gone over."

"Did you ever go to Switzerland?"

"Why, yes, several years ago."

"A woman named Suzette de LaRue filed a police investigation several years ago. Do you know her?"

"Yes!"

"It turns out the hotel where you stayed for a few days fired a young gentleman."

"Oh my gosh, they did? There was a mysterious phone call I received. Also, a strange statement a waiter made to me. It fright-ened me, but I thought little about it."

"Well, it turns out this man was stealing money from many of the guests' rooms. When Miss De LaRue began the investigation, the company fired him. It turned out he moved to the United States. He must have searched for your address before he left. We believe he was out for revenge. Did you hear he moved to the US?"

"Absolutely not, sir. I never met him. The moment the waiter came to our table, I was chatting with Suzette. I never saw his face."

"Well, ma'am, it appears to be the same person. He dyed his hair, apparently, according to photos that were uncovered. Do you have a picture of him?"

Lexi scurried to her dresser drawer, where there was one someone captured while they were out at dinner, laughing one evening.

"Here you go, officer."

He studied the features, the shape of his eyes and lips, and determined it was, in fact, the same person. "Miss, you are lucky he left. He is a dangerous man. After he lures women in and steals from them, he has occasionally raped them."

"*Impossible!* We never had sex."

"I understand. That is why you never suspected him."

"Oh, dear God! I guess losing a few thousand dollars was a blessing."

"There is one other thing."

"What?"

"They found him dead. From what we gather, the investigators in Switzerland had hunted him down for two years. When he mistakenly returned, after stealing your money, he was unaware they had been searching for him. You actually helped them solve a case."

"But wait… you said he was dead. What happened?"

"That is still under investigation. It appears there was a love triangle."

"I don't feel you have the right person."

The officer pulled out all the photos he had and displayed them on the table for her to examine. "Do you recognize this coin? They found it in his pocket. It is evidence."

Her jaw dropped, her heart throbbing, her hands shaking. "It's him. Yes, that is one of the coins my grandmother gave me. It was in the teapot."

"Well, miss, it may have saved your life. This is evidence from your belongings."

The officer got up, tipped his hat, and left her apartment.

What would she do now?

That night, she had a dream. Grandma came to her.

Dear child, I left you the tin because it was to lure the danger away from you, and it did. However, you have a key and a letter to open. I

protected you with the coins because I knew you were in danger. The
key is my gift to you. You will learn everything, I promise. It will make
sense in the end.

Jumping out of her dream state, confused and rapidly breathing,
Lexi could feel the presence of her grandma in the room. She cried,
giving thanks.

"You have always looked out for me. You are my guardian angel.
Thank you."

Her article on Egypt was well received by the magazine subscrib-
ers. Her employer entered her story in a contest. She never expected
to win but prayed she would have that credibility one day.

The following day, Lexi returned to work and requested a meeting
with Marty, her employer.

"Come sit down. What's on your mind?"

"Marty, I desperately want a change in my life. I'm leaving and
will quit soon. I want to move to Italy."

"Hold on, don't jump so swiftly!"

"Actually, it is something I have considered for many years. I
believe it is the appropriate time. I need to modify many things."

"Let's talk this over before you carry out any hasty decisions. The
board and I respect you and your contributions. Perhaps we can
reach another arrangement?"

"I don't have another option, Marty. I've already made my choice.
A different life is what I want." "Would you allow me to take this
matter up with the board? Perhaps we can figure out what we can
offer you?"

"You can work out whatever you'd like. However, I'm moving to
Italy, no matter what."

Lexi got up from the leather cushioned armchair, turned her back
to Marty, and confidently strolled out of his office.

Marty instantly called Stella to come to his office. They needed to come up with a plan, *quickly*.

Italy Café 2014

Alexandra realized the hours had drifted by. Time to call it a day. Graciously, she waited for Marcello to provide her with the cost of for her meal and wine. When the polite proprietor of the café approached Alexandra, he realized something was amiss. He addressed the beauty and asked her if she wanted anything else today.

"*Grazie*, Marcello, you have been kind to oblige me to remain here all afternoon and write. I have appreciated your delightful café, your singing, and your heavenly food."

"You are indeed welcome, lovely lady. Please come anytime."

She nodded her head and paid for her meal.

As Marcello walked away, she wondered what was familiar about him. She absolutely enjoyed his company, and he made her smile. Tucking away her journal in her large purse, she considered another encounter to learn more about Marcello. It would be great to walk after sitting for so long. A nap was in order and tomorrow she had plans to go into a quieter place of this charming country.

Moments later, Marcello went to clean the table. He found an envelope on the ground.

Oh dear, I hope she didn't drop something important.

The envelope had the name "Selena," embossed with a seal. He decided to find Alexandra later and return it to her. Surely, she must be nearby, he suspected. Placing the letter in the pocket of his apron, he was confident he could narrow down the hotel where she was staying after he was done with work.

Alexandra settled in her comfy room, drew the drapes shut, and was ready to relax. After showering, with the aromatic gel, clearing her energy from the day, she dried herself off and wrapped the bathrobe around her.

Lying on the bed, she opened her journal to read some of her previous entries. Casually turning the pages, she landed on the expedition to Peru.

I remember the train ride to Machu Picchu. Perhaps a coincidence, I'm taking a train ride tomorrow morning? Hmm, she thought, rubbing her temples.

While Alexandra drifted off into her world adventures, Marcello became extremely busy serving dinner to his patrons. With no alternative, he realized he would not have time to find her after a late night. He would rise early and conduct his search. It couldn't be hard, he figured. Only two hotels were close by. Undoubtedly, she is in one of them. I only wish I knew her full name.

Alexandra rose before sunrise and took an earlier train. The concierge helped her arrange everything. A few nights at a trullo in Alberobello sounded lovely. She always wished to visit the white city and reside in one of the quaint cottages in southern Italy.

"*Grazie* for all your accommodations and for helping me resolve my plans."

"No trouble, ma'am. It has been pleasant to have you stay with us for a couple of days. I wish you an enjoyable journey to the quaint and historical Puglia region."

She tilted her hat and entered a car standing by to transport her to the station.

Marcello watched the morning sky brilliantly shine upon the city, as he scurried around the town to locate his lovely patron. The first boutique hotel did not recognize his description. Surely, he guessed, she must be at the other one.

Disappointed when he chatted with the attendant at the counter, there was no one who fit the description. He scratched his head and didn't know what to do next. A young woman came out of the office and saw his distraught expression.

"May I assist you, sir?"

"No, no luck today. I search for someone."

"Perhaps I have seen this individual. Please tell me their name."

"Alexandra," he uttered.

"Do you mean the sophisticated lady who wears a hat and carries a journal with her?"

Marcello perked up, barely containing his excitement, "*Si! That one!*"

"Oh sir, you missed her. I can inform you she left the area on a train."

"I found something. It fell out of her journal. I must get it to her. Can you please help me locate her?"

"Well, you must understand we cannot give out information. However, this sounds extremely urgent. I will make an exception. She is headed on the next train to Puglia."

He dashed out of the hotel immediately to catch her before she boarded the train. Racing through the glass doors, he added an appreciative *grazie* to the sympathetic woman, wearing a pleasing smile on his face.

Marcello reached the platform, when a train was leaving. He prayed it wasn't the one she was on. Scrambling to find the ticket agent, he learned it *was* the train to Puglia. The next one was in two hours. Pacing , he had to decide. "Please, may I purchase a ticket for the next train? Where can I find a telephone? I must call someone promptly." He spoke in Italian to the agent.

The agent recognized his troubled look and quickly responded to help him sort things out.

He decided to call Dominic, his cousin and partner at the café.

"Dominic, I need your help!"

"Sure, what is wrong?"

"I have to take a train to Puglia, near Alberobello. A lady ate at the café yesterday. She dropped something important, and I missed the one she was on. I must go on the next train. Please handle the café today."

"No problem. Everything is under control. I detect this lady may be someone who charmed you."

Marcello heartily laughed. He grabbed a coffee and sat down to wait for the next train. His mind wandered. Did I ever meet her before?

New York Staff Meeting

"Good morning, Lexi, can we chat for a moment?"

"Sure, boss!"

"I believe you may like the offer the board and I came up with last night. We went over this several times, and a wonderful opportunity is here for you."

"Go ahead, hand it to me," doubting anything would convince her to change her plans to leave.

"We all agreed you need a change of scenery, a different perspective, and a new start."

She nodded and listened.

"This is what we propose. Ready?"

"Umm, I suppose. But don't expect me to stay in New York City."

Marty had a grin from ear to ear, no dummy to what she desired.

"You are going to remain on staff, and we have planned something you can't refuse."

"Seriously, Marty? I'm not staying! I told you already!"

"Listen to me. We have an assignment in Peru for you and then ...hold on tight!"

Lexi shook her head.

"We are going to pay for your relocation...to *Italy!*"

"What? Are you serious? This is a joke, right?"

"No, young lady, it is not. We don't want to lose you! Since you can work anywhere and virtual work is possible in this generation, why not? Right? What do you say?"

"I'm speechless. Go figure!"

Lexi couldn't believe her ears. Not only was she going to move to Italy, but the company was also going to help her pay for it and keep her on staff, writing. This was an amazing opportunity.

"So? Can this work for you? Starting next week?"

"Wow, trying to get rid of me quickly, I see," she said jokingly.

"We have an assignment for you in Peru. Once you return, you can make your plans for Italy, and we will work along with you the best we can."

"Okay, it's a deal!"

They high-fived each other, slapping the palms of their hands together in the air. "Oh, I would like to take you to dinner tonight. I have some important things to review with you, ok?"

Stella went over to Lexi's desk and with a huge congratulations and a warm smile, placed her hand on Lexi's shoulder, like a proud mother.

"Lexi, I'm so happy for you and glad we could make your dream a reality."

"Stella, I'm speechless. I'm trying to believe it. Marty has treated me so well, it's beyond belief."

"Well, young lady you are not dreaming You earned it, and we want you on staff."

"I could not be happier!" She wrapped her arms around Stella, gave her a huge hug, and started to cry.

Marty shouted out, "Hey you two, we will have no tears. Go to work!"

Lexi had a lot of planning to do, and the next week would be busy. She agreed to remain on staff for at least six months to train her replacement and prepare for her next assignment. Tons of research was in order since she had never been to Peru.

Lexi went to the restaurant promptly at 7pm as agreed with Marty. The hostess escorted her to the table where Danny was waiting.

Confused, rubbing her head, announced "What are you doing here?"

"The question is what are you doing here, sis?"

"Marty told me to meet him here tonight. But I'm confused why I was brought to your table?"

Danny did his best to be quiet, knowing Marty was a prankster. In that moment, Marty strolled over to the table refraining from laughing, he politely said "Hey guys, how are you?"

Baffled, Lexi asked "You two know each other? How?"

They both laughed hysterically and synchronously responded "You don't remember, do you?"

Lexi really didn't get it, yet. She was perplexed, squinting her eyes and shifting the left side of her cheek upwards.

"Sit", Marty said, pulling the chair out courteously for her.

"Ok, guys what's up? I am really at a loss of words."

"Marty, do you want to tell her?"

"Nah, Danny, I think you should have the honor."

"C'mon guys, someone tell me what's going on?"

"Let's get some drinks, first."

Danny began to talk about some childhood memories when Lexi was about four years old.

"Do you remember a silly friend of mine and the games we would play?"

"Not really, I was too young."

"Well, young lady, we were pranksters and I once made you cry. For which I'm sorry," Marty explained.

Lexi punched him in the arm and laughed.

"Well, I guess you do owe me that transfer to Italy?" Everyone laughed, toasted each other and shared some fun memories. Lexi was delighted to know Marty was like another brother. It all made sense why he looked over her.

CHAPTER 17

Peru

Concerned about altitude sickness Lexi arrived in Lima, Peru to adjust to the heights she would experience over the next few days. Her guide and companion knew Peru well and she was told he was a deeply connected soul, intuitive and heart-centered who grew up in the Sacred Valley. She had never met anyone like him and instantly recognized how present he was greeting her. The first day she rested a little, enjoyed a new Peruvian dish at one of the local restaurants and the two got to know each other. Gustavo was a perfect gentleman, and she was surprised how well he spoke English.

"I would like to take you for a walk in our beautiful city. Would you accompany me, Miss Alexandra?"

He was so charming, handsome, and convincing, how could she refuse? Little did she realize he was reading her and was about to change her life. She told the universe her yearnings and it was delivered.

Their conversation flowed so easily while they had some fun getting to know each other on their walk. Once they reached a place to sit, confronted her face to face. She squirmed, uncomfortable with his intensity. His hands caressed her cheeks gently, when she pulled back as he said, "You have much to learn about love." Her initial reaction was to get upset, angry and walk away. No truer words have ever been spoken to her. A serious look within herself may be in order, she realized. Her first reaction passed quickly. "How dare someone ten years my junior, tell me anything about love." Her eyes swelled with tears as her heart pounded. A deep truth resonated within her: Yes, she needed to learn.

Looking into each other's eyes, with no words spoken, just a heart connection, the world seemed to stop. Pure and unconditional… something she was not familiar with, especially from a younger man. Yet something older, deeper, more ancient, perhaps, resonated within her. The urge to leave pulsed through her skin. The instinct to run was evident, but his hands remained on her face, sparking an escalating energy within Alexandra.

It was as though she traveled to another dimension. No way to run, she was grounded in this portal of love. The water fountain at the center of town trickling onto the old stone was in the distance, as she closed her eyes and disappeared somewhere. Transported in time and space, she no longer had any fear, and a sense of calmness was in her heart. His hands were still on her face, only now something was different. She opened her eyes slowly. Where were they?

Lexi fell into his arms, tears gushing down her warm cheeks when she heard, "You have arrived and remembered."

Who was speaking?

In this presence, their souls melded. Something was familiar. His hand brushing her hair softly and whispering, "No love is greater than ours."

Yes, it was time she remembered. Here they were, now in a different country and time, and yet when Alexandra looked up, someone completely different was holding her. Was this the future? Clearly the man holding her had sparkling eyes, and he was older. Confused for a moment, she wanted to understand everything and in one breath; she didn't care. Is this love? Time stood still and at the same time moved rapidly. It was a duality of existence, knowing, not knowing, and wanting this moment to last forever. Alexandra felt herself drifting and watching a scene, as if she was in a movie or was this walking in two worlds, as the shaman mentioned to her years ago?

"Lexi, Lexi," a soft masculine voice with an accent called out. "Don't cry, I didn't mean to hurt your feelings."

Lexi looked up and found herself back in Peru with Gustavo.

What just happened?

"We were in a bed, holding each other. It was surreal. How do I know this person? His kisses are like my favorite dark chocolate melting on my lips. His breath was my breath. If two people could share one breath, connect so intimately; this is what I experienced. I was in the arms of someone else in the future. I don't understand."

"You were shown the capacity of loving and being loved. It happens when you learn about love."

Hmm, she thought. *A magical concept. Is it true? Was I imagining this, or did I truly transport into the future for a moment to experience this depth of caring and connection?*

Gustavo was so gentle and kind. Every word, every touch and every conversation was always caring. They would become acquainted these next few weeks. Being the skeptical one, she didn't allow him any closer and figured it was another adventurous travel romance. After all, she had work to do.

"Are you okay?"

"Yes, I need to rest. Would you walk me back to my hotel, Gustavo? I'm exhausted and tomorrow we have a big day together. I have an important article to send to the magazine about the ancient sites. It will require me to have a clear mind and keep my attention on the goal."

He held her hand softly and walked on the cobblestone road with no words spoken. She unlocked the door to her room. As he turned away, Alexandra said, "Wait, please come in. I want to learn more about love. You know me better than myself, it seems."

He did not respond with words. His lips touched hers like the softness of a snowflake melting. Nothing was rushed; and it wasn't time to figure out what was happening. Alexandra remained in the experience.

Am I crazy? What am I doing? How can this young man teach me anything about love?

Still embraced in an endless bond and connection, he invited Alexandra to lay down on the bed. It didn't matter in this moment if it was an old bumpy mattress that squeaked. Somehow, nothing mattered. They both slept well and that's all they did.

It was early when they both woke up around 6 a.m., facing each other with a smile. Nothing happened or did something shift in a way Alexandra would comprehend later?

The company planned a busy day for them, so they both needed to shower quickly and be ready for the van to pick them up. This was Alexandra's first excursion to Peru and every time she went to another sacred site, there was always deeper insight and memory for her. This time she would consistently hear; "Who Am I?"

"Wait a minute," he said, "Where are you rushing to? Nothing is more important than how we greet this morning, together."

Hmm, she thought. *What does he mean?*

As Alexandra stood naked and chilled on her way to the shower, he summoned the vision of loveliness over to the balcony.

"Look at the sun and give thanks."

"Thank you…got to shower now."

"No," he firmly and softly said. "Listen to the morning, it speaks."

She had to resist her New York sarcasm and learn, right? After all, he was going to teach her about love.

Ha!

A warm, sensual flow of kisses was bestowed upon her neck, his cheek meeting hers as he pointed out the large doorway and opened it. It was innocent and welcomed as a morning greeting.

"Be with me, fully aware of what is happening. See the colors changing in the sky and let us give thanks to the cosmos and the earth, for they love us deeply each day, but many never notice."

Alexandra slowed down her thoughts as he said, "Breathe with me."

His chest rose blending with her back as they synchronized their breath. It appeared the colors were brighter, but she was not going to tell him. There was no separation between them and time. She listened to the symphony from the birds singing a morning song and the trees whispering hello when he said, "You are connecting with the love."

If you say so, she thought.

They stood quietly for a few moments before he intentionally placed his arm around her and turned Alexandra to face him. She peered into his beautiful magnetic eyes She thought he was going to kiss her, but again he said, "Breathe."

What's up with all this breathing ran through her head. But she listened and followed his lead, because there was something magical and etheric about this process.

"Now it is time," he whispered. "Go take your shower."

What? I thought he was going to make love to me. My mind is so confused.

Off she scooted to the tiny and dimly lit bathroom to take a cool shower, as the hot water did not work well. Soon they were in the van, headed to breakfast with a few others. They had not said a word to each other since leaving the hotel. It felt kind of weird. He was different for sure, and her suspicious mind wondered if he was playing her. They arrived at a quaint traditional Peruvian local restaurant to eat breakfast and enjoy a delicious cup of Peruvian coffee.

Ahh, wonderful! The fresh brewed Peruvian coffee caught her attention.

He watched her every move as if he was in her head. He served her, took care of her, and was always right by her side. It reminded her of Tim, but surely it could not be the same.

It was time for their excursion to an ancient place, the "gateway to the gods," Aramu Muro, with a local shaman. Gustavo grabbed two bottles of water, took Alexandra's hand and made sure she was safe; watching the step as she entered the van. She didn't feel like

talking much and leaned against the window watching every building, all the colorful outfits the locals wore, and wondering what the
day would reveal. It was an unfamiliar place. Yet something inside
of her said, *this is going to be revealing and more powerful than you
ever envisioned.*

Aramu Muro was approximately twelve miles away. About halfway there, Gustavo tapped his shoulder and said, "Please rest your
head on me; you are tired."

"I'm fine, thank you."

"Lexi, you must trust me! I am here to provide for you and comfort you."

"No, it's fine. I want to look out the window."

He replied, "I will be here if you need me."

The van abruptly stopped. What was going on? It seemed the
local police wanted to check where they were going. It was a time
of unrest in the country and randomly the militia would inspect
vans, especially when foreigners were present. The group was not
prepared for this sudden invasion.

Hmm, odd, Alexandra thought, as they pointed their rifles in
the van.

A soft voice said, *don't look at them, keep your eyes down.*

This is crazy!

She wanted to get up and say something, but she had to respect
what was happening and not alarm anyone. They spoke in their
native tongue to the driver, and after a few moments of the
exchange, they were gone. Everyone took a huge, deep breath, they
were scared. The chatter began as the group questioned what happened, while others just assumed.

Gustavo assured us, "It's all good." His words provided some reas-
surance; however, Alexandra had never been able to trust a man.

The tension in the van was high, as everyone was concerned.
What if someone had been shot? Oh dear, the thought was awful
as she imagined the blood oozing over the body, perhaps even *hers.*

The van pulled over once again, only this time to purchase some cold drinks for the group. The drive would be a long one to the ancient site due to the condition of the old dusty dirt roads. Everything took longer on these antiquated roads. They were on a relaxed schedule, so the stop wouldn't interfere and shouldn't take long. Alexandra peeked above her sunglasses, on alert just in case. The driver disappeared. Everyone was chatting, but she was paying attention. It seemed to be taking too long for drinks.

"Shall I go check on the driver?"

Gustavo immediately said, "No, wait."

Fifteen minutes had gone by and only Gustavo and Alexandra realized something may be wrong. His eyes showed concern, though he remained quite centered and calm.

"I'm going in."

Moving quickly, so she wouldn't be stopped, Alexandra scampered down the steps of the van. No one paid any attention except Gustavo. When she opened the door, no one was in the little store. Everything was quiet, too quiet.

"*Hola.*" No response.

"*Hola*, I would like to pay for some drinks, *por favore.*" She wasn't sure what language they spoke but thought perhaps simple Spanish may be understood.

Suddenly, Alexandra was gripped by fear. A chill ran through her veins.

I better run back to the van; something is wrong, she thought to herself.

When she went to open the door, someone from behind covered her mouth, picked her up and dragged her through a curtain into a back room. Alexandra saw the driver was tied up and gave her "the eye," warning her not say anything. She was then thrown into an old uncomfortable wooden chair and advised to, "Shut up."

The clock was ticking, and no one said a word. *Where was Gustavo?* she wondered. *Strange he would not come in to check on me.*

A man with a worn, dark-skinned face, deep wrinkles in his cheeks, said, "Don't expect anyone to help you. Your friends have left you."

His rough, menacing voice terrified Alexandra. With a wicked laugh, he then pointed his finger at her and began an interrogation.

"Why are you here?" "I'm on a tour."

"Don't lie to me!" he roared, as he banged his hand on the rickety, old table, where he had also put his gun.

"Sir, I am really here on a tour with the group in the van."

"I have seen your picture. You are an intruder. We know who you are!"

"Please, sir, I think you have me confused with someone else."

Pounding his hand, lifting the gun, and pointing it to her forehead, he asked, "Are you calling me a liar? Perhaps, stupid?"

"No sir, I promise. I just think you are mistaking me for someone else."

"The news says an American woman was in Peru, looking for artifacts. She has stolen many of our treasures."

"It's not me, I swear," she said, her voice beginning to quiver.

He pointed the gun to the ceiling and fired one shot to frighten Alexandra. And he did a good job of it.

She begged for mercy: "Please sir, I beg of you. I am not that person. I have never stolen anything. I appreciate your culture and all the ancient artifacts. I came here to learn."

"Shut up! I did not tell you to speak!" She jumped from the forceful tone in his voice.

He paced back and forth, then whispered to one of his guards. The guard proceeded out of the dark, musty smelling room for a few moments. The driver had his head down, petrified. Alexandra was surprised he did not try to help in any way. Perplexed, thinking of a plan, and wondering where the rest of the gang went, she waited.

"You!" he snapped, pointing at her. "*You* stand up! Tell me what place in America do you live?"

"Yes, sir. I live in New York."

"Humph," he grunted.

"What do you do in New York?"

"I am a writer for a magazine. They send me around the world to write stories about the countries I visit. They are educational articles about the wonderful people I meet, the ancient sites I visit, and the interesting facts I learn."

"Will you write about me?"

Pausing, she responded, "What would you like me to say, sir?"

"I want you to say I protect my people and my country. I protect our heritage and stop the thieves who come to rob us of our cultural gifts. Will you do that?"

"I would love to hear more, sir, if you please. Then I can write it truthfully and let people understand you are *a guardian and keeper of this wisdom*, right?"

"Hmm, yes, I am a guardian and keeper of the wisdom. I like." He seemed pleased with Alexandra for the moment.

The other guard walked back in and handed a piece of paper to the authoritarian man.

He told his guard what she said, and both men laugh hysterically.

Spitting on the floor, he yelled to the guard, "Shut up, you think this is funny?"

He pointed the pistol at his heart and shot him, cold dead.

Alexandra nearly fainted watching the guard's body tremble and bleed out as his breathing ceased.

He wasn't laughing at the man, she thought.

"You see, miss, I protect myself. No one laughs at me. No one! Now, you hear my story, and you remember?"

"Yes, sir!"

He went on to share how vandals killed his parents when he was a young boy. They stole all their goods and clothes and left his parents to die. He cried over their bodies until their last breath. He was six. They ripped the clothes off his mother. His father was tied up and had to watch them rape his mom, while she screamed in pain and disgust. Then his mother had to watch them violate her husband and shoot him in the head after they were done. The little boy hid in a closet quietly until the last bullet was shot. Blood trickled slowly right towards his tiny toes, he took one quiet step back and hoped the blood of his parents didn't touch him and reveal he was hiding.

"I vowed to protect my life and anyone who trespassed onto my property who were not a friend. I will shoot them. Just like they did to my mother and father. I was left alone. I had nothing."

Alexandra began to understand his anger, his fear, and his dominion. It was quite intense and unrelatable to any experience she ever had, thinking; "How could people be so vicious?"

"No one would adopt me. I was unwanted!" he screamed. "I was left on the streets to live and starved many days. My clothes were ripped and dirty and no one cared. People had to protect their own families. They didn't need another mouth to feed. I would press my face up against glass windows of restaurants, waiting for visitors to leave their scraps." He held his hands on the side of his head in pain. "Don't you understand? They killed my parents!"

Touched by his story, she was speechless and concerned. She was sincere. "Sir, may I speak?"

"*No!* I am not done!" He threw his gun across the room, and it hit the wall. Alexandra only watched and prayed for a moment to escape. Out of nowhere came a squeaky sound, like an old, loose wooden floorboard. Everyone got quiet. As she held her breath, Alexandra prayed someone would come to rescue her and the driver.

"Come here!" he demanded. She obeyed.

"Stand in front of me. If your friend is here to save you, I will kill him for invading my property."

Quaking in fear, Lexi could only pray. She wasn't ready to die, nor did she want Gustavo to die.

Meow!! A mangy cat jumped out, startling everyone.

"*Ha!*" he said, laughing. He opened the door for the cat to escape.

At the same moment he pushed Alexandra aside to kick the cat away, someone else grabbed her quickly out of nowhere.

"Quietly step back with me. Don't say a word." The voice was recognizable and eased Alexandra's mind.

He, whoever he was, had untied the driver quietly already. As they got closer to the door, he heard the old man coming back, signaling to the driver to head to the door. The three of them barely got to the door when gunshots went flying across the small shop. "Run to the right and get in the van, now!" Alexandra and the driver ran quickly.

"Wait, Gustavo, come with us!" He looked at her calmly as he walked towards the old man. He understood his people and knew what to do.

In his native tongue, he said something to calm the man down. Reaching into his pocket, he handed him a little money. The man laughed knowing he was understood, as he let Gustavo go.

Lexi briskly wrote a possible story for the magazine:

One must be completely terrified at any age, especially at six, when bandits enter your quiet home and randomly begin to fire machine guns.

The little child, a 6 year old boy, ran into the closet as he heard his mother scream "Please, no, we have nothing!" She did not speak again as a series of shots were fired. The child's sobbing was uncontrollable, however he had to silence himself or risk being killed.

Blood began to flow towards the closet, and the child pushed himself as far back as he could, and remaining silent.

"What is it you want? I don't have much to give!"

"You will give us your life!" Suddenly, sounds echoed through the tiny shack of objects being thrown around. "Worthless," one of the bandits called out in anger. "Now you die, because you are worthless too." The last time the little boy would ever be held by his parents, cared for and fed. He would run away with the clothes on his back to find safety. Numb, never crying, he blocked it all out to survive. He vowed to himself he would never be poor. He would be the guardian of his village and watch over other homeless children.

An hour later and a long bumpy ride, the van arrived at the site. The energy shifted, and the group was no longer afraid but curious and excited. The local shaman greeted them in his native tongue and our guide interpreted the shaman's words.

They were going to partake in a brief ceremony and meditation before walking up to the gateway. But first, a drink of tea, a deep sigh, and some laughter to change the vibe. Alexandra said a quiet prayer, inhaled the fresh air, and was grateful she was alive and safe.

She had done some research prior to visiting this area so she reported back with accuracy in the article for the magazine. She also hoped she might have an experience proving to the readers this ancient site and its legend were very powerful.

"A portal, according to a legend, allowed the Inca priests to be transported to different places of the Inca Empire and to any place of the world. The interdimensional gate, Aramu Muru, also known as *Hayu Marca*, means 'City of Spirits' or *Willka Uta*, 'Place of the sun or gate of the gods.'" The interpreter began to share.

"For many, the Aramu Muru door is a place where a lot of energy is concentrated, and the body and soul are immediately nourished. You also get a sense of being in a safe place, where the body feels free, and all the pressures of daily life go away. A place you encounter peace. For many people, this is a good place to meditate on their daily and spiritual lives, to find the answers to many questions, and return home with more hope and energy."

This monumental structure is older than Incan buildings. It must have been constructed by a pre-Inca civilization. It is literally carved into a huge rock or cliff with peculiar diagonal lines. This is not a building; there is nothing 'inside' or behind the gate. It is carved into a solid cliff, she read this on the internet.

According to storytelling and legends, when the Spanish arrived in the Inca Empire, there was a priest, named Aramu Muro, who belonged to the monastery of the Seven Rays and was responsible for the initiation ceremony and worship of the God: The *Inti*, or sun god. The legend says the door opens only for those people who are spiritually ready to connect to the spirit of Lake Titicaca. But without a doubt, Aramu Muru is a place surrounded by mystery, where people say they have had sightings of strange lights and claim to have had visions of stars or columns of fire or to have heard sounds and feel the presence of a tunnel behind the door.

Alexandra listened attentively to the interpretation of the native shaman. Each person would have a turn to face forward with their body leaning against the gateway. No one really understood, but there was a heightened sense of excitement among them with the thrill of it all.

She observed and waited. Alexandra could hear an inner voice or someone speaking to her from a higher place of consciousness. So, she waited. It took about five minutes for each person to lean their body on the stone. Waiting for something, a connection. Others quietly waited, as some took photos. It was her turn next.

The minute she walked up the slight incline, she felt the energy become more intense, almost electromagnetic. Suddenly aware of other beings on the other side of the wall. The gateway didn't actually open, and the surrounding wall was solid, but she trusted her instincts, followed the instructions, and off she went to another dimension. Her intrigue with time travel or interdimensional travel was welcomed, once again.

She was downloaded with information, in an indescribable language far different from any on earth. She supposed it was providing her something she needed. Lexi had no concept of time, finding herself adrift in some fantastical altered reality.

How did I get here? she wondered. *We didn't use any herbal remedies, like ayahuasca. She disappeared…again.*

In a flash, from inside the wall a puma jumped right through it and into her. She had absolutely no response or fear, only a knowing. It was so real! The graceful animal was elegant. His eyes, his focus and fierceness…She believed the big cat's spirit merged with her. But she didn't understand why.

Alexandra slowly walked back to the stones lined up like a bench. They all sat patiently waiting. They were eager to share and had to be still until the last person returned.

Excitedly, everyone blabbered about their experiences. No one, however, melded into the stone or had a hologram experience. Alexandra wondered if she should stay quiet knowing she was *different*. She wasn't in the mood to be judged. Someone nudged her to share her experience, and afterwards, she asked the shaman what it meant. As he replied through the interpreter, he simply asked, "Were you afraid?" Alexandra replied "no."

The shaman merely gazed deeply into her eyes, smiled, and never said another word. Her curiosity wanted an answer.

What did it all mean? she wondered. *I knew he had the answer. Why wouldn't he tell me?*

As the group walked back to the van, Alexandra was still spellbound and tripped over a stone. Low and behold, her knight in shining armor caught her like a feather floating from the sky. She took her seat in the van, pulled out her journal from her backpack, and began to rapidly and breathlessly write.

I was gone…and no one knew. I entered a portal without knowing how I got there. I saw orbs but didn't tell anyone because I didn't want to sound even weirder. These orbs had images, faces, and symbols floating in an abandoned open space on the other side of the gateway. No one was there except me and the orbs. I know they provided me ancient secrets and, somehow, I understood it in the moment. But how do I access it now? Will someone tell me? Will the orbs reappear and translate it all to me? How silly, of course not, Lexi.

But the answers came almost immediately. *It's in your cells.*

Alexandra was exhausted. She felt drained and turned towards Gustavo; somehow, he seemed to tune in. Tapping his shoulder and gesturing to her to rest her head, this time she was only too happy to comply. She didn't mind as he placed his hand on top of hers and she didn't care what people might say. It was comforting and reassuring.

I am your spirit, your power source, and I came to you today to bring you courage.

Alexandra was instantly wide awake, wondering, *who said that?*

Hours had gone by since this miraculous and mystical experience. Yet no one she asked would tell her the meaning of the puma; they only smiled. She decided to let it go and enjoy the rest of the shopping for the illustrious colorful fabrics the Peruvian women weave. The vibrancy of the reds, oranges, and yellows are like a blazing flame in a fireplace. For the first time Alexandra actually appreciated these bold and passionate blends of reds.

After shopping, she noticed a woman standing outside the factory, hunched over, appearing to be in pain. She was selling jewelry. Alexandra was drawn to her and asked permission to place her hands on her back. She did not understand English, but her friend nodded yes. A smile came across her face, enough to show she had no teeth left but was happy anyway. The friend nodded to Alexandra and gestured with her hands saying, "more, do more for her."

It was in this moment; Alexandra discovered an unusual power spiraling out of her hands. It was more rapid, and her breath deepened. Closing her eyes, she witnessed a dark energy leaving the woman's body. Her intuition was telling her she had been badly beaten, so she prayed silently. Amazingly, within moments she stood up straight with tears in her eyes. The two women hugged Alexandra and walked away, disappearing into thin air. Was she imagining this healing took place?

Nah, I know they were there; I must've blinked, and they turned a corner, right?

When Alexandra returned to New York City to submit her article, the staff surprised her with a huge party. Overwhelmed with how deeply they all cared about her future, she didn't know how to respond. Marty chatted with her about some prospective future projects, and Stella encouraged her to *"find herself."*

Alexandra delightfully explained her upcoming plans for the move, her desire to research the key her grandmother had bequeathed her. She expressed her hope the board would understand the time she would need to heal. Everyone agreed, which made this shift easier for her.

Within a few months, her plane was booked, her villa in Tuscany was arranged, along with some cooking classes at the *Good Tastes of Tuscany Cooking School* for another article she was going to submit.

The final night in her apartment, she cried for every tear she had shed and all the ones she'd held back.

This goodbye was not sad; this one was welcomed.

CHAPTER 18

Paris

Dear Diary, thank you, God for giving me courage. Thank you for helping me manifest my new life. I pray I am able to find happiness. The answers I seek are coming.

She was tired of grieving, for she had far too many goodbyes in her adventurous life. Lexi made the decision to bring true love into her life, heal, and honor her birth name, Alexandra. After all, the name suited her well with her chic and courageous aura.

The last week in New York was rough. Fights with her father over moving grew intense. Alexandra spent many hours frustrated and bawled her eyes out, alone. Tired of being treated like an irresponsible little girl, she gave up the fight.

Alexandra won awards for her numerous writing accomplishments for the stories she wrote around the world. However deeply fulfilling, something was always missing within her. Was she destined to live life single or was something waiting for her, someone she left behind many years ago?

Her father was difficult as usual but, on some level, she understood his need to have her settle down and keep a job. He didn't understand the pain stored inside, the emptiness. Nor did he understand her plan to heal her way. Maybe he did and prevented her from discovering something in Italy?

Perhaps, her strong name guided her to a greater purpose in life. She missed her mom: her best friend, her guidance, and her confidante. Conceivably the only one who truly understood her gifts and dreams.

Alexandra now had to rescue herself and find out what life was meant to be for her. Her voice lessons went well in New York City; however, only a few saw her talent. She kept to herself for the most part. All was set for a voice instructor in Italy, and now was the time to move on. Everything was kept secret. She never even wrote anything in her diary.

Precious moments occur when we take the chance to value life, to acknowledge, to tap into our dreams and aspirations and to realize we can simply experience what is undeniable if we pay attention to the divine occasions right before us ~ Alexandra

Meeting Ricardo

Alexandra may have been delighted on her first trip to Italy at seventeen, but this one was even more enticing to her. All the paperwork for dual citizenship would be completed shortly. Perhaps she would invest in a home, ultimately. Soon she would discover what her grandmother's key would open. Her grandmother had already guided her so closely in life, protected her in many situations, and now that a trust fund was finally released, allowed her to book a first-class ticket.

How does one pack to travel across the ocean? You don't! You purchase what you desire when you arrive. After all, why not? First destination, Paris. Perhaps shopping in the one of the finest places in the world, she would find something divine. She treated herself to this side trip for her birthday and all she accomplished, including surviving the basic rigors of life.

The rumbling vibrations of the engine began, and the air conditioning booted up into high gear.

I'm so glad they provide warm blankets in first class, she purred to herself in delight while snuggling up for her new lifestyle.

"Excuse me, miss, I do not mean to interrupt you, but since we will sleep side-by-side tonight, I realized I should introduce myself." Alexandra practically peed in her pants, struggling not to snort a big laugh. "Oh, my sir, you are correct. That is quite funny. I'm Alexandra and you are?"

"I am Ricardo. A pleasure, my dear Alexandra," he said, placing the emphasis on the "dra."

"Is this your first trip to Paris?"

"No, he responded, I work here sporadically and live in Italy, actually. I fell in love with the region years ago. Three years ago, I asked my company for a relocation. Now, I travel intercontinental and call Italy my home. And you?" Alexandra had a million questions for him about residing in Italy, but for now she would acknowledge his questions.

"This is my first trip to France and my second trip to Italy. When I was seventeen, I fell in love with Italy as well. I love to travel and been to many places, but Italy calls my heart. I am stopping in Paris first to celebrate my birthday."

"Yes, the land of passion and love reaches inside the depths of our soul. No turning back now. Once we are called, we are home. No matter where we live. I must have resided in Italy through many lives. Now I chose to go home. I am able to explore, with simply one little responsibility. Paris is a beautiful option as well." Ricardo avoided sharing the "little" responsibility and promptly continued questioning Alexandra.

"Tell me more about your travel experiences and appreciation for Italy."

"I remembered seeing the gilded bronze Doors of Paradise. Like they reached deep within my soul, as if I were the one who created every panel. It may sound peculiar, but my fingers sculpted every shape."

"Not at all. That is splendid, actually."

"I would love to ask you some questions if you don't mind. How did you transition from America to living in Italy? Were you out of sorts initially?"

"Beautiful Alexandra, Italy is the most embracing place I've been. Once the locals welcomed me into their hearts, they broke bread with me, making me a part of their family. Like you, something causes you to feel you've been part of the culture previously. You will fit right in. Are you visiting or moving permanently?"

"I'm moving. I left everything and merely brought one suitcase. Somewhat bold, I suppose. However, I had to leave behind my past. My boss agreed to keep me on board to write articles and the board agreed to support my transfer. They provided the funds for my relocation." Lexi did not foresee their generosity.

"That is quite an amazing transition, young lady. I like your spontaneity and sense of adventure. Your employer must think highly of you to provide the opportunity to live here. We have some things in common."

Ricardo had been educated in America and was about ten years her senior. He shared his wife had passed several years ago. His teenage daughter had a troublesome time without her mom. Eventually she committed suicide.

Alexandra consoled him, telling him she certainly related extremely well to loss. Another unexpected connection that aligned them. He was of Spanish/Italian ancestry and fluently spoke both languages. During their discussion, he taught Alexandra a few phrases to start her journey. They chatted for hours, toasted one another with a glass of wine, and enjoyed a delicious first-class dinner together. An enjoyable time for them both, like they were destined to meet.

"Well, Alexandra, I suspect you found your home."

He pronounced my name just as I imagined.

"I live in Tuscany. Where will you be going?"

"I'm staying in the Tuscan region as well, thanks to the generosity of my company. I'm going to attend the *Good Tastes Cooking School* and compose a commentary about Italian cuisine. I'm excited for some fun. I understand their culinary classes are remarkable, and they provide their students a rich cultural immersion. I'm certainly looking forward to everything. My company arranged for me to stay at one of their villas. It's called Villa Pandolfini, a luxurious and historical residence. There is a spacious kitchen, gardens, and a marble bathroom. I am so in love with architecture, have been, in fact, my entire life. This is *ahh-mazing!*"

"Oh, and I also arranged singing instructions once I am settled. Something for a little fun."

"You are clearly fascinating. Since you will be in my region, I would love to invite you over for dinner. I actually live close to the cooking school."

"Is that a date?"

"Absolutely! My pleasure, young lady, to pick you up with my chauffeur. We will have much to celebrate together."

I wonder who this gentleman is?

They continued to share many more stories. They had comparable life dreams. *Perhaps*, she thought, *Grandma sent him.* After all, she loved to grant gifts.

The time was passing by swiftly. It seemed like they had known each other for ages. The flight attendant mistakenly inquired if they were on their honeymoon. They both chuckled, and he winked at her. The dynamic electricity between the two was so obvious, they beamed at the remark. The two eventually talked themselves to sleep. Ricardo tenderly placed his palm on Alexandra's while she was falling asleep. She drifted off into her dream world. Her last thought was *I'm saying yes to life this time!*

The flight was more than satisfying. She had enjoyed wonderful conversations with a stately businessman, Ricardo, who understood her. He wore expensive leather shoes and a handsome tailored suit. He captivated her on so many levels, and she looked forward to her first date with him upon her return to Italy. She wondered many things about him but decided to be content for now.

"*Bonjour,*" the flight attendant said while handing out warm towels as the coffee was brewing.

"Good morning, beautiful Alexandra. Such a pleasure sleeping beside you." She smiled and nodded her head. Her main agenda was to brush her teeth and use the bathroom.

"Excuse me, please. I would like to use the restroom." Ricardo stood up and provided her enough room to maneuver, as a gentleman would. Their eyes met for a moment, like the pause between breaths. She turned and seductively walked away to freshen up.

Ricardo had a good morning and smiled. He had not remembered the last time he had such an enjoyable exchange and evening with a woman. The connection felt so natural. He told himself he must remain in contact with this charming smart beauty.

Noticing her coming back, he extended his arm outward to allow her to pass to her seat with ease. The pilot announced they would land in approximately forty minutes.

"Thank you, Ricardo, for being a gentleman, teaching me a little Italian, and being a superb companion on this trip."

"It was genuinely my pleasure. We shall have many wonderful trysts, I am sure. You are my new neighbor." He grinned.

The plane had landed in Paris. First-class passengers had the luxury of departing first. He graciously handed her the carry-on luggage as they walked side by side to the baggage area.

"Alexandra, my driver is picking me up this morning. He is waiting. I would be happy to take you to your hotel."

"Impressive! Are you someone famous?"

"For today, let's not worry who I am. Shall we enjoy each other?" It sounded like a perfect plan to her. She sensed he was kind; she just didn't expect him to be wealthy.

"Tony, I would like you to meet this pleasant beauty, Alexandra, from New York City. She is moving to Italy after her holiday to Paris."

"Welcome. If I can be of service, please ask."

"Hey Tony, I already got dibs on her." They all laughed.

While he had some business in Paris, Alexandra would open herself to fresh encounters. They decided upon a date in Tuscany when they both returned to Italy.

Tony was kind enough to bring her to the boutique hotel. Saint Therese, located near the Palais and other places of interest, and close to the Seine River. Alexandra arranged her birthday celebration feast. With minimal time to explore Paris, she fancied experiencing as much as conceivable.

"*Grazie*, Ricardo and Tony. I shall be in touch with you both soon." She waved goodbye wondering what Paris would teach her.

Upon arrival, the dainty blonde concierge assisted Alexandra with a list of activities she might enjoy, along with restaurants she may appreciate. She didn't have a chance to nap. She sought to revel in all she could consume today.

First stop, comfortable shoes. Conveniently around the intersection was Les Chaussures, a shoe store. The youthful concierge loved shopping herself and shared, "Paris is an international fashion hub. One of the finest places in the world to do some luxury shopping." In fact, the city has virtually every brand you could think of and determining where to shop was almost overwhelming. The temptation to buy some exquisite designer shoes would be a challenge to resist. However, with comfort in mind, she acquired what she expected would be an appropriate sandal for her walks.

The sunlight was dazzling; the flowers were blossoming on this spectacular spring day. Excitement was in the air. She sensed something extraordinary was going to develop, sipping her latte and savoring the fresh crepe, licking the whipped cream off her lips.

Paris was vibrant with passion! Artwork was exhibited along the boulevards, in cafés and stores, and sculptures adorned the promenades. While strolling, she came across some appealing bronze sculptures. Rather intriguing how one artist, Bruno Catalano, captured the surreal personification in his display of "Les Voyageurs".

Quite the enigma, she thought, thoroughly mesmerized by the elusive travelers. Torn between worlds, with body parts literally displaced, and emotions expressed. "Les Voyageurs" represented the shifting of one's viewpoint of life, the world, and in the internal processes of one's thoughts.

"Brilliant!" she muttered.

Time moved swiftly. Captivated and possessed by the vibrancy of the city, she dashed back to her room to shower and change her clothing. She had a date with destiny on the Seine River Dinner Cruise. Little did she realize her thoughts were manifesting far beyond her imagination.

There was a serene ambience on the river cruise. Soft lit candles cast a gentle hue on the one simple red rose in an art nouveau glass vase. The Seine River was bustling tonight while lovers danced by the Eiffel Tower. Alexandra was seated promptly, served a glass of Castel Mouches champagne, ready to celebrate a rite of passage in her life.

While in France, she might as well experience foods she never appreciated. Snails with French-style peas, Parmesan shortbread, and smoked duck shavings were her starters.

Thrilled, she chose a window seat, as iconic sites revealed their romantic elegance. Of course, the Eiffel Tower, erected in 1889, was bathed in golden lights that shaped the giant structure to shimmer after sunset. The splendid views of the Louvre and the Grand Palais were captivating. Alexandra speculated, who would grace the grounds of this exquisite property, and what would it be like to have an encounter with someone you love?

She finished dinner. The staff took memorable photographs of her birthday celebration, and she enjoyed a last toast when the crew chanted happy birthday. Finally, she blew out the one candle burning brilliantly on her chocolate praline dessert, created a wish, and *voila*.

Alexandra wandered along the streets of Paris, like a soft waltz, back to the hotel suite. She realized an erroneous turn was made, while her head was in the stars. As she took in the sights, she saw a striking sculpture of Alexander III displayed across the Seine River Bridge, adorned with art-nouveau lamps and nymphs. Paris showcased the uniqueness of the artisans who traversed the centuries. Locating her hotel was not as easy as she had hoped. The marquees above the restaurants' displayed twinkling lights while her eyes were transfixed on the sky. Wavelengths of light scattered like a painting, projecting perpetual hues of tangerine and lavender.

Concerned now, as the night sky blanketed the city, she spoke to passersby in her limited French to convey her needs but found no one to assist her with directions. She stood calmly on a street intersection, adorned in her decorative bling blouse, calming her mind, and hoping she was nearby.

A chance encounter perhaps could happen, she thought.

"*Bonsoir*, Claudine," a dashing fellow attired in a business suit said. As he rapidly chattered in French, Alexandra did not realize he was talking to her.

He grew closer. "Claudine?"

"No, sir. I am not Claudine."

"Oh, you do not speak French?" he asked in perfect English.

"No, I'm lost, searching for my hotel. Perhaps you can assist me?"

"Mademoiselle, it would be my pleasure to escort you to your hotel. Which one?"

She showed him the business card embossed with the hotel's name.

"I recognize, yes. However, you must first join me. I wish to show you an extremely special place nearby."

Apprehensively, Alexandra replied, "No, thank you."

"Ahh, but if this is your first time in Paris, you must come with me to Jardin Du Palais Royal."

Seriously, was he about to take me to the identical place I romanticized about on the dinner cruise? It can't be! How can you make this up? God indeed has a sense of humor.

He tenderly clasped her hand to cross the boulevard. On guard, Alexandra immediately drew back. "You must be American? *Oui?* Relax, you will love the gardens," he said with a kind smile.

The stroll was short and, as they turned the corner, massive gates opened to the entrance of the Grand Palais.

"Come," he said, as he asked for her hand, "Let's enter the gardens."

Breathless, somewhat overwhelmed, she was surprised by what she saw. He didn't deceive her. Fountains adorned the property, and the benches were crowded with sweethearts who relaxed or embraced with kisses. Was she dreaming?

"What is your name?" "Alexandra, and yours?"

"Gérard. Ahh, Mademoiselle, this is the loveliest spot to take your photo. The flowers behind you create the perfect setting to grace your beautiful smile."

He stepped consciously closer to her like a gentleman and requested that she take a deep breath. "Would you close your eyes for a moment and remove your purse from your shoulder?"

Hell no, her initial reaction. He could steal my purse. Yet, her intuition said *"Listen"*.

She obliged. A familiar touch, one that comes in her dreams often, he caressed both her cheeks tenderly.

He paused; her heart raced. Her body quivered and her knees trembled. She wondered why this man as well was compelled to caress her cheeks. He stepped back gradually, and requested she open her eyes. Relaxed now, her face soft, with a magical essence whirling around her, she seductively smiled as he took the photo.

"This picture is indeed more appealing than the one you had on the cruise boat." "Wait, how did you know?"

"Show me," he said. "They always take one."

Alexandra displayed the picture. And he was entirely correct. "You softened in your element, seducing the camera."

She had no retort for the first time in her life. He stared at her adoringly, while supporting her hand. They strolled through the gardens, filled with pastel colored flowers blooming draped across the gardens elegantly, and with trees and hedges. The sound of music played in the distance, while lovers rested on the benches. He was intriguing her with delightful conversations and was quite a gentleman.

"Alexandra, did you realize when one experiences deep emotions, they must compose them within twenty-four hours, or they will never regain the senses to express them fully?"

"Write? Do you *write*?"

"Yes, and I imagine you do as well. I can recognize an artistic person…The passion that passes through their veins, deep into their soul. I can sense the burning flame of desire, the wonderment, and the deliciousness when their words speak."

Alexandra again had nothing to say. No arrogant remark. No brilliant response. "You seem surprised? It has been many years since you have felt deeply?" "Yes."

How does he intuit these things?

"My dear, allow me to ignite your flame for life. Pleasure is at your service." he took a bow.

It was awkward, though she was curious about what he actually meant, she continued to walk with him, captivated.

"Lovely lady. Shall we learn about each other and share a wonderful evening together?" "I made a wish today. Today is my birthday."

"If I may take the liberty, I imagine you yearned for company on your birthday." "How do you know that?"

"Because you were heard, and I appeared. Events like this don't just happen. There is great energy in our wishes, and when we connect with them genuinely, two people have a chance encounter to bring them to expression. Some may call them soul mates."

He placed his arm around her shoulder while they walked, leaned towards her cheek gradually, and pressed his warm cheek against hers. Slightly turning her head, their mouths now aligned. Energy grew through her belly and tingled all the way up to her breast. Alexandra did not understand what was developing, but sizzling feelings were stirring inside. Something she neglected for several years, something lost in her life.

She would experience a proper "French kiss," sustained for minutes, sighing heavier and surrendering into his arms. She did not want him to stop. As she swooned from the rush of powerful emotions, he held her up and advised they relax at the bench for a moment.

"My dear beauty, passion took your breath away. Fun, do you agree?"

She acknowledged yes.

"Are you married Gérard?"

"Why do you ask such irrelevant questions? You must learn to appreciate the occasion. Be present with someone and don't consider anything else. Be attentive of our time together."

"I guess that is a yes." He grinned and leaned in for another kiss.

What am I worried about? Why do I care? I'm leaving tomorrow and nothing will happen between us. Yes, enjoy the moment. You did not choose to spend your birthday alone. This is a gift.

"Now let's go celebrate your birthday." He escorted her to Le Grand Vefour restaurant, which was closing. Speaking in French to the young man closing the outdoor seating, he pleaded eloquently for the restaurant to remain open, so he could treat "his" woman for her birthday. The young man grinned and agreed. The finest gastronomical experiences in Paris are known to be here.

"Pretty lady, be my guest."

He was most definitely a gentleman. Holding the café chair out for her to be seated, he inhaled her essence. She melted like the candle that burned on her cake earlier that evening.

"Do you enjoy chocolate ganache?" "*Oui.*"

"*Garçon,*" he continued to order in French.

Alexandra was floating and daydreaming, enjoying being his queen and easing into his presence. It was different this time for her. She followed his eyes, his lips, while his hands caressed hers from across the table. No words needed. They simply connected in the moment.

Moments later, two desserts and two glasses of wine were served. One candle and a handsomely sung version of "Happy Birthday" in French. He had won Alexandra over.

"*Merci,* Gérard, that was wonderful!" Applauding him she asked: "What other diverse talents do you possess?"

"Ahh, you yearn to learn of my secrets? Allow me to feed you first, and later I shall reveal another."

By now Alexandra's pulse was beating stronger, her face was flushed, and every touch made her lust for him even more. Gérard arranged a wedge of the cake on the fork and leaned over casually to feed his birthday queen. Opening her mouth slowly and subtly, she allowed the ganache to touch her lips. Her tongue encircled around the side of her lip, savoring the chocolate. He stared into her eyes, watching her, tasting her in his mind and waiting for her to be ready.

Laughter broke the tension as both recognized the seduction was part of the party plan.

"Do you seduce all women on the streets of Paris like this?" "Simply the ones who have a vision for something new in their life."

He told her a bit of historical background about this center and shared that numerous literary artists surrounded this square, a famous rendezvous spot for artisans and Parisian politicals for more than two hundred years.

One more toast. The evening was ending. Their wine glasses met. Alexandra was determined to leave in the dawn and was exhausted.

He stood, peering down at her, he opened his hand, and she grasped it. He drew her near his chest, twirling her around to dance in the Palais gardens. Radiating an enigmatic smile, she fell into his arms. She *loved* ballroom dancing. Naturally they floated simultaneously as if they were on a cloud, every moment in sync, every breath united, never losing their connection as they gazed into each other's eyes.

Alexandra constantly fantasized of someone who would appreciate dancing with her, and clearly, he did. To dance in union is like a field of energy swirling in the air, floating endlessly in the cosmos, playfully greeting the stars.

It was getting late, and the security guards were ready to close the gates. They were kind enough to allow them to finish their waltz and accompanied them out of the gardens.

"*Merci*, Gérard, you made my evening pleasant. Now please show me where my hotel is, so I can sleep for the night."

"Darling, you must dance once more with me. They dance outside, many people, relishing an evening filled with passion, the Parisian's way. Be mine tonight, please."

The offer was tempting, but she was being practical and preferred some rest. She had an early train to Italy.

"I cannot tonight."

"Then tomorrow or the next day. I do not wish you to leave." "I am leaving tomorrow."

"I need to show you Paris, all of it. The way we live here. Everything will entice you and focus your attention on your heart, and then you can write about it. You will experience the genuine emotions, the eclectic side of it all, and you will be alive."

Do I say yes? She thought. *Do I miss another opportunity and regret leaving?* "Walk me to my hotel, please," she whispered.

Like a gentleman, he held her hand and they walked quietly about one block. Her hotel was right where he had promised. Looking into her eyes, holding her close, he did not want to let go, and neither did she.

"Allow me to walk you in safely, *sil vous plaît.*"

They entered the sitting room in the lobby, both engaged in conversation, not wanting the evening to end.

"I must have one more kiss, please, before I leave." Alexandra agreed and contemplated asking him to her room.

Imagine sitting on the sofa, still wondering if this was all a dream, thinking...*what if. What if this is wrong? What if this is right?*

She looked up and across the room was a watercolor painting, with these words scrolled across the bottom. It was surely another *sign.*

> *"Where your treasure is, there will also be your heart."*
> –Paulo Coelho

"The time is getting late. I must go." He sauntered down the step to the front door. One last glance, one more moment. Compelled, he could not resist, one more kiss. They turned around and walked to the elevator. Gérard asked the concierge for the key, and never took his eyes off her. There would be no goodbye tonight.

"Gérard, you were a wonderful gift to me today, merci."

He just smiled and held her, empathically understanding her hurt from years gone by, making him all the more attentive to her needs. Unlocking the door, he suggested Alexandra rest on the bed like a beautiful princess. Nearby, he spotted the large tub and let his imagination run wild with creative ways to nurture her tender body.

"Stay and rest. I will return with a surprise."

He spotted a bouquet on the dresser. Without her noticing, as she was looking out the window, he chose one and took it into the bathroom. As the tub filled, he sprinkled the petals of the fleur-de-lis--a stylized iris, an extremely fragrant flower often used in perfumes--into the warm water. When the bath was ready, he went to gather his beauty.

"Alexandra, I wish to take care of you, to nurture you and relieve you of the pain. Come."

She followed without questioning. Once she entered the bathroom and noticed the flowers, she became emotional.

"Don't cry my love."

"I've never had anyone do this for me."

She slipped off her clothes, and he held her hand to help her enter the big tub. He drizzled the water along her back directing her to breathe and relax. Slowly she surrendered, sighing, moaning in delight, and crying.

"I apologize, I don't understand why I am crying."

"There is no need to apologize. You cry because you feel. Like an invocation, you have ignited a part of you that has died. Let the emotions flow. I am here for you. Passion rises up when you least expect, beautiful woman. I am grateful to have heard your call."

He moved to her feet and caressed them, delicately rubbing the soles. More tears trickled down her cheeks. Gérard moved his hands slowly to her ankles, massaging the soreness away, gliding his fingers up to her calves, which were tender from the rigors of her long walks. She just relaxed, taking it all in, not saying a word. Her moans of pleasure were satisfying to them both.

As he continued to her legs and massaging, she sighed in delight. He sensed what pleased her. He continued to touch sensually to reconnect with her body, her *feelings*, and allow the joyful orgasmic urges to rise up. She deserved it. Alexandra lifted her torso ever so slightly; a tingle ran through her body when his fingers began to explore her more intimately. Delightful moans of appreciation aroused both of them.

Ahh, music to my ears, he thought. *I understand how to pleasure her.*

Alexandra lifted her body gradually, first clutching his hand then placing it on her breast. Their eyes connected. The world stood still while he massaged her breasts. She licked her lips, sighing, immersed in the moment.

"I crave you," she professed.

The tub was spacious enough for two people and Gérard was already half undressed as he disposed of the rest of his clothing and deliberately joined her in the tub. Pausing before her, revealing his own impressive anatomy, she smiled. Dina, her friend from her first trip to Italy, would suggest, "Girl, go for it. He is an Adonis."

As their legs intertwined, their bodies instinctively melded snugly together. His lips brushed hers. The affection ignited and enhanced every nerve sense within them. She touched him, stroked his body where it pleased him, obliging him to slip into her. She gasped.

Calmly and deliberately, he moved with her breath, his body engaging with every rise of her breath while he gratified them both. Her hands grasped his back, a magnified sense swelling within, that orgasmic flash was soon going to erupt with him now. They both squealed, stiffening their bodies, holding onto each other securely and, just like an exhale, they released simultaneously.

Their breath, the sole awareness…The gratification vibrated and spread through every cell. They fondled each other and further enjoyed their intimate, soulful encounter.

Gérard settled in for the night. After an unforgettable evening of sustained affection and lovemaking, Alexandra would have to write about it soon. She never wanted to *overlook* these feelings.

The moon peeked through the curtains, shining on Alexandra's face, as she leaned over to quietly study her lover in his slumbering dream state. Shifting closer to his body, she kissed his shoulder and neck. She touched his face tenderly and whispered in his ear, "I am staying another day."

Since she would travel by train to Italy, it was simple enough to reschedule. Nothing demanding waited for her, so she engaged in the "liveliness" *Joie de vie.*

Wrapping his arms around her, pulling her body closer to his, they merged so easily. He confided back, "I'm enchanted and excited to show you all the enjoyment you are prepared to receive." With that, he blessed her body with morning kisses while she laughed, enjoying every moment.

An hour quickly passed while the ecstasy continued, their heart-rates increased, the feel-good hormones were working overtime, and neither one was in a rush to end it. The rhythmic contractions in her body demanded release. Nothing was rational, but she wasn't troubled. Eventually, she let loose, embracing Gérard as her intimate partner, granting her all the experience she desired. There was no shame or concern, and her pleasure centers certainly weren't objecting.

Gérard had ordered a luscious display of pastries for breakfast. Room service gently knocked on the door at the precise time he requested. Their intimate evening wasn't just lust. In fact, he knew better than to be superficial with this beauty. Her desire was connection.

Alexandra stretched her arms and exhaled with a big smile; her naked body wrapped between the sheets. The aroma of coffee immediately caught her attention. Gérard brought her the brass breakfast tray: a small flower in a vase and her favorite *pain au chocolat* with black coffee. It was going to be a great day.

These two were sensible. They already recognized this relationship was a moment in time to be treasured. They both enjoyed this awakening. They did not mention a word about tomorrow but appreciated the moments of their tryst.

Giggling over breakfast in bed, Gérard became playful with his pastries. He delighted in sensually eating the profiterole filled with sweet custard and drenched in chocolate ganache off her smooth skin. Needless to say, the morning became a delicacy the two would never forget.

The random lovers would have a meaningful, fulfilling day exploring Paris. Gérard would show Alexandra what it was like to awaken all her senses. Every food he chose made her palate come alive, the pieces of artwork they saw in the Louvre and at Montmartre made love to her eyes. Every impromptu dance he engaged in along the promenade made passersby watch their hunger for each other. Parisians were not shy; many would display their affections openly. Surely, she would write about this entire experience in her journal while on the train to Tuscany.

All too soon it was time for their last *adieu*, kisses, and tears, realizing the time had come to say goodbye. Gérard was confident they would stay connected. In her heart this would not be possible. But the radiance on her face convinced him she would return.

"*Au revoir*, my darling. You have shown me what I was missing. Now it is time for our soul encounter to give us both a second chance in life. *Merci beaucoup* for making the celebration of my life more than I ever have imagined. You truly fulfilled a wish from the heavens."

"Alexandra, your sweetness cannot be described in words. Yet I will write how you brought a smile to the chambers of my heart. Perhaps, it is not in the stars to hold our destiny but in ourselves."

She smiled, knowing he quoted Shakespeare.

In silence, they glanced into each other's eyes before opening the glass doors to the world waiting for them. The taxi was waiting for Alexandra, and Gérard looked at his watch, knowing it was time. This encounter was divinely ordained.

Alexandra waved goodbye, thinking A *soul mate found his way into my life, once again, to wish me happy birthday? Or another past-life encounter?*

Gérard walked down the boulevard and life went on.

No, Alexandra was not lost in Paris. She was found.

"*Love does not consist in looking at each other, but rather in, together, looking in the same direction.*"

--Antoine de Saint Exupery

CHAPTER 19

Tuscany

M emories of a time long ago came to mind when youthful Lexi, at seventeen, was determined to travel. She hopped on a train to Florence.

Life has undoubtedly been an adventure, she reflected as she sat back into the contemporary reclining chair. *I wonder what he would look like today and would we recognize each other? How silly. We don't know each other's name. One can fantasize, nevertheless.*

She would ask herself endless times why she would not forget *him.* She pulled out her journal to write.

I truly miss you, Grandma Rosa; somehow, I believe you will be with me every step of the way. This season of life will be beautiful. I don't believe I have ever said thank you for watching over me, guiding me, and leaving me with the wonderful gifts and this key. What will it unlock? You repeatedly have a way of surprising me when I seldom expect it. I am, however, excited to discover what it opens.

"*Alexandra*", I now enjoyed the sophisticated tone of my own name. Finally, emphasizing the "dra." My life is absolutely incredible. One minute I'm slamming the door on my locker in high school and tumbling down into a cave where I meet a shaman, simply to turn up sitting in an Italian restaurant in New York City with some friends. I sing on stage, later I'm told I should study opera. Never had I considered this! The woman in the restaurant was a vocal coach. What the heck, I attended some vocal coaching and now I'm meeting my new Italian vocal mentor to study and teach me how to sing arias.

I inevitably can carry the emotion and embellish the despair and tragedies of life, she added in her newest journal.

With her pen on her cheek, puckering her lips, she pondered the title of this adventure.

She could've traveled quickly by plane, but the high-speed train was the perfect alternative to write about her future and reflect upon her past. Every sign, circumstance, and person was part of the plan.

Poems flowed, thoughts were scattered, and her heart open for the first time in years. My life has taken me in many directions, wandering around, searching. What I was searching for was always with me. Inside! The freedom to be me. The need to express. The courage to heal. It is the strength to fight for myself. The willingness to succeed and the honesty to love. Yearning to be cared for, cherished, and adored. To sing and dance under the midnight skies. To rest beside him in silence and just be. Placing her pen down, softly closing her eyes, she recalled all the goodbyes.

Goodbye, I repeat, and hello to my future. Nice to have you back again, she thought, beaming with delight.

Moments later, she recalled the brief conversation with her mom. The day her dad gave her the "eye" and Mom became quiet.

Hey, Mom, she imagined chatting with her on the other side. *Can I ask you those questions again?*

A faint breeze brushed against her cheek as if the spirit of Mom was comforting her and saying *yes.*

This feeling grew more intense the closer to Tuscany. And that other voice, who said she was my birth mom, has me doing a lot of thinking. Her pulse began to increase, and she placed her hand on her heart. It was warm.

"Can you give me a sign if I'm going to get the answers I have been seeking?" Immediately a man walking down the aisle lost his balance and nearly fell into her lap. *I will take that as a positive sign.*

This was the way she communicated ever since the experience in the Great Pyramid. The energy of thoughts carried quickly in this realm, and she hoped she didn't appear crazy speaking out loud.

"Grandma, will this key open the doorway to my past?" She whispers.

A faint voice whispered through her ears with an affirmative *Yes.*

Alexandra's entire body became deeply relaxed and all the anxiety she ever had simply diminished. She never realized how tense her muscles were. Her busy mind searched for answers. She took a deep sigh and a comforting breath.

Stop struggling, she told herself.

Next, she wrote a note to her dad, unsure if she would mail it.

Dear Dad, another year has passed, and I think of you often. I'm not sure why you refuse to respond to me, but I'm sorry. Please forgive me if I offended you. Dad, you never liked the word goodbye, and I didn't understand, however I believe I do now. I have often been alone, empty, filled with sadness. You would never console me. Perhaps the silence was needed, the space required. Shall I ever find out?

A message nearly hit her psyche over the head.

Prepare now for what never was

The voice continued:

Illusions and reality The truth of it all

We know not, for a source, more knowing has plans beyond our consciousness. Place your faith in God and continue to love, for you have never sinned. It was a lie.

Alexandra's mind got silent. No rambling thoughts, no voices vying for her attention. Complete calm and peace. It was time to rest.

The next several hours would pass by quickly as she slept more deeply than ever before. Even dreams didn't disturb her during this great sense of inner peace.

When the train pulled into the same station, Firenze Santa Maria Novella, many years ago, Alexandra's eyes popped open with an inner remembrance of this time gone by. Suddenly she was vibrant, young again, excited to explore, and hungry for a fresh experience.

The passengers lined up to exit and step down the high-rise steps to the old concrete platform. For a moment, the presence of someone touching her shoulder, caught her attention. A chill ran through her, and her heart throbbed. You will see *him* again, she heard.

She was excited to connect again with Ricardo; he had promised to send a car to pick her up. She prayed she would not be disappointed. He had been home for several days. Arriving sooner than expected, he left a message on her cell phone that a family issue had arisen. Nothing more was said, and she hoped it was nothing serious.

Carrying her luggage through the crowds, she spotted a dark-haired man waving some flowers. "It's him!" Her face flushed like a young girl, she tried to squeeze through the crowd. She just wanted to jump into his arms.

"Alexandra," he called. "I'm coming!"

She couldn't reach him soon enough!

A ray of sunshine sparkled right across her heart. It nearly stopped time. Misty eyed she felt hope, comfort and love pierced through her as they embraced.

"What is wrong my darling, unless it's tears of joy."

"Ricardo, I have no idea what came over me. A dazzling light pierced my heart as you came toward me."

She was speechless. Ricardo also had a great sense of the connection between the two, and she didn't need to explain anything. He quickly lifted her suitcase, put his arm through hers, and escorted her outside to his car.

"I wanted you to myself, so I did not ask Tony to drive us." The most genuine and full smile flashed across her face. He opened the door for her to enter.

"Let's take you to your villa, and then we can decide what you would enjoy, okay?"

"That sounds perfect."

The picturesque hilltop towns; medieval buildings; and labyrinths of rolling fields of grapes, where some of the finest wines produced in Tuscany, took Alexandra's breath away. She remained silent, absorbing in all the magnificence and glorious energy in every cell of her body. It truly was a new beginning.

Occasionally, Ricardo looked her way, delighted with his vision of loveliness and his plans to make her happier than she could have ever imagined. His car slowed down, and he pulled into a long gravel driveway. "This, my dear, is the address you provided. It is your temporary home until I can lure you to mine."

She smiled and believed him. "Thank you so much!" *He was handsome, no doubt, proper and kind,* she thought.

"I feel like I stepped into a fantasy, Ricardo. I'm so happy to be here with you."

"I hoped you would say that. I've been dreaming of you and have wonderful plans to tell you about, but first, you rest, okay?"

"I'm so excited and energized, I don't think I will rest. Would you be interested in lunch? I did not eat during my travels."

"Lets' go! It's my pleasure to bring you to a delightful café here to enjoy a quiet lunch, and a glass of wine to toast your new life. I will show you this beautiful country and one day bring you to my home. How about if I cook dinner for you? It will be our first official date." Alexandra smiled and nodded affirmatively, yes.

Her eyes could not believe the vision displayed before her as they stepped through the private entry to the villa doors. The room resembled something out of a fairy tale. Everything was beautiful and perfectly designed, right down to the bed coverings. The lovely frescoed loggia, similar to an outside porch with large archways, was furnished with handmade table and chairs. It was the perfect spot to enjoy her morning sip of coffee or, better still, a glass of the estate's

Chianti wine, all while admiring the serenity of the Italian gardens and basking in the sunshine.

When you do things from your soul,
you feel a river moving in you, a joy.
—Rumi

"No wonder people say Italy is so romantic. Everything expresses love." "Alexandra, that is because you are a reflection of everything you see. You are love."

She never saw herself that way. Hearing it said this way overwhelmed her, and she burst into tears.

Ricardo quickly embraced her like no other who had ever hugged her. All she wanted to do was remain in his arms.

"There is so much to do. Where do I start? I must call my vocal coach and inform her I've arrived safely. I definitely need to get myself a rental car and go shopping."

"Slow down, everything will work out. You have much to process. Everything happened fast. Trust me, slow down. Freshen up, change your clothes, regroup, and let us go enjoy lunch and a glass of wine. Welcome to Tuscany."

She had to laugh at herself when she remembered the key tucked away in her purse. Quietly, she walked into her room, took the brooch out of her purse, and said a little prayer, thanking her Grandma Rosa. Truthfully, she wanted to jump up and down like a five-year-old, joyfully screaming. She didn't want to scare away Ricardo.

A lovely light-blue sundress with a delicate ruffled edge was her comfortable choice for a lunch date. Ricardo enjoyed his vision of loveliness as her crystal blue eyes nearly knocked him over like a bolt of lightning. Alexandra totally caught his attention, and he was pleased, undoubtedly.

He courteously held her hand and, like a proper gentleman, escorted her to the car, placing a warm kiss on her cheek before closing the door. Something was different about him. Alexandra had waited a life time for a real relationship. One that would support both partners, hoping this was the one.

Ricardo differed from all the other men in her life. He was suave, gentle, and kind and obviously sophisticated and financially stable. Alexandra did not want to depend on any man. However, it sure made her comfortable that he was in a position of financial success.

As these thoughts ran through her mind, it reminded her of Marian, her college classmate. She wondered how she was managing after her wealthy, controlling dad whisked her away to marry someone she didn't love. It saddened her to see her beautiful friend's face give way to despair, with no hope for her own future. Her soul was surely dying. She often wondered why Marian didn't reach out to her. It was probably because her dad and husband controlled every aspect of her life.

Ricardo supported Alexandra's dreams and encouraged her to fulfill them each time they spoke. Over the next few weeks, the two would become more acquainted and develop a deeper bond. Alexandra opened her soul to romance, her heart ready. Every day brought them both more happiness: exploring the countryside, cooking together, and agreeing to respect each other's time, work, and commitments.

Marty and Stella were happy to learn she got settled in and excited to read her article once she completed the cooking classes. Danny had good news too and shared with his sister that he may move to Switzerland for his job. Everyone was happy, except Dad.

Alexandra decided she would reach out once again and invite Dad for a visit to Italy. She prayed he would say yes. Danny told her not to expect much since he was not doing well. He became a grumpy old man, more than usual. She continued to say a prayer daily. A few weeks passed before she received a response.

"You enjoy your life. I have mine. You don't need me, Dad."

Alexandra couldn't help but cry with his one last hurtful comment. It cut deeply, and she would never understand. She prayed for his distraught soul. How could he even be her father?

Dear God, please help him find peace.

Three weeks later, Alexandra was having a blast in cooking school. Covered with flour on her apron, she was learning how to make some pastries when her phone rang. Danny was calling. She excused herself from class to receive the news she one day expected.

"Sis, Dad is gone. He is resting in peace, I hope."

The two siblings realized he was tormented. They said a brief prayer together on the phone. Their sniffles echoed on both ends of the line, but comfort filled their hearts. No longer did either of them have to deal with his abuse, his arrogance, and his lack of love. They tried to understand "his" kind of love, but still it left them empty and longing for it.

"Danny, when are you coming to Europe? I would love a visit with you!"

"Soon, sis, and I will definitely call you. We need some time together. Did you learn what the key opened?"

"Funny you should ask. I have an appointment this week with a property agent. Ricardo found out it belonged to a piece of property. We are going to inspect it soon. I will keep you posted on everything I learn, I promise. You do not know how happy I will be to see my big brother."

They chatted a little longer, said their goodbyes, expressed their love, and discussed their dad's funeral arrangements. They agreed to connect in the evening to complete it all. Since there was no family left, they would keep it all simple.

Later that evening, Alexandra told Ricardo of the passing of her dad. This was a goodbye, frankly, which did not bring her as much pain as she imagined. There was a sense of relief in her and hope that his heart and soul were tormented no longer. She wished she knew more about him. He held her hand and listened, understanding that secrets can often hurt people.

"I don't mean to be cold or insensitive. It's just that he hurt me so much: he didn't support me, he mocked me, and he eventually discarded me. I'm not sad about his passing. I wish he had lived happily."

Ricardo spent the evening supporting her and Danny's decision for a simple cremation. They had to determine where to spread his ashes. They both realized he wasn't going to Italy. Perhaps they would place them along his wife's grave, their adopted mother.

While going through some old papers Danny found in their mother's files, he learned about *another* secret. Alexandra and Danny were at peace for now but had questions and wanted answers.

It was a solemn evening, and she invited Ricardo to spend the night. The two fell a   ns with an unspoken understanding of the

The next few months would fly by rapidly.

Alexandra learned the key and the number on the tag was associated with a property-tax number. As soon as the estate woman identified the property, which had a caretaker watching over the home, Alexandra wanted to rush over and see it.

Ricardo and Alexandra went together along the outskirts of the Siena region. The windows were down in the car, so she admired all the trees and the smell of the fresh air. Once they arrived at the estate, she would learn everything.

An old man met them outside. Mr. Caprese, the caretaker, greeted and invited them into the house and asked Alexandra to sit down at the table in the kitchen. "I have many things to tell you. First, welcome to your home and the family. I am your Grandmother Rosa's brother."

"What?"

"This is difficult, but please listen." He stuttered.

His words were kind, concern was plainly evident on his face, and one could sincerely hear in his voice he wanted to help Alexandra understand from his heart.

"Alexandra, a beautiful and powerful name. Your mother she want for you. She know strength needed. I tell you everything. I try to answer questions."

She listened attentively, occasionally holding back tears. She was confused but waited all these years to learn the truth. Ricardo held her hand the entire time. He wondered if his own family secrets were haunting him during his nightmares.

"Many things happened during the time of war. It split apart families for years. Some, they lose their spouses. You know… things happen." He was expressive with his hands, puckering his lips a little, and tipping his head to the right, with a raspy voice.

"You see, child your mother went on a visit to Italy with Rosa many years ago."

"My mother? Which one? I'm confused. What are you telling me?"

"Your American mother. She wanted child. Her husband not so much. Your dad, want no children. Rosa, she looked for a wonderful family. They can adopt the baby." Nervously Gino began to pace the floors as he continued to explain the story. "A beautiful baby girl born to us. Unfortunately, tragedy fell upon them both. The mother died at birth. The baby was healthy. The father, he struggle to care for the baby. Then he had nervous breakdown. He was not fit to raise another child without his wife."

"*Another* child? Oh, no! Are you telling me--"

Before she finished the sentence, he said, "Yes, you were that angel. Rosa, she make all the arrangements for your family." He tried earnestly to communicate the best he could in English.

Lexi was stunned, but not really surprised. She always had wondered if she was adopted. Ricardo reached out to support her and placed his arm around her.

"But I don't understand why the key to this house. Who is the other child??"

"Rosa, she buy this house. Then, you were adopted You all lived here for a short time."

"What do you mean, *all*?"

"Rosa, she bring your family to Italy." Gathering his fingers together he began to shake them while speaking. "Your father no want to be in someone else's house or life. He was furious. His drinking became habitual, and soon he left. He yell at his wife. He gave your mother an ultimatum. She decided it was best for you all to go to the USA." The room got quiet before Gino continued.

"Your birth father he kill himself. He committed suicide a few months later." His voice shaking as he told her this sad news. "He wanted you both to have a nice home when he met your parents. It was the right choice."

"Oh my God, this is a lot to take in. Why didn't anyone tell us? Why all the secrets? I'm confused."

"Yes, I'm sure it is. Your American father he wanted secrets. He did not want anyone to know. He felt, let's say... inadequate. He demanded they keep it a secret. I have your original birth certificate and the deed to this property. There is a will that states you inherit the house. You and your brother also have a dowry. Grandma Rosa left for you. She always wanted you here."

"I kind of knew this my whole life. Things never made sense. But lies! Why all the *lies*?" she blurted out as she pounded her hand on the table.

The anger she stored for many years, the emotions she held in, were no longer containable. She ran out the door and into the fields filled with poppies blooming, screaming, until she collapsed on the grass.

Ricardo waited a few moments to run after her. He understood well enough about adoptions and family lies. He wanted to give her time for herself. He watched her from a distance, as did Mr. Caprese, who appeared saddened.

When Alexandra sat up, Ricardo rushed over to help her. He wrapped his arms around her as she cried profusely, barely able to stand up and walk back to the house.

"Please, please come," Mr. Caprese called, waving his hand, "Let's make her comfortable inside."

"I want to settle all this now. Show me this house. Tell me about my parents. I want to hear it all, and what is your first name? I assume you are my only living relative now?"

"Yes, yes, I help you Alexandra and answer your questions. Yes, I am your blood family. My name is Gino. I get you something to drink?"

"That would be nice. A glass of wine if you have any, please."

Gino poured the wine he made, slowly, while Alexandra walked around aimlessly through the kitchen, touching the wooden table, the stucco walls, and wondering where her mother had died in this house.

Once she sipped her wine, Gino walked her through each room, and she calmed down quickly. It was quite charming and well taken care of all these years. She learned Rosa had paid Gino, her brother, to tend to the property. When his family died, he lived here by himself and tended to the gardens as well.

When they walked into the nursery, Alexandra stood still and felt the presence of her birth mom. She stood in the center of the room. No one said a word. Falling down to her knees, her head down towards her belly, sobbing, she was aware of the great pain her mother endured. They all stood silently. She could hear the screams of her mother penetrating her soul. More screams, this time gut-wrenching, prompting Ricardo to rush over to her. Suddenly, he stopped, as though a wall stood between them.

Gino stood by the door, sobbing. He was there the day his niece died. It was a sad time that should have been joyous when this beautiful child was born. Instead, she entered through the portal of her mother *from life to death in an instant*. It is no wonder her journey taught her so much about how thin the veil is, that the connections are always there.

She sensed them all in the room from the moment she took her first breath, born an empath. Her brother was young and had gone into complete silence. He didn't use his voice for several years. He lived in shock. If not for his adopted mother, he may have been completely autistic. It was her compassion which helped him overcome this tragedy.

When Alexandra later shared this with Gino, he confirmed it all and said he was not at all surprised she still held the memory within her. She took an exasperated breath and stood up slowly. "Gino, I would like to visit the gardens." She held his hand, turned her head towards him, and smiled. There was a comfort in his face now that didn't exist when she first met him. Gino needed to make everything okay.

"Your Grandmother Rosa, my sister, she had a connection too. She hear from the spirits. She would do what you call a "reading" to let people know their loved ones were okay. Many came to her from all over. You seem to have that gift too. My heart, it says you took on your mama's talents. Your mama's gift, she sang. She had a beautiful voice like a bird chirping through the branches each morning."

Alexandra stunned to learn this. A tear trickled down her face when she realized this was where the passion for music and song came from. That is why the arias had always captivated her. She sniffled, threw her hair back, and glanced at Ricardo. She walked ahead of the men as if to own her own heritage from her grand mama and mother. Now it was time to learn about this property, the land, perhaps her father, and where Danny fit into all of this.

She reached out her hand behind her, as if to signal to Ricardo to come walk beside her on this journey. They glanced over, shared a soulful smile, and just knew their destiny. It was uncanny how well their energy blended and how each understood the other.

Gino described the beautiful valleys in this region and pointed out all the flowers. Her mama loved flowers. Gino was short and stout. A pleasant man with little hair left on his head. He had a little salt-and-pepper mustache and a scruffy beard. His pants were baggy, and he definitely did not have fashion sense.

He said, "*Mangia*, we should have a little something to eat in honor of welcoming you to your home."

Everyone agreed. The property agent later said she would come back to finish the paperwork while they all had some personal time together. They cut an array of cheeses; they broke bread with their hands, ate grapes, drank wine, laughed, and cried until the sun set.

"What would you like to do, Gino?"

"The day would come. I know I have to leave here. But I tell you this, Alexandra, this is my heart. This is my home." The old man had tears trickling down his face; barely controlling his sobbing.

"Then you shall remain."

She looked at him and he appeared surprised. He never imagined there would be such kindness extended to him. He worried for many years he might be homeless. Alexandra recognized this was his home and for years he tended to it with his loving hand.

"We're family, Gino. I want you to remain here. I want you to be safe. Grandma Rosa didn't just give me this house. She gave it to our family. I am happy to have you here. I wish to learn more about you. Perhaps, one day, I will move in, but you shall remain and guard it for the family. How does that sound?"

He put his head down, bowed solemnly and softly said "*Grazie, bella, Grazie.*" He was humbled by her generosity.

Alexandra was happy she made him happy.

Everyone was getting tired, so they called it an evening. They would tend to the legal matters the following day.

Gino mentioned he had her original birth certificate. She was glad to hear he did because she needed it for her dual citizenship. When she applied, they informed her the one she had was not authentic. She didn't understand and argued with the agents, but she patiently waited until she arrived in Italy to do further research. And it was easier than she thought. Now she would become a citizen of Italy. If she purchased any real estate or decided to live there permanently, all would be fine.

She turned to Ricardo and just held him. There was a secret he had as well. Perhaps one day he would share his. The two of them drove quietly through the rolling valleys. Alexandra sang some songs because she needed to be comforted by melodies. It had been quite an emotional day. She experienced more in the past few hours than she had in her lifetime. Looking over at Ricardo, she felt he needed to release something. He welcomed her into his home as if she had been the princess who had lived there forever. Tomorrow, he would tell her of his little concern.

"I need to speak with you about something important tomorrow. Will you have time to listen?"

"My dear one, I will always have time for you. You have been here for me. I was brought here now for you."

He just looked into her eyes with disbelief that someone cared so deeply. After thanking her, off they went to the bedroom to dream, to sleep, and to sink into each other's arms…to be blessed by a comforting love. It was tonight that Alexandra would learn that Ricardo had nightmares. She ·   ll her, in his time.

The sun glimmered across the fields of sunflowers. A glittering sheen on the curtains, blowing gently with the breeze past the wooden shutters reminded Alexandra of the days when she ran through the curtain in her mother's room. How she missed her conversations, long night talks and wisdom from her. It was a glorious day. No matter what these two had to face, they looked into each other's eyes the next morning and smiled. Somehow things were going to be better. Those eyes always spoke to them.

Alexandra rose first and surprised Ricardo by preparing the coffee. She made some divine pastries, which she learned to create in cooking school. Before Ricardo made it into the kitchen, she whipped up breakfast and had coffee ready.

He reached out across the table to touch her hands. "I have a secret."

"We all do," she responded.

"Alexandra, several years ago, I was married once. My wife died of cancer. It was not an easy time for us. Just like you, my grief runs deep in my heart. Sometimes I don't understand why God took my wife and my daughter. We adopted her because we couldn't have children. She was loved so deeply by both of us but didn't know we were not her birth parents."

She listened attentively as he continued.

"You see, my daughter could not handle the loss of her mother. She grieved deeply, lost in an abyss. I couldn't make it better for her. The more I tried, the more she cried. The more she cried, the more she eventually numbed her emotional pain with drugs. Her depression was out of control." He paused almost unable to contain his emotions. "Her self-esteem went down the drain as she tried to keep up with the generational times, posting selfies on Snapchat with sexy clothes, lots of makeup, and kissy lips to impress people." He shook his head and looked down at the cup of coffee. "It became harder each day for her to smile, to keep up with the façade. All the clothes she once wore were gone. Now she was dressing voluptuously, like a slut." Holding back tears, he continued. "She ran away several times. I was so distraught; I could not find her and was afraid I had lost her. The pot, the drugs, and the alcohol consumed her, and she never saw how much it controlled her life. She eventually got pregnant." Pausing for a moment, the two were in deep silence.

"Alexandra, I was out of my wits. I felt like a horrible father." His voice became solemn. "I didn't know how to take care of her. Travel frequently made it harder, and when I returned home, it was always worse. I am afraid to do it again. I just don't have it in me."

Alexandra tipped her head slightly, curiously. "What do you mean? Do it again?"

"My daughter, Trinity, committed suicide several years ago. The baby's father is also a drug addict. His mother tried to care for their child, but she is single and not financially capable. She contacted me last year to tell me the severity of the situation asking for more money. We have been negotiating care for Selena, my granddaughter. I want a better life for her than my daughter had. What can I do?"

She gently tapped his hand, acknowledging his story, and asked, "How can I support you through this?"

"I often think this is a payback because I was not able to save my wife or raise my child. If Selena is my second chance, how can I do right by her?" Ricardo, feeling distraught, shook his head, "I don't know what I need. She's a beauty, by the way, like you. My job takes me to so many places. How will I care for her? I can hire a nanny, but I don't know if I'm emotionally capable of dealing with her grief and the fact she will be a teenager soon."

"We will figure it out together." Alexandra assured him.

They had much to figure out and tomorrow Alexandra was ready to learn more about her own family secrets.

*Of all the books in the world,
some of the best stories are found
between the pages of your passport.*

—Anonymous

CHAPTER 20

Secrets Revealed

"Gino, what is my real name?"

"Caprese."

"Why didn't my mother tell me?"

"Occasionally she try. Your father want no connection back here."

"Well, that explains why he wouldn't come when I invited him to visit me here before he died."

"He promised to never come back."

"Why did you not reach out to me sooner?"

"Rosa told me, wait. She said, right time comes. When your mother gave you the ceramic teapot, she called me. I made sure everything is good, maintained, you know and I waited."

"How did everyone know I would trace the house with this key?"

"Well, if you didn't, your mother, she gave me with a way to contact you. I was told to allow you several time of months. Up to one year to figure it out, and you did."

"I guess something was off. My heart home called me back since my first visit. The voices, Grandma's supportive whispers, always knowing, and now Mom recently communicating with me from the other side. This explains many things.

Lexi continued, "this house reminds me of the archways in the New York Public Library, which always fascinated me. I *remembered* on some level. Everything guided me here," she continued.

"As a young child, I would go into my mother's jewelry box and be intrigued with this mosaic brooch. Do you recognize it?"

Nearly falling to his knees when he saw the brooch, his face appeared shocked.

"Yes! That is your birth mama's. It was gift. Your adopted mother save for you."

"It has been a good luck charm for many years. I never understood and thought it was my mother's. Then I thought it belonged to Grandma Rosa. Now you tell me it belonged to my birth mother?"

"*Si*, yes! She loved it dearly." Struggling to get his words out correctly, he continued. "When she got pregnant, she told Rosa if she had a little girl, this would be for her. It would symbolize all the shattered pieces in life that would never break you down. Your mama had a very hard life too. Everything can create something beautiful, she said, when we change our perspective. She saw signs in everything. Somehow, she guessed you would need this one."

"That is amazing. I always see signs and symbols, hear messages, and never let all the tragedy in life break me."

"That is the courage your mama passed to you."

"*What!* Courage? I received courage at a sacred place in Peru. A mystical experience which filled me with a powerful energy."

"My dear young child, you are what they call, *gifted*."

"Gino, I could talk to you for a lifetime. I believe you are the connection to my past, which will help me with my future. *Grazie* for everything you have offered so far. Most importantly, you gave me my birthright, and now all my doubts have vanished." Alexandra embraced Gino with a warm hug. He didn't want to let go.

Later in the day, the property agent and the lawyer met with the family to settle the estate and dowry for Alexandra and Danny. There would be a great time of celebration and healing. Gino, ecstatic, drank an entire bottle of wine by himself, laughing and dancing, and thanking Rosa too.

Little did anyone realize Rosa was quite wealthy from all her real estate investments. She kept the secret well. The family would now be taken care of and not have to worry about their future. Alexandra hoped for no more surprises.

A New Life

Ricardo's life was about to change drastically once Selena arrived. He wanted to do something fun with Alexandra first and scheduled a romantic getaway. Her cooking classes would end soon, and her article would be submitted to the magazine. He hoped she would make the time. They expected Danny to arrive in another month and life would get busy, he predicted.

Alexandra rushed into the house excitedly announcing, "Ricardo, I'm officially a graduate of the Good Tastes Cooking School! I can't wait to write about the fun I had, the delicious recipes, and how I hope to encourage others to take advantage of this amazing opportunity. I never imagined how much I would enjoy cooking, beyond my expectations. I never liked tiramisu until I made their recipe. This is the best from the first taste!" Her smile said everything.

"I have wanted to do something special for you. Are you free this weekend for three days?"

"Of course. What do you have in mind?"

"A surprise. You've worked so hard this past year, dealt with so much stress, and soon our lives will shift again. First, I want you to move in with me."

"I never thought you would ask! *Yes! Yes!* I would love to! Marty will be happy he won't be required to pay rent on the villa any longer."

"Then it is settled. Let's move you in immediately and then pack a small bag for our getaway."

The idea both intrigued and excited Alexandra; she loved the idea of a secret getaway. The next few days were busy...packing, moving, preparing for Selena's arrival, Danny's trip, and their romantic getaway.

Alexandra also thought about singing. Her voice lessons were going well, and while she mentioned little to anyone, she was fulfilled beyond her dreams. It was something she may want to pursue further, maybe to the point where she would give up writing. Many decisions had to be made.

But first, a lovely getaway. The car was packed. Ricardo had everything planned for the surprise weekend. Tony, his driver, agreed to watch over the house, and Gino offered to stop by and water the plants.

"Where are we going?"

"Ahh, you *really* want to know?"

"Please, *please?*"

Ricardo laughed and gave her a sneak preview. "How would you like a romantic candlelit four-course meal each evening?"

"As long as I don't have to cook!" she laughed.

"Then jump in the car and let's drive through the rolling hills, pass the medieval towns, capture some memorable photos, visit a historical cathedral or two, and head towards the Adriatic coast!"

"*What?* I have never seen the turquoise, teal and sapphire colors of the sea! This sounds marvelous!"

Ricardo thought of everything. He packed a picnic lunch, had a bouquet of wildflowers for her, a bottle of champagne, her favorite chocolates, and a surprise gift he would give her the night of their romantic interlude. The weather was perfect. He put the top down on the convertible, and drove quickly across the country to a boutique hotel.

Several weeks prior to their adventure, he had by chance met a lovely English couple when they were visiting Tuscany. He heard about their place, and how they restored it in the "other Tuscany" called Montelparo, located in LeMarche. It would be a perfect getaway for the two of them.

The owners were excited to host them and planned a lovely time at their inn. *Hotel Leone* offered a captivating magical setting, luxuriously designed rooms, and sumptuous food prepared on site.

At the back of the restaurant, down an old stone staircase, deep under the foundations of old Montelparo, was a wine cellar. This curious old vault was the perfect place to preserve the hotel's wine collection. Madeline, a co-owner, had hand-picked superb wines from all over LeMarche to showcase the main wine-producing areas. She mentioned to Ricardo they had award-winning *tre bicchieri* (Gambero Rosso's prestigious "three glasses") wines from the region, and some fabulous wines from some smaller and lesser-known producers. He had the perfect bottle waiting for them in their room with the balcony overlooking the terrace and the beautiful view of LeMarche.

"Ricardo, I want to tell you something."

"Yes, my beautiful angel. What is it?"

"I am so blessed to have met you. Our connection is so amazing, and the love in our relationship we exchange is like the wind. You can't see it, but you can feel it."

"Beautiful Alexandra, you are the love of my life. I want to make you happy. Because, when you smile, my heart smiles. I knew the moment I saw you; we were destined to be together."

Alexandra leaned over the stick shift and kissed him tenderly on his cheek. Resting her head on his shoulder she called out, "Thank you, Grandma Rosa."

"Yes, thank you, Grandma," Ricardo repeated.

Alexandra remained quiet for about half an hour, wondering what is the possibility Ricardo was the young gentleman on the train so many years ago. *Hmm, I wonder.*

"Did you ever propose to a woman on the train in Florence?"

Ricardo looked at Alexandra curiously and laughed. "Why do you ask about my romantic adventures?" "I was curious if you ever met a young woman on the train and proposed to her?"

"I can't say I recall, unless I was half-asleep or drunk."

She realized it couldn't be him, because Ricardo was multi-lingual, and the other young man did not speak English.

"That was an interesting question. Are you writing a romance novel?"

"No, but many years ago, when I was only seventeen, a handsome young man with dark hair and brown eyes proposed to me in Italian, when the train stopped at the station in Florence."

"And... you said no? Did you break his heart?"

"I didn't respond. The train was getting ready to pull out of the station, and I had to get off. A lady passing by told me what he said. I panicked, waved goodbye, and got off the train."

"Quite a story and fascinating experience. You never connected with him again?"

"No, I often wondered, though, if I would ever recognize *him*."

"Well, now you have me. So, no more wondering, I adore you!"

"You adore *me*?" A huge grin covered her face from ear to ear.

"Yes, my secret is out. My plan is to make you the happiest you have ever been."

"*Ooh, la la*, I like the sound of that Ricardo!"

The two laughed and shared their deep feelings for one another, more secrets and their plans for the future. The time went and before they realized, Hotel Leone was right before their eyes.

Alexandra immediately fell in love, not only with the hotel but also with Ricardo. The owners pleasantly greeted them, welcomed them with open arms, and told them they already had a lovely lunch prepared for them out on the terrace.

"Please tell us if we may assist and do anything for you. I hope you enjoy your room, the lovely time here, and the delicious home-made meals and wines we have planned for you," Madeline expressed.

"Absolutely!" they both replied simultaneously.

"This room is absolutely magnificent, Ricardo! Come on the balcony with me. I'm already in love." "With me?" he asked

"Well, if you must inquire," she said, spinning around to face him, "Yes, I'm madly in love with you, dear, handsome, and brilliant man."

"You kept this a secret?"

She coyly nodded yes.

"Well, I have a secret too!"

He leaned in to kiss her and said, "Let's go."

"You tease!"

The next few days were absolutely magical and romantic. The boutique hotel was perfect. The atmosphere, the hospitality, the food...not to mention the connection between these two lovers.

It was the final evening, and Ricardo played it cool and mysterious each day, not revealing his secret until the moment was perfect. The two gathered for their candle lit meal and toasted each other. Ricardo pulled out a beautiful blue velvet box with a bow from his jacket pocket.

"Alexandra, this is a gift...from my heart to yours."

She excitedly opened it, shocked to see the most exquisite heart necklace engraved with "*Listen to your heart, trust your intuition.*"

"How did you know?"

"Know what?"

"I have written almost the same words most of my life in my diary. Did you peek?"

"Never once. I suppose we are more connected than we both imagined. Can I place the necklace on you, please?"

"Ricardo, this weekend was perfect in every way. Every kiss, every laugh, every touch...and now *this*."

The couple radiated a deep soul love, and the people saw it in their presence. They were excited about creating a future and thrilled to bring Selena into their life. They were practical and aware of the challenges, and Ricardo understood Alexandra's dreams to pursue her singing. He did not want to interfere with her goals and promised he would have all the help needed to assist with raising Selena.

Alexandra agreed to be available when he had to travel and care for this child. She wanted her to grow up feeling loved and supported.

It was something Alexandra had always wanted in her life, a child. Ricardo whisked his love into bed as soon as they arrived home later in the evening. It was the first time they truly surrendered to each other, feeling safe enough to let go and experience the merging of their love. Exhausted from the drive, they fell asleep in each other's arms peacefully.

Time was flying by and lots of preparations for Selena's arrival were made. Alexandra was a bit nervous because she understood completely if this young lady did not want a surrogate parent.

CHAPTER 21

Selena Arrives

Alexandra was out of town when Selena arrived. There was an unexpected change in schedules and Ricardo was totally apologetic. He did not want her to shift her singing engagement in Sorrento. When he heard her sing alongside a violinist at a local restaurant, it took his breath away. He instinctively decided, she must pursue this gift.

Selena's grandmother, Sylvia, from New York, urgently contacted Ricardo to fly her over immediately. Her son, Eddie, was being released from prison. Selena did not need any drama. The decision was made to have her arrive a few weeks sooner. She was concerned Selena's father might cause trouble and ask for more money. He filed for adoption and didn't need any trouble either. Eddie never wanted Selena anyway. Ricardo often wondered if he was the legitimate father, probably not, he assumed.

Ricardo gave Sylvia a handsome deal as well to be rid of her son's involvement with Selena. Eddie was part of the reason his daughter committed suicide. The two young teens smoked pot and were stoned frequently. Eddie would slap her around and tell her she was worthless.

Selena, now eleven years old, arrived after a red-eye flight, looking disheveled and exhausted. She recognized her grandfather and ran into his arms crying.

"Selena I'm so happy to welcome you to your new home."

"Papa, I'm so scared."

His heart nearly crushed as he attempted to reassure her everything would work out well, in time. He wished Alexandra was here because he was already frightened, he would fail. On the way home he had an honest conversation with Selena and confessed he was scared. She looked at him curiously, asking why.

"My dear beautiful child, I failed once, and I don't want to repeat it again. I've been thinking constantly how I can make a good life for you. You deserve the best."

"Papa, I hope everything is better for both of us," she reassured him.

Ricardo said a silent prayer hoping her words were truth, asking God for the strength to help him and provide the support she so desperately needed. He wanted her to be healthy and happy, and he didn't want his past to ruin anything. When they arrived at his home, Selena stood in awe of the beautiful place where she would live.

"Is this truly where I will live, Papa?"

"Yes, my dear. This is your home. Come, I will show you your bedroom. I hope you will like it."

The next few hours the two caught up on many things and shared their deepest fears. Ricardo wanted to create trust and honesty in this relationship. Selena wanted the same. She hadn't seen her dad for a few years, since he was in prison and confessed, she didn't want to be battered by him, like her mom. Ricardo had no idea she was abused as well.

Quickly changing the subject. "Would you like to go shopping after you rest?"

"Oh Papa, I would love that! I need some new clothes, please. Grandma said to ask, but I was afraid. She never had much money and I never asked."

Ricardo was furious. He damned well knew he gave that woman plenty of money. She didn't keep her end of the bargain; therefore, he would consider cutting her off soon. First, settle Selena in her new home. Ten thousand dollars a month was more than anyone needed. His blood boiling, he was infuriated.

"You don't ever have to be afraid. And yes, we will get you something you like to wear. When Alexandra returns, you may want to shop with her. She is an expert at clothing."

"That sounds nice," hesitantly responding, but wanting to please her papa.

Selena noticed a photo of the two of them and asked Papa many questions about Alexandra. He did his best to prepare her for when they met and hoped they would eventually have a wonderful connection.

"I understand this is brand new Selena, and we all will have to adjust. I just want you to be at home and be honest with us, okay?"

"Yes, Papa, I can do that. I hope she will like me. I tend to be shy with strangers."

"She has a way about her that makes people comfortable. I'm sure you will find your way to connect with her. No rush, okay?"

"Thank you, Papa." The two embraced in a gentle hug.

It turned out well, having this personal time together before Alexandra returned from her concert in Sorrento. It gave Selena time to relax, tour the area with her papa, and get comfortable with her new environment. She enjoyed Tony and found him funny. Gino came by to welcome her to the family and toured her around the property Grandma Rosa left to the family.

"I love these flowers, Gino. May I take some home, please?"
"Absolutely, young lady." Ricardo smiled and was pleased the men were helping her adjust. The phone rang; it was Alexandra.

"Hello, my darling, how is everything?"

"It is wonderful, and we are waiting for you to come home soon."

"Well, I have good news! I'm arriving tomorrow. The owner of the restaurant took ill, and they had to cancel all the entertainment."

"I'm sorry, but I'm really happy you are coming back tomorrow. Selena has been asking many questions about you. She is afraid you won't like her. I told her you would take her shopping."

"I'm sure we will get along soon enough, and I'm more than happy to take her shopping. Good night, my love. I look forward to seeing you both tomorrow."

To be honest, Alexandra had her own fears and doubts. She didn't have much experience with children, but she related to them, given her own childlike ways and insecurities.

She is here, as promised. Now is your time to help this young one.

The whisper faded away as Alexandra fell off into a dream state.

Meeting Selena

Ricardo hired an au pair to take care of Selena, which startled Alexandra when she returned home. "Hello, Miss Alexandra, I'm Sophia. It is a pleasure to meet you."

"*Buongiorno*, Sophia."

Ricardo quickly joined them to conduct a formal introduction. Alexandra was surprised and uneasy being greeted by a stranger in her home.

"Alexandra, I'm so happy you are home. I employed Sophia yesterday to assist us here and to help with Selena. In all the commotion, I'm sorry I did not review the decision with you."

"I understand, but I am rather surprised. The help, I'm positive, will be welcomed."

Ricardo grabbed her baggage and walked with her to the bedroom for a private conversation.

"Seriously? You overlooked discussing this matter with me? It's not like you took in a stray cat! How can you keep secrets from me?"

"You're right. I've been so anxious of doing things wrong, and now I have disappointed you. It was foolish of me to bring someone into our home without considering you."

"Very foolish, Ricardo, and yes, I'm disappointed. I'm all about clear communication because once it leads astray, it continues downhill. How am I to trust you?"

It never crossed Ricardo's mind this would be a trust issue. The two had a heated discussion. Alexandra did not wish to create any issues with Selena, so she settled down and remained open to this opportunity. After all, she was exhausted and on edge from a tiring day of travel and she had said she would support Ricardo.

Ricardo called Selena from her room to properly introduce her to Alexandra.

"Selena, please meet my dear partner and love, Alexandra."

Selena was extremely shy. She barely got a soft hello out of her mouth and preferred to hide halfway behind Papa.

"Hello, lovely young lady. I've heard wonderful things about you! I also understand we need to organize a shopping spree. Would you like to do that soon?"

Selena just bowed her head and nodded yes.

"Come, ladies...my pretty women. Let's look at what a marvelous lunch Sophia has created for us."

Ricardo did his best to initiate conversations. Selena had a few comments, she was nervous. Alexandra, at a loss for how to approach a preteen, gave it her best shot.

"I think I will go unpack my suitcase, take a little rest after my shower, and meet with you two afterward?"

Ricardo rose like a gentleman, helped her out of her chair, kissed her on the cheek, and went on to finish lunch with Selena.

"Is there something you want to do today? I heard you liked the gardens Gino showed you. We should get some flowers to plant."

Her eyes lit up, as she smiled.

"Then we have a date."

"Sophia, please tell Tony we will need the car for a little adventure."

The afternoon flew by quickly, and Selena did indeed enjoy picking out tons of flowers to plant in their gardens. The two laughed together and they enjoyed smelling the array of flowers. Ricardo was hopeful he could make this little girl's life pleasant.

Over the next few weeks, everyone had an adjustment period. Selena had some difficulty welcoming Alexandra into her life. Alexandra decided not to push anything, remembering how she wasn't understood as a child. Ricardo was lost in his desperation to please everyone.

"Selena, I have an idea you may enjoy. When I was about your age, someone gifted me a diary. A secret place where I wrote anything I wanted, including all my feelings. It felt like a safe place for me to empty my heart, my hurt, and my disappointments…and to write my dreams."

"Really? It sounds cool."

This was the first time Selena actually engaged in a conversation with Alexandra.

"Come, let's go to the store and find one that you will love. Does that sound like a good idea?"

"Sure."

Tony drove the two ladies into the city. He stopped by the perfect shop with many types of gifts.

"Alexandra, I think I like this one. May I have it?"

Surprised that Selena chose a red journal, she replied, "You absolutely you may have it. Let's go pay for it now."

On the drive home, Selena asked Alexandra to show her how to use the diary. It was the perfect segue to helping this young lady. They had a chuckle or two before they arrived home. Tony smiled as he drove them home. He knew the two would definitely become good friends.

Months flew by and the two ladies were doing well bonding. It was time for Ricardo to take a business trip. Alexandra was nervous to take on the sole caretaker role. The two of them discussed matters with Sophia and Tony. Everyone agreed to support each other while he had work.

"Selena is fortunate to have so many loving people in her life," Sophia responded.

"Alexandra, can I show you something I wrote in my diary?" Selena came running down the stairs from her bedroom.

"Why, yes," she said, surprised. "It would be my honor to listen to what you wrote."

Selena reached out for her hand and led Alexandra back to her bedroom. They sat on the bed like two friends when Selena began to read.

I don't remember my mama. She died at my birth. I somehow know she is here with me. I don't like my dad; he is always mad. This is why I had to leave. Papa is kind and I know he cares a lot, but I feel lost. My fears will go away when I write in this book.

Alexandra cried and hugged Selena close.

"Do you understand these feelings, Alexandra? Papa said you would."

"Absolutely. I had a mother but learned just last year she was my adopted mother. I always had a notion I was not her child, but no one told me the secret until my adopted parents died. When I was born, my birth mom also died. My birth father went insane with grief and eventually killed himself. My journal saved my life."

"Wow, you *do* understand. Maybe that is why I am here, because you will help me. Do you think angels sent me here?" Alexandra's heart warmed in the knowledge she could help this child.

"Yes, I believe so too. Selena, people come into our lives in many ways to help us. Even our birth mamas continue to guide us."

"I believe that too. I think I can hear my mama. She likes you."

"I have an idea…let's go get gelato!"

The two jumped off the bed and found the perfect café to eat their favorite flavors of gelato. They talked for hours, bonded, laughed, cried, and came to understand each other. Alexandra was ready to be her mentor, guide, and friend. When they were done, Selena walked over to Alexandra, took her hand, and, with a sincere tone in her voice, said, "*Grazie*. You are my angel."

By the time Ricardo arrived home, the girls were hanging out dancing around the house, laughing and enjoying each other's company. Their home was joyful, and everyone was working towards healing their relationships. Selena understood Alexandra would have to leave occasionally to pursue her singing, and Ricardo was glad everyone was so content. Now, if only his nightmares would go away.

Two years went by when Ricardo received word about Selena's dad who had died. He, too, committed suicide. He had no words and would ask Alexandra to help him share the tragedy. Now he would cut off the remaining excessive funds which were never used for Selena. There would be no more black mail.

"Selena," they called. "Come into the library to meet with us."

"Papa, I have something to tell you."

"We do too, but you go first."

"Daddy came to me in a dream. He said he has no more pain."

The two adults looked at each other, curiously, and now had to break the news.

Papa proceeded, "Selena, it seems your daddy was telling you he went home to heaven, where he would be at peace. Your grandmother just informed me as well."

"Papa, I'm happy for him. He was always in pain and very sad. I couldn't talk to him. It made me cry all the time. In my dream, he was happy and healthy. He said he was sorry for hitting Mama."

Alexandra and Ricardo glanced at each other, knowing God just made their job a little easier.

"Selena, is there anything you may want to do to honor your dad?" Alexandra asked.

"I think I'm going to write him a poem. Maybe we can plant some flowers for him and bury the poem. Does that sound good?"

"That sounds perfect!" they replied together.

Selena spent the night in her bedroom composing her poem. She asked to be excused from dinner and was granted her privacy.

The next morning, she came to breakfast with a piece of paper in her hand, "I want to read something to everyone. Here is my poem."

Too Many Goodbyes

I came into this world alone and every time I wanted to be held and comforted in your arms; you weren't there. I had to say goodbye before I could speak, filled with an emptiness my heart didn't understand.

God, I never understood why I must go it alone.

Goodbye, Daddy, you were never really there. Your pain is now gone. Goodbye, Mama, I hear you from afar and feel your love.

Goodbye, Grandma, across the miles. I may never see you, but I will write you. Goodbye, sadness, my aching heart needs to heal now.

Hello, world, and thank you for my angels. Hello, life, for the opportunities waiting for me.

Hello, people I want to meet someday. I may touch your heart when you need to say goodbye. Life may have too many goodbyes... Only to open our hearts to many new hellos.

I love you, Mama, Daddy, and God. Oh, and I love Papa and Alexandra, Tony, Gino, and Sophia too. Rest in peace daddy.

Alexandra and Ricardo clasped each other's hand. Everyone in the room had tears trickling from their eyes. Selena was standing proud, wise beyond her thirteen years, and ready to face her path. Her poem was one anyone of them could have expressed; Selena did it for them all.

"Is this okay?" she asked.

Without uttering a word, everyone nodded their head yes. Ricardo reached out to hug this wise angel child and kissed her on top of her head.

"Sweet child, your heartfelt poem is more than okay, it's *brilliant!*"

A small ceremony was in order. Selena would pick her flowers to plant. Everyone would shovel a scoop of dirt to represent the community of love that stands by us. Selena asked Alexandra to say a prayer and help her bury the poem. Ricardo filled the hole with the flowers and watered it. Then they all said goodbye.

Selena adjusted well over the next year and was happier than ever. Alexandra became her confidante and mentor. Ricardo felt peace in his heart. Soon she would celebrate another birthday.

Life as a teenager was just beginning.

Hot Air Balloon Ride

Ricardo and Alexandra continued with their heart-to-heart talks, building their relationship, their trust, and creating a wonderful home in which Selena would thrive. He was adamant about demonstrating what healthy relationships looked like and how a man should treat a woman. He began with Alexandra, who was open to the idea.

One evening after dinner, Selena surprised them by playing the piano. Alexandra was familiar with the song and asked if she may sing along. Selena smiled and nodded yes. Ricardo was thrilled, listening to his favorite girls, and he vowed to himself to support their dreams. Alexandra made another vow, silently to herself, *I will remain open to his love.*

Since Alexandra and Ricardo both enjoyed cooking, the two would create meals together, singing and dancing all the while, when eventually, Selena wanted to join in the action. In typical Italian fashion, they had friendly fights over who could make something taste better. Passions flared, with their hands motioning in the air; voices escalating; yes, food fights occasionally happened; and, in the end, they laughed and enjoyed their meals together. Let's not forget, they had to sing over their creations, too.

One evening, Selena, who had been studying classical music all year, surprised them with a romantic melody. Ricardo reached out to Alexandra to dance.

"I have another surprise for you."

"You do? I still remember the last one."

"You shall see tomorrow."

Ricardo winked at Selena, while dancing with Alexandra. She helped him plan the surprise. Sophia happily agreed to watch her while they went off on an adventure.

Evening came and the partners were delighted to share their upcoming rendezvous together in the morning. Alexandra completely forgot it was her birthday, so this would be extra special. Embraced in each other's warmth, they cozied up in the large king-size bed, left the shutters slightly open for a cool breeze, and snuggled under the comforter. Ricardo had become an amazing lover, filled with genuine passion, a gentle touch, honest words, and warm kisses. He always treated her with respect and became a wonderful provider in many ways. It was one of those mornings filled with stillness and blessings. The sun was barely up when Ricardo nudged Alexandra to get up. Moaning and groaning, she said, "Are you crazy?"

"Perhaps…but trust me. Rise and shine, my dear."

"Oh my God, seriously?"

He dragged her gently out of bed, notified Tony to be ready with the car, and the two drove to Siena. Daybreak was cresting through the valleys and over the mountains and soon the light began to shine brighter to eliminate the darkness and shed a golden glow over the rolling hills.

"Where are we going?"

"Well, since you always like to look up into the sky, I planned the perfect birthday gift, my darling." Just then, they pulled into a field where a hot air balloon was being prepared for a morning liftoff.

"Ready for a new perspective?"

Alexandra's jaw dropped. He always knew how to catch her off guard and surprise her in so many ways. What she didn't know was that this surprise was only the beginning.

The balloon floated across the valley as the sun rose over the cypress treetops. The morning was crisp and chilly, and Ricardo snuggled up behind Alexandra. He wrapped his arms around her waist, and kissed her neck, hugging her to keep her warm. His heartbeat connecting with hers. A sense of gratitude warmed his heart and he felt blessed.

Approximately forty-five minutes had passed when the balloon followed its "tracker," which guided them to a landing zone. The ride was surprisingly gentle, and the landing took place in a field of wildflowers. Alexandra was in awe, speechless, and grateful for this beautiful opportunity. She was escorted out of the basket and back on the ground, where a champagne toast and a feast of delicacies awaited them both.

Once the balloon was deflated, and everything was set up, including a small wooden fold-up table with heavily hand painted blue flowers and two chairs, Alexandra and Ricardo were served. Ricardo held her hand and, with a champagne glass in his other hand, looked deeply into her eyes.

"I have a toast to propose," he said.

"Alexandra, like the sun that rises over the hills, my heart elevates in your presence. Like the air that fills my lungs, you fill my life each day with your love. Today, I propose a union of our souls. Will you walk in this life with me and be my wife?"

He placed the glass down to present her with the custom ring he made for her tiny fingers.

"Yes, *yes*, I will walk with you forever on this journey."

The ring fit perfectly. The staff applauded, and the lovers reached across the table for a celebratory kiss. They concluded with a rendition of "Happy Birthday" to the new future bride.

They would make wedding plans over the next year. With two busy work schedules and their travels, they barely had time to think about a wedding. But Selena and Sophia had some ideas up their sleeve.

CHAPTER 22

Sorrento

Alexandra had a rare opportunity to sing a romantic aria composed by Puccini at an event in Sorrento. She would need to arrive two weeks prior to rehearse with the violinist. It was a dream come true. The opera house featured many popular singers, and its owners would surprise her and tell who was the main feature once she arrived.

The beautiful venue, Correale Museum of Terranova, was bequeathed to the people of Sorrento, where the three tenors, Carreras, Domingo, and Pavarotti, toured and recorded for years. They introduced opera to an audience that had little experience of this genre.

Alexandra was in for a tremendous surprise. She was chosen as the brilliant, new soprano singer. The show's organizers chose Puccini's popular aria, one every soprano needs to have in their repertoire, for her debut. It translates to "Oh my beloved father," with heartfelt lyrics of a family feud, making it a moving performance. She would begin practicing at home each day to prepare for her rehearsals. Nervous, excited, and unsure if she could carry this great honor out well, she promised herself she would sing for all the families and their fathers.

When she met Salvatore, the violinist, his music captured her every cell and made her blood flow with passion. They were a perfect match. Placing her back against his to feel the vibrations and tones of the notes, helped her. She felt confident and safe to bring forth the deep emotions to reach people's hearts and souls. Their connection required no words. Everything was melodic as if they were one melody. They didn't understand what overcame them, when every emotion drenched and invoked tears to the ones listening, grasping every note within their souls, but it inexplicably hit a cord in their own lives.

There was no doubt this would be accomplished. His music, her voice, two hearts with synchrony…and the audience gave them two standing ovations. They threw flowers on the stage and bouquets were handed to her while they were both overwhelmed with gratitude and tears. They shared a genuine embrace of two comrades who knew they would stand together on many more stages, sharing their gift to the world.

"Ricardo, they loved us. I'm overwhelmed with gratitude for all the blessings bestowed upon us. Please come see the next performance, my love, and bring Selena."

"Yes, I will come to support you and Selena will surely enjoy the musical performance. She's become quite the protégé, following your footsteps."

Ricardo and Selena indeed came to witness this grandiose and stunning performance. He had a twinge of jealousy when he saw them leaning up against each other, back-to-back. Selena admitted later she was concerned about all the time Alexandra would have to spend away from home.

Once they all arrived back home, Ricardo expressed his concerns and fears. Alexandra completely understood, reassuring him the passion was in the music, not between their hearts. She had one love, and it was him.

It didn't take long for her voice to be recognized as one of the great sopranos to grace the local world of opera. Many offerings came, which she gladly accepted. It meant; however, she would be mostly traveling through Italy for at least six months.

Ricardo kept his word to support her dreams. Selena was sad, and the house became quiet in her absence. The wedding was postponed.

Her tour was just about over when she received an emergency phone call from Sophia. "Please, miss, you must come home. Selena has run away."

Distraught and frightened for her soon-to-be adopted grandchild, she immediately notified everyone that she had to leave. Ricardo waited for her anxiously at the door when she arrived, fell into her arms, and sobbed. "I failed."

Tony, Gino, and Sophia explained the details. Ricardo was so saddened he did not mutter a word without breaking down. Apparently, Selena had met a young boy at school. With the absence of Alexandra on tour and Ricardo working, she needed attention and craved love, so she ran away with him. Gasping for breath, hoping she was okay, Alexandra asked if the police knew.

"Yes, they have been notified. We are not sure where the two ran off to, and he is a few years older than her. A friend at school said they saw them smoking a joint, kissing and laughing, but nothing more." Sophia explained. This reminded Ricardo of his own daughter's past, and he feared for Selena.

"Thank you, everyone. Now we put our prayers and hearts together to find this sweet child and hope she is safe." Everyone nodded, and Ricardo fell down on his knees in prayer.

The next few days were tense, and Ricardo wasn't functioning well. He would go out for long drives in the country, hoping to find her and lost himself. His nightmares became more intense. He would cry out for help, but never explained anything to his wife. Alexandra was helpless, not able to ease his mind and called every person they knew. Maybe they would spot their golden brown-haired beauty with stunning blue eyes somewhere at a local café drinking cappuccino.

It was late one evening when the phone rang unexpectedly. It was the police, and they had found their lovely Selena. Ricardo and Alexandra went down to the police station to pick her up and bring her home to console her, to provide her with attention, support, and love. They almost didn't recognize her. Selena was sullen and withdrawn. Quiet, with her head down, she chose not to say a word. The young man was not found, and no answers were available. Apparently, Selena found the police station and asked for help.

Everyone was quiet on the ride home. She ran to her room, shut the door, and locked it while Alexandra held Ricardo in her arms and thanking God, they found her safe.

"Alexandra, if anything happens to her," he sniffled, "I will not be able to handle it." She nodded in an understanding way and prayed the child would always be safe.

The next few weeks required a lot of patience and understanding. It seemed Sophia was the one who would reach Selena this time. She was a runaway teenager herself in the past and tried to share her concerns with Selena. The young teenager was not in the mood to listen to anyone. With the underside of her hand, she lifted her long hair and brushed it off her shoulder, closed her eyes, pouted, and walked away.

"Selena," called Alexandra. "May I come in?"

"Do what you want! You always do."

Alexandra was not used to her being sarcastic, but she related. Opening the door, she entered the room and sat on the bed to open a conversation.

"I'm just concerned, and while I don't proclaim to understand anything, I would like to know what you were thinking."

"What was I thinking? You left me! You didn't think to tell me how long you would be gone? You just left! You left Papa and everyone. You didn't say goodbye!"

Alexandra was not expecting that response at all. She took a deep sigh and asked God to help her respond.

"You are right. I didn't realize how irresponsible I was, Selena. Can you forgive me?"

She put her head on the pillow and sobbed like she had just lost another parent. Alexandra placed her hand on her back, stroking it and running her hand through Selena's hair, the way her mother comforted her when she was a child.

"Please don't leave me ever again! Please!" she bawled.

Alexandra did not consider this young woman felt this way and responded, "I will never walk away like that again. I promise I will invite you on my travels if you would like to come. Okay?" Sniffling so much she was barely breathing, she mumbled, "fine."

The two women made an agreement to be open and honest, and Selena agreed to go to counseling with Alexandra. Ricardo, in the meantime, shut down and isolated himself. He was angry and felt like a failure once again. There was another concern on his mind, no one knew; it dealt with work. The only way he processed his emotions was to take his sports car on long drives through the winding roads of Tuscany.

They still had a wedding to be planned, and Alexandra wanted to confirm it was still on when Ricardo was calmer. He hesitated at first as Selena barged into the room and begged him to marry Alexandra.

"I want her to be my real grandma, please Papa." He agreed.

To remove the stress of a large wedding, Alexandra suggested an intimate one with their small family. Ricardo agreed it would be wise, and Selena danced around the house, grabbing Tony and Sophia to dance with her.

The life energy was back in their home, and everyone held hands and prayed for a good life for all. Alexandra agreed she would only take local singing engagements so she didn't have to travel far, and she would see if Marty wanted her to write again for the magazine. Just as she announced her decision, Sophia handed her an envelope from the United States.

"Wow, Marian! I can't believe it! She wrote!" Rapidly tearing it open, she read through it quickly. "She's coming!" shouting to everyone.

The note said she had read Alexandra's article about Peru and contacted Danny, which led her to Italy. At the end of the letter was a PS: *I'm probably going to knock on your door soon.*

"Everyone, she's already on her way. Look, it says it right here. We must prepare a room for her!"

In two days, Marian arrived, and the two friends embraced each other tightly. They spent hours catching up, the details of her divorce from the evil man who beat her, the death of her father, and the sadness her mother endured for keeping secrets too.

"Dear Marian, I'm so glad you came here. What are your plans?"

"I have no idea. Perhaps you could give me some suggestions. I'm lost, honestly. I have money, but no confidence."

"Oh Marian, you are a wonderful writer. Maybe you can get a job with the magazine too. I will ask Marty. He would happily take my recommendation."

"I never considered that possibility. You mean I can travel and write like you did? How fun is that?"

"Yes! Let's put a call into him tomorrow. For now, we need some girl time. I want to take you and Selena out for a tour. Would you like that?" The two ladies chimed in together responding *yes*, and they all laughed together.

After stopping at medieval villages, exquisite cathedrals with stained glass windows, and ceramic warehouses, they found a delightful café, where they all agreed to get a cappuccino. Selena asked to sit at a table by herself to write in her journal while the friends chatted.

Across the table, a young man with dark, curly hair spotted Selena. He was sitting with a group of friends, all appearing to be American. Selena ignored him and kept writing. The young man desperately wanted to say something to her when his buddy elbowed him and said, "Go for it." "I don't know what to say." "Try hello or

Buongiorno," they said, laughing.

Selena looked up to see the boys giggling and noticed the handsome young man. He appeared tall and athletic and had bright blue eyes like her.

Nervously, he tried to say hello in Italian and not look like a fool. "Bongorno," he said, mangling the greeting. He definitely had difficulty with the pronunciation. She smirked and replied, "*Buongiorno*, are you American?"

"Yeah, we are visiting for a soccer game."

"That's cool. What's your name?"

"John."

"Nice to meet you, Giovanni."

"Ahh, that sounds better than John," he chuckled. His friends teased him, chanting "Giovanni" while Selena laughed.

John or Giovanni was very shy and didn't know what to do next. He really wanted to learn more about her. Alexandra watched the courtship and just allowed it to flow so Selena might have a little fun too.

"What are you reading?"

"I'm actually writing in my journal," she replied.

He whispered to his friend, Eddy, next to him. "Dude, I don't know what to say next. Man, she is hot."

Shrugging their shoulders, the inexperienced boys realized they did not know how to charm this beauty. Alexandra tapped Selena on the shoulder and said, "Time for us to go."

"*Ciao*, Giovanni," she said, waving. "Maybe we will see each other again."

"Chow," he replied with his American accent.

"Damn, dude, she wants you!" All the boys laughed, immaturely teasing Giovanni. He liked his new name.

221

Alexandra helped Marian get her first internship, which made Marty happy because the magazine needed some fresh blood. He even suggested Marian do an article on her perspective of being a single woman exploring Italy solo. Alexandra loved the idea and offered to host Marian until it was time to leave.

Selena was healing well and wrote in her journal about Giovanni. She hoped she would bump into him again and possibly have a conversation. Ricardo, buried in work, was dealing with some hard decisions about his company and wondering what the future would hold. He was also preparing legal paperwork for Alexandra to officially adopt Selena. He wanted to make sure they always had enough money to be cared for, if anything was ever to happen to him.

The next month flew by rapidly. Marian had her story and was on her way back to the USA. Alexandra was so happy to reconnect, and the two friends would rebuild their connection.

Selena did, in fact, meet up with Giovanni one more time before he left for home. They enjoyed a cappuccino, and she took a walk with him to get gelato. He was a little older and Papa probably wouldn't approve, but she knew he was leaving soon.

"Selena, can we stay in touch? I would like to text you or sometimes call." She was thrilled and quickly jumped at the opportunity to give him her cell phone number. "Great, I promise I will text." "Me too."

When it was time to leave, Giovanni attempted to give her a hug. Realizing he was so much taller than her, he bent down, when she surprised him with a kiss.

"I'm never washing that off."

"*Ciao*, Giovanni. I want to hear from you again."

"Cool."

The two would stay in touch through text and an occasional phone call. Selena liked him. Papa was just glad they were thousands of miles away.

Texting Giovanni before bed, Selena wrote, *Maybe, one day I can visit you in America.* He responded with hearts and smiley faces. She drifted off to dream.

The Wedding

Several months flew by before the couple would organize their intimate marriage ceremony. If not for Selena, many more delays would happen. She was determined for these two to finalize this union. Her relationship with Alexandra grew stronger, and she adored her. Her papa always seemed under more stress but wouldn't speak of anything.

This concerned Alexandra since their relationship always genuine and open and was tense now. He claimed wedding jitters stressed him, a teenager, and a lot on his plate with the law firms he oversaw in New York and in Europe.

Alexandra asked Selena to be her maid of honor, and Marian flew back to be her bridesmaid. Danny and Suzette flew over from Switzerland to witness their happy day.

The gardens exquisitely decorated by the hands of the ladies made every detail, all the more charming. The couple spoke privately early in the morning about their vows. They both seemed happy, relaxed, and ready to begin this next chapter of their life together.

A harpist played Pachelbel Canon D, in the gardens. The glamorous bride wore a white fascinator hat from the '50s, tilted slightly over one eye, creating the mystery and intrigue she so loved.

Ricardo, always well dressed and handsome, waited for her alongside the minister under the garden trellis, adorned with white and pink flowers. Marian and Selena walked down the aisle, charming all the single men. Alexandra, ready to marry. Finally, a beautiful caring relationship of love. She wanted to help him.

They recited their personal vows, acknowledged their love, and agreed to be husband and wife. The photographer captured the most genuine loving smiles from the two, the delicate touches of their clasped hands, and the intense connection in their eyes when they both said, "I do."

After a champagne toast, the party began.

The couple would take a quick honeymoon to Paris for a few days. Both of their schedules busy with deadlines. They agreed to schedule an "official" honeymoon to Croatia or Greece, soon. Selena would be sixteen soon, and they wanted to celebrate this passage of life. Danny and Suzette announced they would soon be getting married, and Gino now with a partner who made him happy. All appeared well in Tuscany.

The couple discussed Selena's future while they went to Paris. Ricardo wanted her to attend proper schools and receive a good education. Alexandra wanted to ensure her creative side was nurtured. Yes, they would be parents or grandparents to a child gifted to them by God. This brought contentment to both of them.

Now Alexandra finally understood the message she received when she lived in St. Lucia. A very important person did come into her life, and only Alexandra's experiences of loss may help Selena understand this journey. Her mystical experience in Peru gave her the courage to walk through this lifetime. The healer helped her open her heart so this union would happen, and the shaman in the cave reminded her to pay attention in life. Each person she encountered helped her develop into the person she became.

Yet, she still wondered about *him.*

The Tension Rises

Life was grand for several months. Each evening Ricardo began to wear a concerned look on his face again. He would mumble in his sleep, toss and turn, occasionally shout out for help and wake up tired. His trouble mind took over his life.

"Dear man, please tell me what troubles you."

"No! I deal with a lot! We shall discuss things later. Please let me figure some things out first. I have no patience right now. Go!" This tone of voice was not typical for him and disconcerting.

While Alexandra did not like the secrecy, his sudden bursts of anger, she became extremely concerned. She agreed to give him one more week, and then, she said, he must open up to her. She always respected his position, didn't pressure him, and honored his need to do things his way.

Selena got caught up in teenage drama and Alexandra saw some inappropriate things being posted on social media, like Snapchat. Immediately she demanded the sexy photos come down. This is not appropriate for a young girl. She knew if Ricardo found out, it would bring back horrific memories; she wanted to protect both of them.

"My generation does this," she replied with an attitude.

"Well, I do not approve. The things on these networks are fake. They don't build self-esteem; they only destroy people."

Selena broke down crying.

"It's true, what you said. I am not good enough. I don't like all this makeup, and I'm embarrassed of my body. But I can't stop. The obsession became an addiction. Every day you are competing to be accepted. I hate this! Yesterday, a girl committed suicide. Someone posted disgusting pictures of her hanging herself. I wanted to die."

This new piece of information understandably alarmed Alexandra. "I have no words, frankly. But I do realize this is not healthy for anyone. I have an idea. Come with me on a trip. You love art and photography so much. Let me take you to some places. It will lift your sadness."

"I can't."

"What do you mean you can't?"

"I have school and…and…" "And what?"

"I have a boyfriend. I can't leave him." "Young lady, school can wait and a boyfriend…well, if he can't wait, more will be available someday." "No, I don't want to go."

Alexandra had nothing else to offer at this point. She explained to Ricardo about the things happening at home, he barely listened. Sophia tried to find solutions and Tony remained on the lookout for something to offer. Gino offered to let her come to the family home for weekends and learn about the Italian ancestry.

Selena said no to everyone and every idea. They all witnessed as the months went on, her moods becoming more unpredictable. She slept more than usual and didn't want to eat. Something definitely was wrong, and no one seemed to be able to help.

"I'm a teenager, leave me alone." And alone is where she chose to remain for the next several months.

Alexandra and Ricardo finally sat down for their conversation about her concerns. Nothing was revealed which would satisfy her. He reassured her there was no need for alarm. Unfortunately, her intuition told her the lies being told and trust was breaking down. The family wasn't working together, and Alexandra remained hopeless. She was extremely concerned for Selena, as well.

Dear Diary, I have not been diligent about my writing in a long time. Perhaps when we are happy, we don't share those emotions, and when we are sad, we drip our tears on the paper feeling sorry for ourselves. I thought I made the right decisions. Everything felt right, even welcoming Selena into my heart. Now I don't have a clue what to do or what to expect...but no one is talking to me from the other side.

Alexandra took the small pouch out from her dresser drawer and held her birth mother's brooch. As she looked at the shattered pieces of glass which created the bouquet she called out , *why am I being drawn now to observe these broken pieces?*

Ricardo never came home for dinner that evening and did not answer his phone. Tony said he would try to reach him, but no response. They called Gino to find out if they were drinking their bottle of wine together. Nope, no one contacted him all day. This concerned Alexandra deeply.

The time has come

"What does this mean? Someone tell me!"

Silence, once again.

She cried, not understanding why. Her fingers ran across the broken pieces of glass, each colorful shard creating a flower. Always curious, even as a child, how something so beautiful was created with broken parts and pieces of nothing, became exquisite. The sheer curtains blew with the breeze the same as during her childhood. The presence of someone at the doorway, watching her, definitely palpable tonight. The doorbell rang. Tony ran up the stairs to retrieve Alexandra and begged her to come downstairs.

"What is so urgent?" "Please, come now!" he desperately called out.

He held her hand as they briskly walked down the marble staircase when she spotted two policemen standing in the entry hall, under the chandelier. Her knees shook, her stomach churned, and an overwhelming sense of despair filled her heart.

"Madam, we regret to inform you we found your husband's car overturned on a narrow road."

"Where is he?"

"The car exploded, and we cannot find his body anywhere yet. The coroner is looking for clues and the investigators are already at the scene."

"What happened?"

"We don't exactly have those answers yet. I'm sorry."

A loud scream came from upstairs when Selena overheard the news. She fell and slid down the stairs, sobbing uncontrollably, while Alexandra did her best to remain calm.

"*No!*" she cried. The gut-wrenching scream echoed through the halls.

The policemen let themselves out. Tony and Sophia stood by to support Alexandra and Sophia, but they really didn't have a clue what to do either. Everyone crying, confused, sad and helpless.

Hold her, the soft voice whispered. *You both need to hold each other now.*

Alexandra complied as she always did when the voice advised her.

Their heads leaning into one another, their bodies limp, they wept uncontrollable tears. Nothing made sense.

The next few weeks brought no conclusive answers about the tragic accident. The car, totaled in the explosion, and nothing found in the debris. Alexandra searched their rooms and his office to see if he left any clues. Selena remained in a deep, dark depression, unable to cope, as Alexandra did her best to remain calm for Selena while she dealt with her own grief.

Every morning when the sun rose, she asked God tons of questions. No voices were speaking, no insights, no clue as to what happened, and Ricardo never came to her in a dream. Each day harder to help her granddaughter. Ricardo left both of them well taken care of for life with his investments and his life insurance policy. But the money meant nothing if he was gone. Alexandra went in circles, calling out to her angels, guides, ancestors, and Jesus. No one came around. She shut down with anger, disappointment, and lost faith.

Tony did his best to keep the house in order and Sophia would be let go soon. Alexandra considered selling the house and moving into her Tuscany home she inherited with Gino. Many decisions needed to be made, but for now, both women cried every single day.

"Selena, it's Alexandra. May I come in?" "No!"

"I thought we could chat about doing a little ceremony. One like you did for your dad. The poem was beautiful. When you want to talk, I am here for you."

No response.

Sophia kept an eye on Selena and made sure she ate, even if a little. Tony polished the car almost daily, lost without his friend. Danny came for a visit to help Alexandra settle the estate and provide some comfort.

"Ricardo, I am aware the veil is thin and perhaps my anger is keeping me from hearing you. Please, I beg of you, lead me to a sign so I can help Selena, and we can understand what happened."

You will know soon, a voice whispered

"Thank you, God."

Remember, everything is not as it appears.

"Let me think… He spent a lot of time in his office for months. No one from company headquarters reached out. Strange, something must have gone wrong."

Alexandra decided to become a sleuth and called Tony to help. She never got involved in questioning Ricardo about his business and didn't know the name of his company. With all the personal details, articles, classes, and performances, her plate full, not to mention the time and energy to raise a teenager.

Tony didn't ask many questions of Ricardo either, he told Alexandra. He thought perhaps, an international law firm. The hunt began. Some large law firms survived more than one hundred years and then fallen to pieces in a matter of months or weeks, she learned. No doubt a collapse happened. However, no one called about Ricardo's death, or they didn't care. Something is really wrong.

Selena snuck down the stairs quietly and went into the kitchen. She confided in Sophia she wanted to go back to America. Her friend, Giovanni, said she could visit, and maybe she would visit her real grandmother. Sophia didn't think this was the best idea and advised her to speak with Alexandra. Pouting, she turned abruptly, walked up the steps, and slammed the door.

"What was that?" called out Alexandra.

"I'm sorry, miss, Selena was upset."

"Tell me what happened."

"She wants to go to America and see Giovanni and her '*other*' grandmother. I told her to speak with you."

"Oh goodness, another problem on my plate," Alexandra said, screaming. "I don't need anything else; you hear me, God?" She continued to search through everything in the office for hours. Nothing provided a clue.

The estate lawyer called and said all the paperwork is prepared and in order. A sufficient trust fund was left for Selena as well as for Tony, Gino, and Sophia. Ricardo definitely wanted everyone to be taken care of, the attorney mentioned. Ricardo, a multimillionaire, according to his assets, shocked everyone. Alexandra just walked away with no interest in his inheritance. The lawyer left abruptly and did not chose to answer any questions, replying there was urgent business elsewhere. That's when her heart told her something is wrong. Nothing was accurate and everything mysterious.

Ricardo's body, never discovered, the family decided to gather some photos, say a prayer for his soul, and plant some flowers. Alexandra sang a beautiful aria, one truly from her broken heart, and Selena stood emotionless the whole time, with no eye contact with anyone.

A full moon rose in the sky, the stars twinkled and everyone was more emotional. Alexandra, about to fall apart and needed to do something promptly to pull herself together.

"I need a trip," she said. "I must leave here!"

Rummaging through her luggage, she found a piece of paper which had fallen to the floor. Nearly fainting when she saw a note signed by Ricardo, while she sat on the bed. How did the paper wind up in her suitcase?

"You were everything to me and will always be my love. Please look over Selena. I have provided everything you will ever need. I knew eventually when you had to travel, you would find this note."

"What the hell?" she screamed. Sophia and Tony ran up to the room briskly to see if everything was all right.

"Miss, may we come in?" No response.

"I cannot fucking *believe* this!" Tony opened the door cautiously.

"Are you okay?"

"No, I am *not* fucking okay! Read this! The bastard hid his illness and knew he would die."

Tony, confused, Sophia, shaking, and Selena ran down the hall to find out what all the commotion was about.

"Alexandra, what are you yelling about?" asked Selena. "Your papa *kept a secret*, and he never told me!"

"What do you mean?"

"He had cancer. Progressive cancer, inoperable cancer. He didn't want us to help him as he withered away." Her heart ached. She had enough. How ironic he would also have cancer, like his late wife, she thought.

"But the accident? He died because of the car accident?"

"Yes, but he was going to die soon anyway and never said a word." Selena came over to place her arm around her grandmother to console her. "I want to get out of here. Selena, do you want to come with me on a trip?"

"I can't."

"Again, with the I can't. I will never understand your reasons."

"I can't because I'm afraid."

"Child, there is nothing to be afraid of. I will take care of you."

"I am afraid to be close to anyone now. I'm afraid to leave this house. I'm afraid of everything."

"Oh, dear child, don't waste your life being afraid. Traveling has always helped me receive answers. I need to go for a little while. I hope you will understand. Sophia, Tony, and Gino will care for you as well. Danny is coming too. You won't be alone. I'm not leaving you!"

"I understand. You have had a lot to deal with. Please go, and when you come back, perhaps we can both go visit someplace together. I'm thinking about colleges and remembered how much you thought I would love Paris."

"Sounds like a plan. I will take the train to Rome. y tears must release my sadness and I will write my emotions in my journal."

Everyone agreed she needed to go away for a while. The next morning Tony drove her to the train station. Selena hugged her tightly and cried. Sophia and Gino assured her they would take care of everything.

The house somber now. Danny would be arriving soon. Gino and his lovely partner went back to the family home. Sophia had to make a decision with her life, and Tony, lost without his best friend.

Rome 2014

Alexandra lost the spark in her heart, no desire at all to shop. Aimlessly walking the streets for hours in Rome she passed many of her favorite boutiques. Nothing intrigued her. She understood nothing. The time for her to go was now.

As she sipped her wine before her day ended, she said her gratitude prayer and knew she had many blessings for all those wonderful years she spent with Ricardo.

She missed him *so* much. There were some lovely years together although he was taken too soon. Selena brought joy and purpose in her life too. Everything, so perfect…but alas, one must move on. Would she ever receive the answers she sought when he never returned home? Would she learn the cause of the car accident?

Her dreams took her back to the days when her name shone in lights. Elegantly standing on stages in several towns for festivals, weddings, and concerts, she curtsied before her audience with poise. Many times, Ricardo sat in the front row with a huge bouquet, once his jealousy was gone. He truly did love her, but he felt he wasn't *the one*…the one she longed for in her heart.

The colors rolling along the hedges…everywhere
Creating a balance, a soothing feeling of gentleness
To touch it – a softness
A reminder that we are fragile
Complexity – as life runs through each vine
The miracle of creation
Simplicity – in its form
Beauty – that we all possess.

—G.COPPOLA

CHAPTER 23

Puglia

The ride to Puglia went by quickly. Every memory sped by in her mind when the face of Marcello appeared. *He was a kind man*, she thought. *I must visit him again one day.* She had no idea he was on his way to find her. She thought about the letter she wrote to Selena earlier in the day.

Dear beautiful child,

I've been graced with you in my life. While we are not of the same blood, we are with each other's soul and that never dies. Listen to your heart - follow your intuition.

Love, Grandma Alexandra

She sobbed, wondering how she may help this child when she returned home.

Later in the evening, after arriving at Puglia, Alexandra stood in the dark room of the Trulli and removed her dress. Naked, she was startled when she heard someone by her door. She saw a pink envelope had been slipped under the doorway from the dimly lit hallway, which provided enough luminescence for her.

She became curious. She did not have friends or any acquaintances in this quaint region of Alberobello, Puglia. Her evening journey had exhausted her, and now she was tense from this unexpected intrusion. Her visit to this quaint town was a last-minute decision as she felt like she needed quiet time for herself and wanted to explore a less popular region in Italy. The fourteenth-century whitewashed huts, known as "trulli," captured her curiosity upon her arrival. Concerned now as to whether someone was lurking outside the door, she observed a faint shadow disappear into the night. Hesitating to pick up the letter, the sheer curtain, which draped across her fairy tale setting, suddenly blew inward with a burst of wind, making the quiet night seem even mysterious now. All she wanted was peace, a time to grieve and determine what to do with her future.

The charming Trulli with its vintage furniture had a romantic essence. The intricate needlework, a historic form of filet lace, draped the custom crafted wooden tables, where a complimentary bottle of white wine and two glasses stood. Looking over at the two glasses, Alexandra remembered their toast the day of the hot air balloon ride.

A small porcelain table lamp caught her attention. A unique antique Italian Capodimonte lamp, two delightful cherubs on a whimsical pedestal of colored flowers, originating in the eighteenth century. Similar to one Ricardo had in his bedroom. The lamp was out of place, but lovely nevertheless.

She cautiously opened the wine from the Masciulli winery and sat in the soft velvet tufted chair. Much of the furnishings all seemed a bit grandiose for the fourteenth-century huts, which were designed for a simpler life. She had read the trulli were constructed as temporary field shelters and storehouses, or permanent dwellings, by small-scale landowners or agricultural laborers.

Just as she settled down, the church bell from Saint Anthony's rang so loudly, the tone vibrated through the limestone walls. This was definitely not the peaceful evening she had envisioned.

As she bent over to pick up the pink envelope, the phone rang.

"*Buonasera*," the concierge said as she answered.

Damn, those phones always make me jump!

He called to extend an invitation for brunch, assuring her the meal would be *favolosa*!

She sipped her wine; the delicate hint of fruity aromas had a harmonious blend to this smooth elixir. It relaxed her as she slowly closed her eyes. Her head melded with the soft, fluffy pillow as she faded off to a magical dream state.

The letter was never opened.

The early morning light did not disturb the sleeping goddess, when the bells from the church startled her out of her dream state. *Oh dear, I must get going.* She realized she never opened the letter and now had no time to read. She was late for the brunch. *I'll put it in my leather bag and open later. It's probably just a thank-you note from the hosts of the Trulli,* she thought.

Gathering her belongings and taking one last look at the beautiful view from the terrace, she took a deep, fulfilling breath to begin her glorious day. "Goodbye Ricardo, I hope you are happy wherever you are." She danced around towards the arched alcove, she drew the curtain that wrapped around the bed, and rushed through the old wooden door, past the stone flowerpot, cascading with colors of yellow, pink, and greenery. She decided the day was going to be magnificent. Only today no one would recognize her. Her wide-brimmed hat shaded her face, and she had anonymity. She was not going to grieve any longer. Too many years, too many goodbyes.

Not far beyond was the Ristorante Trullo, there was a long table waiting for guests in the outside garden. People were gathering for brunch, hugging, laughing, and kissing, delighted to connect with each other, when they noticed Alexandra. The whole place quieted, as if their breath halted in midair.

A gentleman shouted, *"Lei é arrivata!"* (She has arrived.) as the server escorted Alexandra to the head of the table. Whispers amongst the crowd asked, "Chi é lei? (Who is she?)

Tossing her head, she lifted the wide-brimmed straw hat to reveal her face when the letter fell out of her purse. A gentleman leaned over to pick up the envelope from the stone courtyard walkway. He looked up into the deep sea of her blue eyes once again.

"Non hai aperto la mia lettera, bella?" (Did you not open my letter, beautiful?)

Curious eyes all turned in their direction from the enormous table, wondering what was going on.

"*Buongiorno*, Marcello! What are you doing here?"

"I came because you dropped your letter. Once you left the café, I thought there was something familiar about you. I could not sleep, so I had to find you and followed you here. I had to tell you my love has always been for you."

"Wait, you *love* me?" she asked.

"We *met* each other once before! It's all in the letter I slipped under the door last night."

"That was you?"

"Yes, at first, I could not believe myself. I questioned my memory and imagined the impossible. However, your eyes, the sea of blue…I never forgot that day, many years ago." Curious, she listened.

"I had no name for you. I remember your eyes. Something familiar. Your beautiful energy, captured me on the train. I never really understood."

"The train?"

The crowd, captivated by their conversation, was sitting on the edge of their seats, now realized who she was, a well-known local opera singer. Their curiosity peeked wondering why she was being courted by this man.

Her heart had been sad for so many years. Now, with Ricardo's death, she found singing difficult. Every aria expressed a passion and torment which pierced the hearts of her fans and loved ones. Her audience always understood the deep longing, the hard journey, the losses, and her quest to be reunited one day with her love. They would embrace every melodic note she sang.

Alexandra slowly stepped closely to Marcello, held his hand, and said, "I do remember now. I remember your espresso colored eyes. I was writing about them yesterday at your cafe."

"*Si*…and you sat writing about *me*?"

"Marcello, I am astonished, amazed, and blessed. My heart had to heal. Now you are here. I don't understand!"

"God had a plan. We never forgot."

Fifty years ago, she had jumped off a train, a young girl traveling through northern Italy, when a handsome young man attempted to detain her after a long journey from Switzerland to Italy.

He would ask the same question today.

"*Vuoi sposarmi?*" (Will you marry me?)

The very words she didn't understand when she was seventeen. Her eyes lit up brighter than a full moon night with glistening stars. Her smile could fill an ocean with joy. Everyone was waiting for the very moment they could cheer her on, only this time for her happiness.

"I will, *yes!*" she announced with exuberance.

As if by magic, the bells of St. Anthony rang joyfully through the air. Everyone stood up and applauded this enchanting couple's reunion. The symphony swirled through the air, touching every heart. Everyone connected with this powerful love. Her song was heard. They ate, drank, and laughed. Then he handed her the letter he found.

"Oh my. I'm so glad you found this. I wrote the note for my granddaughter, Selena. I want her to have this one day."

"Then I am glad to find for you. This magic brought us together."

Alexandra looked up to the heavens. Everyone was watching over her, she imagined Ricardo too. If she had not met him, she would not have Selena in her life. If she didn't have Selena in her life, the letter would have not been written. If the letter never fell on the ground yesterday, Marcello would never have found her. And if Ricardo didn't disappear, this reunion would have never manifested.

Yes, signs are everywhere, and Alexandra now understood her life journey. This time, however, she wanted a happy ending.

Marcello and Alexandra remained in the quaint village for two days. His cousin was happy to run the café and everyone at home was delighted to assist with Selena and the house. She didn't tell them all that happened, but somehow, she had a knowing they sensed the magic. Selena texted her to say, *I love you.*

They had so much fun getting acquainted, eating, sipping wine, and shopping. They wandered down each narrow street tenderly holding each other's hand. A soul love never dies. The tenderness was peaceful. This connection would always lead to finding one another, no matter how hard the journey may be. Always meant to be, the longing is unexplainable when one knows. This is the way a true soul mate remembers.

One day you will tell your story
of how you overcame what you went through.
It will become part of someone else's life guide.

—G. COPPOLA

ILLUSTRATION BY MANDY ASQUITH

CHAPTER 24

Their Future

Q uickly they decided their future. They both had waited for this moment for over fifty years. Alexandra would help Marcello in his café for a while. Selena would be going off to college, and nothing was left for Alexandra to do back at her home. Gino was pleased to remain the caretaker and supported her decision. Danny loved the idea, knowing how long his sister had waited for this love.

Many days were spent in Rome at Marcello's café, and now Alexandra was singing happy songs with him. No more tragic stories or emotional arias. Her time had come to celebrate. The patrons adored them, always referring more customers to the café.

Marcello was getting ready to pass the café onto his cousin. The time had come. He was so glad he had studied English all those years so he was better able to communicate with his sweetheart the stars sent to him. He had deeper faith than most people. He prayed she would return. He never gave up faith.

Alexandra was delighted he wanted to settle in the Tuscany home. Gino was happy he would have more family to serve. It always made him have purpose. Grandma Rosa was smiling because all her signs brought them to this moment.

But, for tonight, this mature couple looked forward to an evening of tender lovemaking.

He brushed her hair away from her eyes and kissed her cheeks. He always had a deep longing to care for her since the first time he laid eyes on her. The years kept them both in pretty good shape, yet their bodies had different needs now. To caress and know the warmth of each other's body was a gift, a treasure…and to feel their hearts beat together was magical. They were content with the gentleness shared between the two of them.

The whisper spoke: *Be happy now.*

"Yes, Grandma, I am."

Marcello didn't question her because he understood all too well… they both had guides watching over them.

CHAPTER 25

Welcome Home

The next few years would bring everyone much happiness. Gino was overjoyed to have them in the home, along with his delightful and jovial partner, Margherita. Like the old days when his family was alive, Gino once again had joy in his final years. Alexandra wanted to learn more about the family, and he happily shared a few stories. It brought her much comfort to understand all her feelings during life; yet, she new there was much more to learn.

Marcello enjoyed tending to the garden and mostly watching Alexandra move gracefully past him. Her scent always made him feel alive. Occasionally, she would tease him and gently brush across his body to see if she could light him up. He certainly was aware what she was up to, and the afternoons were delightful, running off to the bedroom like two teenagers in heat.

Selena was doing well and sharing her thoughts about her future. She hoped her grandmother would approve and help her in some way. She was almost completed with college. It took a little longer than expected because of the many family needs. Danny and Suzette were planning more family trips and enjoying a "real" family, finally.

Alexandra had found a wooden chest in the old home several months back. Tucked away in the cellar, even Gino never went down there. She was ready to open and find out what was inside. It was time for Danny and her to find out about the secrets.

As soon as she had a quiet moment, she planned to explore its contents. She got emotional seeing her birth mother's initials carved into the wood G.C. Sitting quietly in the dark, musty room, her wrinkled hands rubbed across the top. One tiny tear flowed, but it wasn't time to open it. Perhaps tomorrow, she thought.

The "lovebirds," Alexandra and Marcello, brought cheer to everyone. Even Marian stopped by for quick visits to fill herself up with genuine love and friendships. She loved her assignments with the magazine and had the opportunity to do a lot of traveling. She told Alexandra her favorite place was Hawaii. Selena's ears perked up and said, "Hawaii is on my bucket list."

While the whispers became less frequent, Alexandra always had a sense her loved ones were nearby if she needed them. She expressed her gratitude in her journal before going to sleep one lovely evening as a full moon illuminated the night sky.

Dear Diary, I'm grateful for this journey we have had together. When I read each entry, I realize my journey may have not always been the easiest, but I would not change anything. Well, maybe. Nah, if I did, my beautiful Selena would not be in my life. Please take care of all my loved ones, angels, guides, and spirit family. My heart is full, and I am grateful. Our journey is nearly done, but we live in peace now. For now, we sprinkle fairy dust on each soul and allow the magic to unfold.

I know you – in your darkest hour and in the light,
I see pain so deep – piercing through you.

Why do you suffer, when you could find peace?
Is it the only way you believe life can be?

Darkness – around you, that you've created –

Sadness, in your heart – letting no one in.

Confusion – everywhere –
mixed messages, scaring us away…

I know you - because I have been in
the darkness of death, consumed by it.

Never run away from the shadow
that follows you.

—G.Coppola

CHAPTER 26

No More Espresso

Marcello patted his hand on Alexandra's tenderly. The birds whistled joyfully, and the two gave a big yawn and contented sigh simultaneously. Every single breath they took was united. They were tranquil, reveling in the moments to snuggle in each other's arms. Life was simple and easy. The large king bed with the fluffy down comforter was an open invitation for lazy mornings. They regularly began their mornings with a prayer of gratitude and a tender kiss. Marcello consistently had a way of making Alexandra smile to start the day. She had no objections.

Gino stopped by their room about thirty minutes later. Every morning, his routine was the same, to lightly knock and announce to the lovebirds, "Breakfast is ready."

The aroma of the espresso, which Alexandra learned to appreciate, was always distracting. You couldn't resist following it down to the kitchen where Gino regularly had fresh pastries prepared in a basket wrapped with a colorful cloth.

It was strange, thought Gino, not one of them answered the wake-up call, but he assumed they were otherwise engaged in their passionate embrace. Twenty minutes passed by, and still no movement from upstairs. He wondered if they stayed up too late and fell back asleep. Frequently those two acted like youngsters. They snuggled, chuckled, and tucked away under the covers until almost noon.

Marcello, growing older, wasn't moving as fast. Alexandra didn't wish to call attention to the aging process, so she would play along with Marcello and curl up longer. Gino, older than both of them, really didn't want to go back up the stairs, so he waited.

"Those sweethearts are certainly having an enchanting morning," Gino chuckled, moving slowly, he arranged Alexandra's favorite fresh flowers in a vase on the table. Alexandra always enjoyed having colorful bouquets gracing the home. She once said it reminded her of the colorful bouquet of flowers on the brooch and made her feel like the five-year-old who pranced around.

Ten more minutes and Gino became concerned. Something is off. He sensed it. Unless, of course, they are in the shower playing. He giggled to himself. He shuffled upstairs slowly and listened by the door, but he didn't wish to intrude just in case their intimate morning had extended. Knocking delicately on the door again, he called out to them. No answer.

Grinning to himself, he imagined they escaped for one of their rendezvous, like two teenagers, not feeling the need to tell anyone. Hesitantly, he turned the brass knob slowly to open the door. There they were, embraced, sleeping. He felt awful he intruded. Distressed he would disturb them, he stepped back quietly.

He quickly became aware of a peaceful presence. It filled the entire room. He paused, and as crazy as it seemed to him, he sensed angels everywhere.

"Alexandra," he whispered, walking over to the side of her bed.

"Alexandra…Marcello…*Buongiorno*, lovebirds."

Marcello didn't move. Engulfed by a pink glow around their bodies, he quickly detected they weren't breathing. He cried out, "Alexandra, Marcello…*No!*"

Falling to his knees, he put his elbows on the edge of the bed and his palms across his eyes. He realized they were eternally together, and this made his heart glad. He knew their wishes, and it was time for their soul journey to continue.

Somberly, he stepped out of the room. He closed the door so they had privacy, as if he didn't want to interrupt the sacred energy he witnessed.

The stairs creaked as he made his way down to make the necessary calls. He never recognized how loud they were until today, when the home had such a tranquil aura. His first call would be to Selena.

In honor of their lives, he sat sipping espresso and toasting their journey, their love. The elderly man was emotional. Now close to one hundred years old, how many more breaths would he take?

Selena arrived quickly from her night away with friends. Gino didn't have to say a word. She came up behind, draped her arms around him with a loving hug, kissed his head, and said, "I know." Gino sniffled, grasped her one hand, and cried. "Go, be with them. Your grandmother is waiting."

The room still had an element of angelic energy. A sweet scent swirled in the air, possibly from the flowers in the garden. Selena knelt beside the bed, soft tears in her eyes, grieving but also happy to have known these two beautiful people. She placed her hand on grandma's heart and said a prayer. A graceful soft breeze flowed through the curtains.

"I'm not saying goodbye," she told her.

She swore Grandma smiled when she heard a whisper, *The note.*

Looking to see where a note may be, she turned her head to notice an envelope on the end table. Before she opened it, she felt the energy of all the splendid spirits in the room. She realized everyone was watching over her now, and she wondered if Alexandra perceived they both would pass on together.

Gino entered the room and remained with her. They chatted, and he stared into her eyes. He may never be with this beautiful child again.

"It was your grandparents' hope for you to experience a full and passionate life. Everybody is proud of you. Be certain to finish your education and go visit Giovanni."

Gino was the only one she spoke to about him.

"You must find out about this connection. Something has kept you two connected. Like your grandmother, you had one brief encounter with him, but neither one of you let go."

She knew his words were true.

Suddenly, a soft whisper said, *Follow your heart; your intuition.*

"I will, Grandma."

There was clearly a journey waiting for her to explore, and she recognized it was time. Nothing would hold her back. Ricardo and Alexandra would leave her everything. Some of it was in a trust fund which would be released when she was older. She would never have to fret financially. She had a plan when it was time. One which would benefit children who lost their parents. First, she would travel to visit Gino.

Danny, Gino, Suzette, and Selena held a small celebration-of- life service. Alexandra and Marcello would be laid to rest out in the family cemetery on the estate. The headstones were mostly chipped, falling over, and dirty. But the poppies were in bloom. They are symbols of sleep and regeneration on a spiritual level, poppies sym- bolize the eternal life of the soul, including reincarnation. They remind us that death of the physical body on earth is just a step in the evolution of the soul.

Danny and Gino agreed they would clean things up and make this resting place elegant, with lots of flowers. Gino wanted a con- fidential chat with Danny. They went down into the valley quietly. "Danny, I'm not sure I will be able maintain this place. I'm tired and old."

"No concerns, Gino, we have sufficient funds for us to employ someone and for you to live here. I have a notion Selena won't be living here very often for a while."

"Thank you for understanding. Your family has been extremely kind to me."

Danny saw Gino's limp was worsening, and he offered to get him medical care and a cane. He didn't want to put anybody out in any way and politely declined the offer.

"Please, let me know if you require anything. Suzette and I were considering staying for a couple of months. Is that okay with you?" Gino smiled and replied, "Yes, of course. Family time makes me happy."

Honestly, he was glad he did not have to be alone. His beautiful Margherita had passed away suddenly in her sleep a few weeks prior, which deeply saddened Gino.

In the next few months, Selena would prepare for her trip to America. Giovanni was texting her every day now. He was excited to see her again. He was so shy when he visited several years ago; he thought he made a fool of himself. In the meantime, he pursued his athletic career in baseball during college and later focused on his business degree. He wondered how they would get along now. In a few months, they would both understand more.

All was peaceful in the home now. Mornings weren't particularly busy. Gino relaxed and drank his espresso and listened to the birds. Danny made certain, once he moved back to Switzerland, a housekeeper looked over him and the home.

It was a brilliant day. The crisp air and leaves were sparkling from the dew. Selena came running down the stairs and yelled out, "I forgot about her pouch with her good luck charm. *Look*! The brooch! It's *mine*! Thank you, Gino, for leaving it in my room with a note."

Gino waited a few weeks before he brought it to her. Alexandra had requested when the time came give the pouch to this lovely child. Selena would receive it exactly when it was meant to be. It was the divine time, for sure.

They remained around the table, recalling Alexandra's story.

"She would tell me when she was a little girl how she would creep into her parent's bedroom. Tiptoeing past the white sheer curtains blowing in the breeze so no one would hear her. She played and imagined the curtains were angel wings," Selena reminisced.

Gino and Danny nodded and smiled. The story never got old. "Go on," Gino encouraged her.

"Oh, and she loved to dance like a ballerina and twirl around to the music from her mother's jewelry box. Deliberately, she would lift the lid and the music would play. She hoped no one would hear it. But she constantly felt the presence of someone near the door. She would remove the blue velvet bag and carefully pull out the brooch. Her tiny fingers would feel every bump and shape of the broken glass which created a gorgeous array of flowers. Her favorite was the blue. I can understand why this remained with her for over sixty years. She called it *'shattered pieces.'*

Just then, everyone thought they heard a whisper.

The magic is beginning.

Laughter echoed in the country kitchen. The wind blew the curtains, and a breeze brushed by each of them as if someone had hugged them hello. They all smiled and knew who had come for a visit.

CHAPTER 27

Epilogue

Selena, you may not be my blood, but you are my soul. God granted me the most beautiful child to watch over. If there is one thing I can leave you, it is my love and if there is any wisdom I can share, be you, all of you and experience this life the way that fills your heart. And when you love, put God and yourself before another and always listen to the signs. For when you listen, you will hear the whispers I send to you, and you shall journey with me once more.

Listen to your heart ~ Follow your intuition. Love, Grandma

Now in America pursuing her Giovanni, Selena was delighted to see her curly-haired, blue-eyed, handsome beau. Giovanni wanted to show her New York City and take her to Little Italy. She wanted to learn more about her mother's past. Her curiosity was growing immensely. Some things didn't line up.

Selena wore the beautiful heart necklace her papa had given Alexandra. It would always remind her of the most important thing of all… love.

Danny found the wooden chest and wondered why Alexandra had never shared it with anyone. He brushed the dust off, unlocked it, sat by himself rummaging through its contents, and cried.

Secrets

Families have secrets. Some protect us, some hurt us,
and some we will never *ever* find out.

Acknowledgments

Nothing gets done alone.

Each of these individuals helped in their way
to make this book come to life.

To *Kylie Murray* aka Selena and *Mikey Murray*
aka Giovanni, my grandkids.

Thank you for having some fun with me creating those characters.

My Family ~ you love me no matter what crazy adventure I go on.

Patty Pascua, you encouraged me to write this book
and held my hand every step of the way.

Candy Thomen, you always come through for me with beautifully
designed covers. This one is fantastic!

Rodine Isfeld and *Patricia Black-Gould* your cheer leading
gave me the energy to be tenacious.

Mandy Asquith, thank you for the lovely illustration
of Alexandra and Marcello walking each other home.

Alexa Bigwarfe, your coaching and Women in Publishing School
helped me find many resources including

Michelle Fairbanks who designed this lovely interior layout
and held me together through the end.

To every person in my life that helped me weave character
traits throughout this story, none of this is possible without
the people I meet in life.

GLORIA COPPOLA specializes in helping others find their true purpose. She has endured several personal losses and overcome financial challenges, as well as battled with depression and self-doubt. These experiences led her on an inner journey to self love and have given her the ability to engage and empathize with those who have lost hope.

Working along with shaman, kahuna, and her mentor, Bob Proctor, Gloria learned more about her soul's purpose and unique gifts. It guided and taught her how to receive and align with the frequency of love—and love feeds our souls.

Gloria loves to travel, which inspired *Too Many Goodbyes,* and offers annual writing retreats in various locations around the world.

She enjoys engaging others to live their soul-driven life and empowering them to live an inspirational life both personally and professionally. Her soul purpose consultations are life changing for those ready to seek guidance from this level of consciousness to find the truth of their purpose.

Gloria is a visionary, an award-winning author and educator, and International Professional Life & Health Coach. She received a humanitarian award for her non-profit services with the massage community and has been a featured writer for various holistic magazines and spoken at several conferences across the United States.

"It's a beautiful thing when you inspire a life to make personal and professional changes they love." – Gloria

CONTACT: Gloria@Gloriacoppola.com
www.PPP-publishing.com

BOOKS:

Both Ends of the Rainbow
You were Born to Love
Women Standing Strong Together
The Path of Awakening
Breakthrough, Wisdom of the soul
Awakening the consciousness of humanity
Coming Soon - Lexi's Journal - She Hides Her Tears

CONTACT: Gloria@Gloriacoppola.com
www.PPP-publishing.com

Made in the USA
Middletown, DE
11 August 2022

71175660R00158